After a career in non-fiction, radio, film and TV, Helen Townsend is now concentrating on fiction writing. She lives in Sydney with her family, and commutes to Lake Macquarie for sanity breaks. She has been married to the same husband for longer than she cares to admit and they have three children. *Curably Romantic* is Helen's seventh novel and reflects her interest in relationships, working life and perceptions of Australia and Australians.

curably romantic

HELEN TOWNSEND

HarperCollins*Publishers*

HarperCollins*Publishers*

First published in Australia in 2002
by HarperCollins*Publishers* Pty Limited
ABN 36 009 913 517
A member of the HarperCollins*Publishers* (Australia) Pty Limited Group
www.harpercollins.com.au

HarperCollins*Publishers*
25 Ryde Road, Pymble, Sydney NSW 2073, Australia
31 View Road, Glenfield, Auckland 10, New Zealand
77–85 Fulham Palace Road, London W6 8JB, United Kingdom
Hazelton Lanes, 55 Avenue Road, Suite 2900, Toronto, Ontario M5R 3L2
and 1995 Markham Road, Scarborough, Ontario M1D 5M8, Canada
10 East 53rd Street, New York NY 10022, USA

National Library of Australia Cataloguing-in-publication data:

Townsend, Helen, 1947– .
    Curably romantic.
    ISBN 07322 6957 1.
    1. Midlife crisis – Fiction. 2. Single mothers – Fiction.
    3. Mothers and sons – Fiction. I. Title.
A823.3

Cover and internal design by Darian Causby, HarperCollins Design Studio
Cover illustration by Lloyd Foye
Printed and bound in Australia by Griffin Press on 80gsm Bulky Book Ivory

6 5 4 3 2 1   02 03 04 05 06

In memory of Lucy

Chapter 1

Let me define middle age. It's when every day goes on forever, but life as a whole seems remarkably short. You're not happy, but not unhappy. The problems you once dreamed of solving — your fatness, your house facing the wrong way, difficult kids, your short legs, the career stuck in the mud — have become entrenched. They no longer have the sweet agonising edge of youth; an edge so sharp a solution seemed inevitable. Hope now appears in occasional flashes between forgetfulness and denial. You're sustained by vague, romantic dreams which you know will never come true. Your carefully honed talent for repression works to prevent you examining these dreams. Only on a few sadly nostalgic days do you realise your waist is getting thicker and your mother is older than your grandmother ever was.

Then, something happens. In the great sludge of middle age, there's a change, a revelation, an awakening. Because you're not young any more, it doesn't happen with flashing lights and chiming bells. In the case of Leah Jarrett, it took a year. This is her story of that year.

I was halfway to fifty. Which is not twenty-five. According to my sister Taz, you start counting again when you're forty, so the halfway point is forty-five. But whatever way you look at it, I was on the downhill slide. Some place in my head I was eighteen, dancing all night, probably drunk, full of sex, with a life ahead of me. But that was only a shadowy dream. In reality, I had three kids, an ex-husband and a job as an infants teacher. I hadn't had sex for ages and when we did folk dancing at school, my feet hurt.

My mother, who is seventy-three, says everything speeds up the older you get. The days just flash by, and then you're dead. She says this with triumph as if this applies to me, but not to her, because she is immortal.

You should be over your mother by the time you're forty-five. My two daughters already seem pretty much over me. "For God's sake, get your hair coloured properly!" my mother says at the end of her happy birthday phone call. "You're forty-five now!"

I know, as I know with every birthday, that my sister Taz will give me a surprise party. So it's hardly a surprise, more like a pre-arranged set of facial expressions. Surprises, Taz thinks, add to the wonderful unpredictability of life. She's into spontaneity, unpredictability and risk taking – in theory at least. But when you have grown-up children, you don't need surprises.

I really feel like Taz's little sister, despite being size sixteen, despite having been married and having had the three kids. I feel that bulk and marital and reproductive activities should confer some status, but to Taz, these achievements are a kind of carelessness. Taz is a size twelve. She has no children. She was married briefly to dreary Malcolm, who was quickly sinbinned out of the marital bed with a penalty kick because he wanted sex. So it's odd given her distaste for the whole reproductive business that my sister both adores and corrupts my children.

"Mum, Mum, Mum," chanted Genevieve, my oldest daughter, calling on the morning of my birthday. "Happy birthday. Do you want a kitten? The cat had kittens this morning. So it's the same date as your birthday. It would always remind you. Mum, please say yes."

"Darling, that's sweet of you but ..."

"You're going to say no ..." You could almost hear the pout forming. Genevieve is twenty-three and has a medical degree. It always amazes me that one of my children is a doctor, because producing doctors doesn't feel like my sort of thing. If she'd become a teacher, like me, or a dental nurse, I would have thought that was in line with expectations. But Genevieve is one of those self-created people. She decided she was going to be doctor when she was four and immediately worked out the TER score she'd need to achieve her goal when she was eighteen. After that, it seemed remarkably straightforward. Which is not to say she is mature in other areas of her life.

"I don't want another pet," I said.

I already owned Lucy, who is a digging Labrador of considerable charm and destructive tendencies, and a savage cat called Jack. Having Jack is like having a stalker living in the garden. He observes me, follows me and when I least expect it, pounces.

"Mum, you're just saying that."

"Why would I just say it?"

"All right," she said. "Happy birthday anyway."

Sam, my seventeen-year-old son, was doing Year 11. *Doing* sounds too active. His only chance was to absorb it through his skin. He came in, breathless, while I was having breakfast. I wish he'd been out having a morning jog, but he'd run out of cigarettes and had been down to the Seven-Eleven. He handed me a bunch of service station flowers. "Happy birthday, Mum." I tried not to think that he'd probably swiped them from the bucket outside after getting his fags. I tried to think it was good he remembered my birthday. In a moment of unexpected tenderness, he put his arms round me and kissed me. "You're a great mum."

I tried not to think he must be involved with a car stealing racket.

In contrast to Genevieve, Sam makes me feel it is quite nice that I am past the perils of being young.

The other child, Maggie, my twenty-year-old daughter, did not ring. She was lost in India, not heard from for two months. She was only lost in my mind, not in hers. She never thinks of me whereas I think about her all the time – flashes of Maggie, I call them. Not unlike a migraine. I feel insecure about Maggie. She never needed me and I can't be absolutely sure she likes me.

"Are you coming to Taz's tonight?" I called along the hallway to Sam.

"Taz?" he answered, as if the name of his favourite aunt was totally unfamiliar.

"She's asked us over for dinner."

"Dinner?" Another difficult concept.

"For my birthday."

He emerged, alert to the possibilities. "I gotta get an assignment in. Filthy's coming over. Sorry, Mum." He was out the door. He meant that he and Filthy had to play the stereo really loud and smoke a lot of cigarettes.

Forty-five. I looked in the mirror in my bedroom, which confirmed the forty-fiveness. I thought I had that mirror tamed, but it also confirmed size sixteen. It confirmed my clothes were bought at the sales, and from Target, or a combination of the two. It confirmed that not only had my beautiful red hair faded, but the beautiful red dye that I put in two weeks ago had also faded. It confirmed I had lines round my eyes and my mouth settles into a turned down slump when I'm grumpy. I was grumpy. I didn't want to look like this. I wanted to be gorgeous.

I smiled. That was better. My mouth looked pretty, my teeth white and even. I ignored the faded hair dye. My eyes are a good, deep blue. Which is great, except sometimes people think I wear contact lenses and don't realise I have genuinely beautiful eyes.

I looked at my watch. I had half an hour before school started.

That was enough time for a cry.

Years ago, I found that if I needed a cry and had time for one, it was better to be done with it rather than hold out hoping I might cheer up. When I explain this to people, they think the grief and despair may not be real, or they decide I am full of self-pity. But take my word for it, I can make time for a cry, put the make-up on and be in time to sweep my class of sweet infants into their lines, up the stairs and sit them down ready to sing like tiny angels. And be in a lot better shape for the day.

It's called controlled crying. They do it with babies. You let them cry for ten minutes so they get used to the idea of abandonment. Then you go and pick them up, so they learn that eventually mothers do give in.

The reason I was so sad on my birthday was not only that I had fading red hair and knew I had unlovely wrinkles forming in parts of my body I could no longer see. There was more. My divorce had been finalised on my birthday ten years before, which made it the tenth anniversary. I was not over it. I stopped telling people how bad I felt because I knew they felt a sort of repulsed pity for a woman who has grieved too long, cared too much. For a marriage long over. Divorce is pretty everyday stuff, except mine never felt like that.

It was one of those old-fashioned arrangements, where the Ex got the money and I got the kids. These days, I hear smart young women get the money *and* the kids. Some time in the future, she'll get the money and he'll get the kids. And if we do that for two thousand years then we'll have an historically level playing field.

When the Ex went off to live with Miss Pouty Lips, he moved to a condominium on the Gold Coast and bought (with a mortgage in my name) a very modest house for me and the kids. This house is made of particle board and fibro. It is in Banksia Close, which is in Grevillea. Grevillea is one of those made up suburbs which are common in Sydney, arising from old factory sites or reclaimed rubbish tips, ironically named after native vegetation, with matching streets. Grevillea is an oldish new suburb, so it hasn't got the dramatically distressed socio-economic profile of the really new ones. But it isn't Point Piper either.

I moved down the social scale, the Ex moved up.

The Christmas after the divorce, the Ex sent us the dog, "for the kids". Lucy, dear Lucy because I do love her, reduced the garden to a dirt patch, ate the remote control and put a dog-shaped hole through one fibro wall while in pursuit of a ball. She has a sympathetic and compassionate nature, along with an egalitarian instinct to sabotage any status related improvements round the house. She has become more controllable as she gets older, and often I feel she is my one success in dog/child rearing. Especially, because unlike the children, or the cat, she is uncritical and truly loves me, and takes her worm medication when requested. I have a neurotic horror of intestinal parasites.

"I want to make sure you and the kids are okay," the Ex told me when he sent Lucy. And because it seemed important that the Ex and I should remain civilised and friendly, in case he should ever come back and be in love with me again, I let him get away with his bad treatment of me and think that the kids *were* okay. We would live in Banksia Close and the children would never go to a fancy pants school, which suited me fine because I was never that sort of person. It wasn't so much *our* modest living conditions, but the fact that he and Miss Pouty lived in a swank Gold Coast apartment. People said, "Oh, you wouldn't want to live there. The Gold Coast is so vulgar," but I thought I could cope with vulgarity and an ocean view.

I lost sight of emotional reality. Keeping this warm and fuzzy relationship with the Ex, I neglected to notice that deep down I wanted to make his life as sad and miserable as mine was, perhaps even worse. I had stabs at planning misery for him, but really, I couldn't accept he'd gone and our cozy little life together was gone – the love, the jokes, the kids in their pyjamas, the picket fence with the rose growing over it. Not that it had been exactly like that, but there had been moments.

My sister believes it is banal to fall in love with the Australian suburban dream. But I didn't care about being banal — I wanted it. It wasn't the lace café curtains or the fake leather lounge or even the kids' pictures on the fridge; it was the warmth, the fun, the security of it. That was the romance. Having a husband who loved us, the kids with scrapes on their knees and funny sayings you could send in to *New Idea* and win a scratchie.

"So basically," said Taz, "you're talking about your standard margarine commercial?" Yes! Exactly! With the Ex and me right there in the middle of it.

When he left, I should have got hold of all his money and used it to have him run over by a man called Stan with missing teeth. I should have had his heart professionally broken. And the same goes for Pouty. Instead, I merely fantasised about convenient accidents for Miss Pouty Lips such as bumping her head on the bottom of the canyon when she took *my* children bungee jumping.

I had met the Ex when I was eighteen. He was my first boyfriend. I loved him. Truly, madly, deeply, neurotically. And he loved me. Until Pouty Lips came along. But then, I *kept* loving him. Sometimes I think I loved him more after the divorce than when he was around. By then, he didn't love me at all.

Sam was just seven, Maggie was ten and Genevieve was thirteen. They bravely hated Miss Pouty Lips, but in their hearts, they blamed me for the move to Banksia Close and the loss of their father. Their hearts were broken, but they're over it and I'm not.

That birthday morning the controlled crying wouldn't stop. I had been about to play the Beach Boys "Do you love me, do you, surfer girl, surfer girl …?" with that mournful melody, but thankfully Sam had connected the speakers to his devil worship music system so I was spared that bit of extra crying. I love the Beach Boys. It seems to me there's a Beach Boys' song for everything that happens in my life. I was still sniffling as I ran out the door in my sunglasses, all too aware that I couldn't teach kindergartners in sunglasses. You could do adolescents, and they'd just think you were trying to be trendy, but your average six year old knows a broken heart when they see one.

I ran past my neighbour Katie with a wave and a stab of guilt because our grass was so long that we had no flowerbeds showing. Katie, known in our house as Katie Bless You, because that's her signature phrase ("Bless you Leah! Bless you darling Sam!"), has been so good to me over the years that I almost hate her. She doesn't notice the hatred. It never occurs to her that hatred could be part of the infants teacher/mother/housewife territory. She still comes in for a coffee and says gaily, "Oh dear, I can never leave the house without making the beds, can you? It's ghastly to be a slave to housework, isn't it?" She doesn't notice that I'm not a slave to housework. I feel okay about unmade beds until Katie Bless You says that.

"Bless you, Leah!" she cries as I run past, while I despise her for her floppy, flowery gardening hat.

I'm late. My comrade in arms, dear old Mrs Took, who's been bending over kidlets for so long that she's got a permanent stoop and extra long arms, has covered for me. She's taken them up to the music room, pretending it's what we do every Friday. I'd do the same for her of course, but teaching is the only thing in her life, so the ten years we've been teaching together, I've only had to cover for her once. She has a wonderful heart and soul.

I'd forgotten that this was the induction day for next year's kindy class and their parents, so almost immediately, we had to hand the children over to the second class (in every sense) Miss Snitch — really she's Miss Smith, but Snitch is the children's nickname for her and describes her character perfectly. The kindergarten teachers had to be on hand to induct children and parents, and answer questions as to whether the school has a violin program ("Sorry! We're a *public* school,") and whether we keep perverts in the toilets. Little Oliver clings to my hand. "I don't like second class, Miss. Could I be your special helper?"

"Not today, Ollie," I say. "But after recess, we'll read some *Fabulous Mr Fox*."

"Have you been crying, Miss?" he asks.

"Only a bit," I say, encouraging him into the jaws of the second-class tyrant. "Now, you be good for Miss Snitch." I wonder all the way down to the assembly hall whether I said Smith or Snitch. Maybe that's why the bitch will never give me a break with playground duty.

When I get to the hall the parents and children who start next year are being shepherded about by the Principal, otherwise known as the Twisted Sister.

"Now! We want all our new *little* people for Grevillea Public School who are coming next year to sit down the *front*," the Principal booms. Her name is actually Miss Siskay, which she has printed in nice big letters on a Busy Bee badge on her enormous bosom. "And our new *big* people," she says, beaming at the parents, "you can sit on our very *special* chairs that our very good *Year 5* people have brought into the hall for you." She feels she has to emphasise a couple words in every sentence or they'll lose the plot.

It always amazes me at this point that the parents don't rush out and start looking for another less vomit-inducing school. Every year it feels worse. The gap between the rhetoric and the reality widens.

"We're a *caring* school," Twisted Sister goes on. She says "caring" like it's a word the parents may not be familiar with. "Caring *and* sharing." I can't listen. I realise the controlled crying wasn't such a good idea. It wasn't controlled enough. Under all the sadness, there's anger at my crummy life, anger at being at the mercy of this woman because I'm a casual teacher. I'm a marginal commodity, despite my years of loyalty to Grevillea Public.

"We have a *program* here," she rambles on, "so *every* child has the ability to maximise his or her potential. And, we have programs in place to ensure there is no *gender* discrimination." She says "gender" like it's a daring, sexy thing to say, but she doesn't mention her hatred of wayward little boys.

There'd be no need to go on about this primary school version of the thought police, except for what happened next.

"And this is Mrs Leah Jarrett," she says proudly, signalling me to stand up, as if she'd brought me up by hand herself. "She's one of our very *dedicated* kindergarten teachers. I know that some of you have heard of her. Some of you may have had *older* children in her class. She's done a *wonderful* job at this school."

The past tense of that sentence should have signalled something was up. But I didn't get it until she delivered the body blow.

"She *may* be working here next year from time to time when we have staff off sick, but we've got a new *permanent* kindergarten teacher, Miss Baker. Please stand up, Miss Baker."

I stared open-mouthed at Miss Baker. I should have realised that she wasn't a parent. For one thing, she had long nails with pink nail polish, and she lacked that dragged down look that anyone with a live-in pre-schooler has. She was young and bright and enthusiastic, if a little overdressed (pink silk blouse, white linen skirt, pink high heels) for the classroom.

"Miss Baker is a new *graduate*, and she's done a *very special* degree about helping our little readers who might be having trouble."

It flashed through my mind that "helping little readers who might be having trouble" could not have been the title of Miss Baker's thesis. It flashed through my mind that I didn't have a job. It flashed through my mind that maybe I could get an economy contract out with toothless Stan and look after the Ex, Miss Pouty Lips and the Twisted Sister in one body blow. I felt old Tookie's hand clutch mine – a warning as well as a show of support. This was horrible, unbelievably horrible. I only had a couple of years till the Twisted Sister retired. It was only two or three years till I got permanency. Now, I'd have to start again, contacting schools, doing odd days, ingratiating myself with principals, teaching kids I'd never see again.

I'd advise all parents to give controlled crying a miss as a technique for dealing with emotional distress. Or for putting babies to bed. All that controlled crying I'd done in spare ten minutes here and there over the years hadn't been enough and the residue came flooding out there and then. Even before the parents had gone, tears were sliding down my face. The Deputy Principal, Weenie Sister, stooge to the Twisted

One, was looking daggers drawn at me, but by the time I was out of the hall, even the pressure of Tookie's gnarled old hand on my arm wouldn't stop the tears. Someone shoved a tissue at me, but when I put it to my eyes, it dissolved.

"Go up to the staff room," said Tookie. "And don't try to teach this morning. I'll be up at recess."

I put my head down on the staff room table and sobbed. The tears must have dissolved the lacquer on it because it seemed a lot stickier than usual. I used all the paper towel and then cried on a damp tea towel. I heard the recess bell, and felt the sympathetic pats of the staff on my back, an arm round my shoulders.

"Go home," said Tookie. "You can't teach. Go home and I'll come round and see you tonight."

"My sister's giving me a birthday party," I sobbed. "She'll make me go."

"What time?" she asked.

"Eight o'clock." I started to think about my party and my sobs decreased. Switching off reality, I created a vision of riotous hedonism. "Fun, fun, fun," as the Beach Boys sing it.

"I'll be on to the Federation at lunch time," said Tookie. "So I'll be round your place at three-thirty. Now off you go."

The Federation is the love of Tookie's life, in addition to teaching. The Federation is there to ameliorate all the great injustices of life – for teachers at least, and she has faith in it as a radical fighting body. Its failures, in her eyes, are due to the right wing stooges who inveigle their way on to the executive.

The bell went. Tookie gathered up her books. The Twisted Sister came in, followed by the glamorous

Miss Baker, who looked scared by what she realised was a loaded gun situation. "We had *no-one* supervising the lines," Twisted said, giving me the evil eye. "Seeing as *you* decided to absent yourself. Really," she went on, "this is *totally* unnecessary."

My tears stopped. I looked up at her. Hatred shone out of my red eyes.

"What did you expect?" said Tookie to Twisted, looking her straight in the eye. "After what you said and how you said it?" She was the only teacher with the guts and seniority to point this out.

But Twisted wasn't having it. "I think it was *especially* unnecessary," she said to me, "in front of *parents*. I understand you're *upset*, but *really* . . ."

"It was totally unnecessary to tell her you were getting rid of her in front of the parents," said Tookie. "There are protocols."

Miss Baker tried to shrink herself as Twisted puffed herself up into super principal mode. Twisted was a tinpot dictator, a mean, vindictive, ugly, bitter middle-aged woman. I didn't believe in her any more.

"Why can't you talk like a normal person?" I demanded. "Even kindergarten teachers don't carry on with the crap you do."

She stared at me, stunned mullet style.

"And don't you get it?" I asked. "Don't you get it that no-one in this school – not a single child or teacher or parent, has the slightest *respect* for you." I began to mimic her. "No-one *likes* you. We call you the *Twisted* Sister." Tears filled her eyes, but I felt no pity. This was like bringing the school bully to account and I was on a roll. "That's your *nickname*. You're all puffed up with *piss* and *wind* and your own flatulence." There was a thought in the back of my mind that this was not the thing to be saying if I was to be getting any teaching at Grevillea Public next year. It wouldn't help getting a reference from Twisted either. But the insults just kept coming. "You're out of date. You've got no bloody idea about education. And all that sucking up to parents wears off pretty bloody fast when they find out how *vicious* you are." Sam would have been proud of me. Except that wasn't necessarily a good thing. "You abuse your power. Your ideas about education are crap." Miss Baker disappeared. The Twisted Sister was red in the face. Tookie gave me a thumbs up as she walked out the door.

After school, Tookie had come round to tell me that she had the Teachers Federation on side. She said it as if it was great news, but I knew what the outcome would be – all the fuss and bother about one teacher and one principal would end up principal one, teacher nil. That was the nature of things. I supported the union, but I was heavily embedded in the life management technique that if I ignored what was going on, it might go away. I was grateful to her but, in truth, I didn't want to be bothered by the union taking my side.

I fed Tookie some of the Eat U Rite (read semi healthy) choc chip muffins I'd been eating steadily since I got home, and gave her a cup of tea. I didn't want to talk about what had happened, but Tookie was up on her hind legs quoting by-laws and regulations and international protocols. I had to pretend to be enthused, because all we teachers feel bound together, us against the system, goodies versus baddies, underpaid and overworked. Which is partly because the only thing anybody outside the profession ever has to say about teaching is, "Lovely long holidays you get, don't you?" So I nodded and cooed while Tookie raved on about the unfairness of my life.

She did say though, "You might try a bit of bridge mending with the Twisted Sister. Just for your own good."

I wasn't going to be in that.

Soon after Tookie had gone, Sam came home with the sleeve ripped out of his shirt. When I asked him what happened, he said, "At least I'm not on drugs," and then laughed in this awful way which made me suspect that he was. I had to suppress my fantasy of how nice it will be when he leaves home, and remind myself what a sweet child he once was.

I knew I'd go to the party Taz was organising (even though there probably wouldn't be any riotous hedonism) because I needed to get drunk and forget. I looked in my wardrobe and thought my clothes couldn't be any worse if I was unemployed, which I was about to be. Basic black. I'm lucky I look good in black although you can't wear it to school because little kids like nice flowery things which you can't wear to grown-up parties. I decided to wear my slinky black T-shirt with a run down the front which I'd made with my car keys one drunken night, but which could be hidden with a long scarf. And I'd wear my black trousers and the shoes that hurt but look good. I wiped my eyes and decided I'd forget about Twisted and have a wonderful time with those members of my family, unlike my wayward son, who still loved me.

Although he had said he loved me that morning. I remembered how he used to say it all the time when he was three. "Mummy, I wuv you." Back then he was totally

16

sincere and didn't want money or anything. Now I could smell his cigarette and he was playing that awful mother fucker, mother fucker music. He said not to take it personally but I did.

Despite the horror of the day, I went to the party feeling okay. I pretended to be surprised that it wasn't a dinner party. I pretended to be happy even though it was my forty-fifth birthday and I'd just been fired from a job I'd had for ten years.

❀   ❀   ❀

I love a party, but I can never give myself one because it would seem unfair after I've forbidden parties for Sam. I once allowed Genevieve to have one and they wrecked the new carpet, which still bears the scars even though it was advertised to "last a lifetime", which it will have to, despite the stains and burns that now adorn it. I used to love kids' parties with the smiley-faced iced biscuits and dinosaur cakes and pin the tail on the donkey. Of course that's dead territory now.

This was a cocktail party, Taz's favourite kind. The drinks looked beautiful, with olives and cherries and umbrellas and they were being handed round by a waiter about Sam's age. This boy was charming and solicitous, and I tried to work out whether it's because he was paid to be or whether these are qualities some young men have naturally. He handed me a canapé. I knew I would eat too many, but I reminded myself that this canapé and the cocktail I was embarking on was forgivable, considering it was my birthday and I'd lost my job. It wasn't pure greed.

Taz's apartment is beautiful. It's daring, because she likes to think of herself as adventurous, although in reality she's pretty controlled. It's got lots of Uluru red with azure sky ceilings and Aboriginal artworks that are dusky and sensuous. The fruit in the fruit bowl were wild bush oranges. You never see bush oranges at Coles because they are too expensive to eat, as well as tasting pretty disgusting. I tried one last birthday.

Taz is beautiful too. I inherited the short and stubby genes. She got the tall and willowy ones. She was wearing burnt orange and a green belt round her tiny waist. Her name is actually Tania, but no-one calls her this except my mother, who always introduces her as, "Pronounced — Tania, as in *lasagne*, my daughter," to which Sam always replies, "Pronounced — Tanya, as in, *can ya?*, me auntie."

Taz has lots of mirrors round the apartment, so she can keep checking her angles. She does little adjustments with discretion. She is extremely vain, but she is proof that using very expensive French cream for fine lines round the eyes really does work.

The apartment was filled with people. Despite the fact it was *my* birthday, I hardly knew any of them. I had met them at other parties Taz has thrown, but they weren't *my* friends. Taz doesn't understand that the people I work with and the people in my neighbourhood are actually my friends. She's an unashamed snob. I'm elevated only by virtue of being her sister. But I like meeting these people and seeing that even rich people with fantastic jobs are unhappy, or shallow, or hopeless. Or in my lighter moments, see that they're good-natured and kind and not different from me, even if they are thinner and richer.

Taz's dress was low cut, and her boobs were pushed up. She looked like she was advertising her sexual charms, but it was for display only. She has a great laugh.

She has red hair like me and she behaves like she's a fantastic extrovert. I've made her sound shallow and superficial, but she's not at all. She hugged me wildly and presented me with a man.

"I'm David," he said, "and you're Taz's sister Leah." He had a nice smile.

Taz whispered in my ear. "He's madly in love with Rosanna. But she's trying to get rid of him." Rosanna is Taz's very attractive and very promiscuous flatmate. Taz and Rosanna were at school together and Rosanna is almost like another sister to me, except her Catholic upbringing made her promiscuous, whereas Taz is still stuck with Catholic prudery. Taz didn't like what she called "the sex bit" of her marriage. The sex bit seems to be Rosanna's favourite activity.

Rosanna intimidates me because she places great stock on people *having* "ideas" and *discussing* "ideas". She's culturally intense. Evidently Taz is very open to "ideas" and I sort of ride along on her coat-tails, never confessing that my notion of a good idea is a long hot bath on Saturday night, or making Eat U Rite choc chip muffins for breakfast on Sunday. I love reading, but I can never tell them what I'm reading because they either look down their noses at me, or ask me what I thought of the poetic sub-text, when I either think it's a great yarn, or that it isn't.

"Do you know Rosanna?" David asked. He had blue eyes. I am a sucker for blue eyes. Otherwise, he looked a little battered by life, paunchy, and dressed in a way that didn't quite gel. There was a mad light in his eyes, but I had no illusions, especially with Rosanna in his heart.

"I know Rosanna very well," I said. I'd had this conversation before.

"Mother..." yelled Genevieve from across the room. "Happy birthday my darling mother." She is truly beautiful, this child of mine. She has long, dark red hair, blue eyes, perfect features, is tall and has fantastic milky white skin. She is incredibly clever, which seems unfair in one person, until you realise she is very short on basic things like intuition, tact, the ability to empathise, sympathy, kindness and common sense. Nevertheless, she is good fun.

"You put on such a tantrum about that cat," she said. "You could be nicer when I went to so much trouble to think up a good present."

"If they were born this morning ... Really Gen, it's pretty obvious."

She smiled. "Okay. I bought you this anyway." She handed me a small box. It contained a silver chain, hung with a small amethyst. It would have been perfect except I'd given it to her for Christmas last year. I'd gone to a lot of trouble to choose it, but I'd known when she said, "This is really nice thanks Mum," in a flat voice, and put it back in the box that it would never be round her neck.

"Thanks darling," I said.

"I've got a new bloke," she gushed. "He couldn't come tonight." She acquires blokes in the same way other people buy magazines. She has them round for a while, finds them boring and chucks them.

"That's good."

"He's poor and worthy," she went on. "Your type." And looked David up and down.

"What do you do?" asked David politely, after Genevieve bounced away.

"I'm a teacher. Infants. What do you do?"

"I'm a journalist," he said, "on a downhill slide."

"What else do you do," I asked, "that doesn't pay you or depress you?"

"I'm crazy about classical music. That's how I met Rosanna."

Now all I knew about classical music was that what I used to think was classical music, like Frank Sinatra and Vera Lynn, wasn't at all. Classical music is what they play on ads for really expensive cars on TV. However, I am an amateur expert on music produced by Phil Spector and music made by the Beach Boys who, unfortunately, Phil never did produce. But when I mention my expertise to anyone at Taz's parties, they look at me as if I am a professional molester of their cultural privates. ("Help me Rhonda!") So I certainly wasn't going to try it on David, who was a lover of the classics *and* Rosanna.

"Rosanna used to play the cello," I said, pitying him. He was dying to talk about her.

"I could imagine that," he said. "It's a very sexy instrument."

"It sounded bloody awful when she played it."

"Maybe she needs a different teacher. She's musical. And very knowledgeable."

I was sad that the only way I could keep him talking was with gossip about Rosanna, because it defeated the purpose.

"She's over the cello," I said. "She gets over things very quickly. Rosanna likes something one day, and something else the next."

"Oh," he said.

"I'm still not over my divorce," I said, "and that happened ten years ago." I don't know why the divorce popped into the conversation. I guess because it was my birthday and my divorce day and I was already a bit drunk. I never mentioned my failure to be over the divorce to Taz because it made her cross. I never said it to the kids because I didn't want to set a bad example to them. And I never said it to my mother because she always said, "He wouldn't have gone if you hadn't got fat, after you had Sam." And other people seemed to be either newly in love and happy (it would be cruel to disillusion them with a divorce story) or long out-of-love man-haters, who believed I should *hate* the Ex, and were prepared to do it on my behalf. People think it's healthy to hate now, more healthy than it is to love. Love is seen as more of a neurosis, unless you're a celebrity and have the million-dollar wedding. And even then, we're really waiting for the split.

"I'm not over my divorce either," said David. I looked at him, surprised he was still there after my little private reverie.

"How long ago was yours?" I asked.

"A year."

"Mine was ten years. Exactly. Today. That's the only reason I mentioned it. I don't talk about it usually. It's pathetic, not being able to get over someone after ten years."

He smiled. "My wife was over me in about two minutes."

"It's the difference between being the leaver and the left."

"I left her," he said. "But maybe that was wrong. Maybe I should have tried to make it work."

"Not if she got over you in two minutes," I said. "It would have been silly to stay." I sounded like a first grade teacher dealing with a first grade problem, like someone's pencil being touched by someone else's elbow. He didn't seem to notice.

"I'm an agoniser," he said.

"Me too." I understood being an agoniser. "Agonisers are the most sensitive creatures of the human race," I said. "I agonise about being an agoniser. And I'm into micro guilt about the kids. Have you got kids?"

"No," he said bleakly. "She didn't want them. And I didn't realise I did until it was too late. We weren't suited at all really. I sort of died emotionally in the marriage." He cast a look at Rosanna. "I'm just getting over it."

"She's not crazy about kids," I said.

"Kids are something I should have done. I don't want to have them now. It's just one of the regrets about the marriage. One day you wake up and you realise you've become a person you don't like much. And you've spent a lot of time becoming like that. And it's not only your own time you've wasted. It's the other person's too. That's why she was so angry when I left. The waste of it. It made me feel really guilty."

Now this wasn't exactly a flirtation, but all this talk about guilt and agonising was giving me warm feelings. Or maybe it was his nice blue eyes. We were having the conversation, but there was also the old emotional sub-text ticking away in my brain . . . *he seems nice enough not to notice how big my arse is; I'm sure I could have sex without him seeing it; I could fancy him; he seems kind; why don't we go to bed? I haven't had sex for years; it used to be nice, better than childbirth anyway. If Sam goes out Saturday night, I could ask him over for dinner . . .*

It was all over in a second. There was Rosanna, smiling at him, and though he wasn't exactly drooling, he had the bewitched and enchanted look men get round Rosanna. I began to feel that my T-shirt was sitting tight around my bulges. I wished I hadn't eaten so many canapés.

"Come on everyone, happy birthday now!" There was my sister with an exotic cake she'd made for me. "Happy birthday..." Taz started singing and everyone joined in and David took the opportunity to put his arm casually on Rosanna's shoulder as if that was what you did when there was community singing and Genevieve winked at me and looked so stunningly beautiful that I felt a thrill of motherly pride that my life hadn't been quite wasted if I had produced this devastating if heartless creature. And Taz put the cake down and came over and hugged me and said, "What's up, little sis?" in the really kind way she does when she knows I'm in shit, and I blew out the candles and made a wish, not a very imaginative one, just that my life might be more fun. And then I played mother and cut up the cake and gave them all a piece on the stylish china plates, while thinking using serviettes would have saved on the washing up.

❀　✺　❀

"Sue them for wrongful dismissal," said Rosanna after everyone had gone and we were sitting there at three in the morning, just Taz and Rosanna and me, and Genevieve asleep on the floor. Taz had made me tell her what was wrong while Rosanna got rid of David. Genevieve had been going to make us coffee but fell asleep instead.

"The Federation said they're going to do something," I said. "But really, I haven't got a leg to stand on because I'm a casual."

"I'm going to say something," said Taz. "And I don't want you to overreact."

A sure indicator for overreaction on my part.

"It's the best thing that ever happened to you," said Taz. "You need to take control of your life. Teaching isn't a job for a grown-up, especially teaching ankle biters."

I was about to launch into a defence of my chosen profession, but I remembered the Twisted Sister and how she made my life a misery. Mind you, it wasn't personal, she liked to make everyone's life a misery unless they were the child of a doctor, or the spouse of a doctor. "Dr Murray, Dr Jones..." She'd recite doctor parents' names as if she was about to go into a trance. The Twisted Sister didn't have a fine eye for social distinction, but she had great respect for the idea and she knew the approximate outlines. Her staff were at the bottom of the barrel, just below the luckless single parents. Of course, I fell into both groups. And I'd burnt my bridges by telling her home truths regarding her character.

Taz thought I did teaching for the holidays. But even when I thought about the hard bits and the sad bits, it still felt like part of me. Like Carrie, the autistic kid who'd been in my class. I tried and she tried but she'd had to go off to a special school anyway. And Andy, who was knocked around by a succession of step-fathers but had something bright and beautiful, which made me think he'd make it.

I thought of our class pet project of breeding mice so we could learn about mummies and babies and how we'd ended up with three healthy baby mice. We cooed at them and carried on until mother mouse ate the three babies one night, leaving the little, pink back legs. They were discovered by two five-year-old girls who'd probably be scarred for life by the experience and would never be mothers.

"Or they might *eat* their babies," Sam had suggested.

I thought of playground duty and craft afternoons and the percussion band, and parent–teacher night and end of year reports. I thought of the child protection trainer who told us we couldn't cuddle upset kids any more in case we molested them, and the safety regulation that meant we had to dismantle the beloved fort in the playground, and the cut in resources that meant we had no reading support program, and picking up papers in the playground. And I suddenly felt as if Taz was right and it wasn't a job for a grown-up.

"So," said Taz, "you'll have to start looking for a job."

"At the end of the year," I said. "There's still half a term. She doesn't want me to go straight away."

"Of course she doesn't, the old bitch," said Rosanna. "So give her a taste of her own medicine. Leave now."

"Yeah," said Taz.

"But I couldn't," I said.

"Why not?" they demanded so loudly that Genevieve started. I put a cushion under her head and she slumped back to sleep.

"I can't leave in mid term," I said.

"Why *not*?"

"Because of the kids," I said firmly. "I can't just walk out."

"You just said you were casual."

"I am. But not to the kids. I'm their teacher. They couldn't get someone at this time of year. They'd be stuck with a string of teachers."

"Leah," said Taz, "they're kids. They'll grow up. They won't remember. Shit, the only clear memory I have of kindergarten is a teacher with black curly hair and gold earrings who was called Mrs Black Sambo, which just shows the complete inaccuracy of the human memory below the age of ten. You should leave."

I felt very drunk and very sick of canapés. Taz gave me a leather-bound copy of *Great Expectations* for my birthday because she thinks Dickens isn't as shameful as some of the things I read and she's trying to get me a full leather bound tastefully embossed set, over time. The last one, *Tale of Two Cities*, I had to replace, because Lucy has almost as much taste for a leather-bound Dickens as I do, which Taz would never understand. So the *Great Expectations*, while a great present, was also a burden and made my head spin with the thought of Lucy finding it under the bed, and then me finding it in the garden, and then having to find an identical replacement before Taz came to visit again.

I have these times when I'm scared I'll forget my name and I imagine I'm losing my mind. At least I think I imagine it. I reminded myself it had been a stressful day and I had had a lot to drink. "I will leave," I promised. "But not till the end of the year."

But Taz and Rosanna had lost interest. They chatted about David in a dismissive sort of way and about how beautiful Genevieve looked and played with their cat.

I lay on the couch. I was too drunk to drive and tomorrow was Saturday and it was such a soft couch and I had one child looking angelic right there with me on my birthday. It was ten years since the divorce I hadn't got over and I'd just lost my job. But I felt a sort of calm. Cried out after the controlled crying. I began to imagine a different life might happen to me. I'd stay to the end of the year because you can't desert your class, but even if the Twisted

Sister offered me Year 5 for the next year (unlikely), I'd refuse. Someone would offer me a fabulous job. I'd be good at it and get paid heaps of money, and move house and go overseas and get a new car. The imagining of it whooshed through me like the wind.

Then I fell asleep.

Chapter 2

Children wait to become adults. The elderly wait to die. But in middle age, having struggled for security and comfort, we create an illusion of permanence. So when things end, the middle aged cling to their illusions and scratch their heads in wonder.

The reality is that things end all the time — jobs, relationships, bargains at the mall after Christmas.

Leah clings to the belief that things should be the same, even when they are bad or uncomfortable. She sticks at things, because of the comfort of sameness, because of her belief that change can be avoided.

Being an infants teacher, I'm pretty familiar with the dazed look and its psychomotor consequences. After my birthday, I developed the dazed look for my own protection, locking myself into a state of watertight denial about my looming unemployment. I could not bring myself to schmooze up to the Twisted Sister and apologise.

Eventually I rallied, with a kind of rabid flamboyance, characteristic of teachers in trouble. We did more class singing. We ran in circles and danced in lines. My voice got louder. We put on plays with elaborate staging and costumes.

As the final term of the school year drew to a close, I became hysterically Christmassy. We made Santa hats, pom poms, chains of streamers, cards for mummies, daddies, grans and grandads, for dogs and cats and the occasional guinea pig. I decorated the class Christmas tree, which I got illegally from a state forest, and drove to the school with it sticking dangerously out of my car window. I gave the treacherous mother mouse a special Christmas bed. I received an inordinate amount of cheap soap, cheap jewellery and room deodorisers in gratitude for my year of toil. I organised the school picnic and carol singing, and powered through speech night. It felt as if the Twisted Sister owed me fifth class the following year. She said nothing. My denial of my future unemployment began to fray. I began to feel even crazier.

I realised on the second last day that the next day might be my last at Grevillea Public. But I was cracking hardy. Nuts, in other words.

"Now all remember tomorrow is mufti day," I reminded the class. "So you don't have to wear your uniform. You can wear *whatever* you like."

"I'm wearing my pink party dress, miss."

"Gorgeous!"

"I'm going to wear my new shoes Dad got me."

"You'll have to show me how fast you can run."

"You never wear mufti, miss."

"She wears mufti every day."

"No I don't," I said. "I have all my school clothes and I'm really sick of them. They're just like a uniform."

"Wear mufti then," said one bright spark. "Wear your party dress."

"Wear your pyjamas," said the class wit.

"Ohhhh," went the class at this genius suggestion. "You're not allowed, are you, miss?"

They were right. I was not allowed. But I did. A fine rebellion, the last thumbing of my nose at the Twisted Sister. Or maybe the first stage of mental disintegration. But the next morning, I got out of my car in the staff car park dressed in my Santa pyjamas, my faded yellow chenille dressing gown, my fluffy blue slippers, with Genevieve's old teddy bear under my arm. In about ten seconds, I was surrounded by a mass of screaming, horrified, delighted, ecstatic and hysterical children. The Twisted Sister poked her head out of the office window and withdrew it in shock-horror. Sure enough, there was a note for me in the staff room at morning tea.

"*Dear Mrs Jarrett*," I read to the staff who were in about the same state of uproar about my pyjama attire as the children had been.

"*The policy of this school is to encourage the educational and personal development of its student body. Inappropriate dressing undermines not only our dress code, but also these goals we hold so dear for our students, as well as encroaching on the dignity of the entire staff. It also undercuts the authority of the principal to uphold the dress code appropriate to the school culture of responsibility and dignity.* They're all arguments in *favour* of wearing pyjamas."

"I must agree with the principal on this one," said the Snitch.

"If you must, you must," said Tookie, and the Snitch flounced out.

"*I therefore request you to go home and change into more appropriate attire. Mrs Took will take your class for the hour after recess. Yours sincerely* et cetera, et cetera."

"Are you going?" asked someone.

"No," I said. "Why should I?"

So that day I worked in my pyjamas. The kids loved it; their parents thought it was hysterical. I was out with a bang rather than a whimper, maybe missing the point that I was actually out. That night, I went home, had a large gin and an Eat U Rite choc chip muffin and tried not to think about it.

❀ ❀ ❀

The other string to my employment bow was a job I had on Thursday nights at Target, which I'd had ever since the Ex left. It was an easy job of putting things back on the shelves that customers had strewn about, re-ticketing jackets, dresses and shirts which people returned after they had worn them to just one party, and thrown on the floor for a week, before they panicked and realised they didn't want the item or couldn't afford it. Not very different from laundry duty at Banksia Close.

When school finished, I asked the floor supervisor for full-time work. She looked at me as if she had no idea who I was, but she signed me up till after the New Year sales.

Thursday nights was one thing, the Christmas rush on your feet all day was another, but I enjoyed the air of panic. One day, I remembered Harriet whom I'd met at the school re-union five years ago. She'd been in my roll class, undistinguished in any way, and I was mortified to find she'd become chief buyer at a big department store. She earned a mint, had an in-residence husband and a perfect baby daughter called Chloe. She had looked about ten years younger than the rest of us and we hated her. Now, I found the memory of Harriet irresistible. I would become Harriet. If she could do it, I certainly could. I was positive I'd done better than her in a maths test once, and when I got a high salary like her, I'd look slick too.

I approached my supervisor. "Have you got any training programs?" I asked. "To become a buyer?"

"We don't call them buyers, dear. Merchandise co-ordinators."

"So is there training available?"

"Yes. We have lots of programs – they're running all the time." She was busy, showing one of the pimply kids how to do the pricing, so I left her. But I felt a warm glow in my heart. I'd leave teaching, rise up the ranks of retail. I saw myself swanning back to Grevillea Public, smart and size twelve, to lunch with my former colleagues.

Alone at home, with only Lucy as my confidante, it was harder to embrace such dreams. The arrival, just before Christmas, of Sam's end of year school report emphasised that dreams mostly don't come true.

"It's quite good," he said optimistically, as he does every year. "I mean it's not fantastic but . . ."

Just when I thought I was over the post-natal depression.

Sam's academic progress or, more accurately, the lack of it, had worried me so much that earlier that year I'd sought professional help. I wanted to get Sam motivated or organised or whatever it was he needed to be, but the psychologist redefined the problem.

"I'll help you manage your anxiety about his progress," she said, "because *your* anxiety may be fuelling *his* anxiety."

I had thought Sam's lack of anxiety was the problem. And the psychologist had so many degrees she should have been unemployable. But she pointed out gently that I'd had Sam for seventeen years and my results weren't impressive. I needed a new perspective, new techniques. I'd tried hard with Sam, but my childrearing strategies have tended to be reactive, rather than contemplative.

From the psychologist I learned that I should not be ridiculously encouraging. Avoid saying things like, "Oh great! Thirty-five percent is a *big* improvement on twenty percent." And especially to keep the sarcasm out of my voice.

I learned not to be judgmental and punitive, as in, "You've got to stay home Saturdays, stop smoking, keep your room tidy starting *now*, study three hours a night, and not act like a *loser*."

Not to project, painting pictures of Sam's future heroin addiction, crime sprees and Thai jails.

Not to be angry, hysterical, possessive or demanding.

The loss of these favourite stock diatribes left me literally speechless.

"Oh," I said, when confronted with a list of desolate, despairing comments by his desolate, despairing teachers.

"I knew you'd be shitty," he said.

"I'm not shitty," I said. "I don't know what to say."

"You always used to say I could do better," he said.

"But I don't know that you can," I said.

"Shit!" he said and went to his room and played the mother fucker music very loud. It was times like these I wished his father was still around. I would have another adult to despair with. Or even better, Sam and the Ex could have a heart to heart talk, from which Sam would emerge saying, "Gee Mum, you *are* right!" Or simply exert the alpha male authority and make him stop the music. But in the absence of the Ex, I went into my bedroom and shut the door. Nothing like despair to put you to sleep.

"Sorry, Mum." Sam fell back onto my bed. "Were you asleep?"

"Almost."

"I'll really try next year. I'll try to try anyway." There was a note of despair in his voice.

I began to think about the youth male suicide rate.

"Do you want a job at the shop?" I asked. "They've got a few jobs going through to New Year."

"No," he said. "Actually, I'm even going to stop working at KFC. I've gotta study."

But however good his intentions were, Sam wouldn't study. It was so hopeful and hopeless at the same time. He'd be worse off without KFC because one thing he had going for him was fast food experience continuously from the time he was fourteen.

"Who'll pay for your cigarettes?" It was a wicked way to try and manipulate him to keep his job, but it's all that came to mind.

He was silent. I could sense he wanted to talk. I wanted to tousle his hair or take his hand like I used to when he was little, but I waited.

"I might go and stay with Dad for the summer," he said after a few minutes. He grinned at me. "You know, get out of this wicked environment, all *your* bad influence, Mum. Turn over a new leaf."

I was silent.

"Do you mind, Mum?" He looked at me. "You know, last year, it hassled Dad, because I trashed the boat. But this year, I thought maybe I could do something for him – like paint the house, or do the garden stuff. You know, something." His voice had an edge of desperation, which was completely justified, because he didn't know which end of a paintbrush was which, didn't know a weed from a rose, whereas his father was meticulous about such things.

The relationship between Sam and the Ex had been a constant thorn in my side. Sam always did something dreadful when he went to stay with his dad. I primed him to be good and tried to smooth things over with the Ex when things went wrong. I guess I had always blamed Sam because he wasn't exactly relaxing to have around. The girls had been mostly easy, whereas Sam had a high level of primal discontent. He broke things by looking at them.

But I'd had Sam around *my* house for seventeen years. I'd loved him, fed and clothed him, taken him to school, gone on holidays, worried about exam results, bad company, crooked teeth, the bully in the locker room, which were a whole lot of things the Ex didn't have to worry about. He just had to make a phone call every so often and take him on holiday once a year. But then, the Ex yelled at him for breaking things, spent time with Pouty Lips and favoured the girls. In the last few years he hadn't even taken time off work when Sam was there.

Sam looked young, and uncharacteristically innocent. All this, I suddenly understood, was the Ex's fault, for not being with us, for not being Dad. It was a revelation. It wasn't my fault. It wasn't Sam's. It wasn't happy families. It couldn't be, because the Ex wasn't there. He'd never tried to be there for Sam.

"He's gone to the States," I said. I delivered this news deadpan. "He's gone for Christmas and he's staying most of January. Jackie wants to see her family."

Silence. The Ex made regular trips to the States. He had taken Genevieve when she was sixteen and Maggie the next year. Every year, Sam was convinced it was going to be his turn. But it never was. He sat on my bed, his back to me, slumped in despair.

"We'll go to the coast, Sammy. I'll teach you to drive."

Suddenly, he was on his feet, his fist through my mirror, blood all over his hand, yelling with rage, pain and frustration. I grabbed him as he smashed the mirror again. I felt the strength of him, the rage. But there was still enough little boy in him to get him to the bathroom, to run his hand under the tap, to get the larger splinters of glass out, to staunch the bleeding with a towel, to bundle him into the car. To do the mother thing despite the horror of it. He sat in the car, clutching his hand to him, tears pouring down his face. "I don't want to go to Dr Saunders," he said angrily, "not like this." He meant the tears, not the glass in his hand.

"I'm taking you to casualty at the hospital." I felt grey and weak, as if *I* was in shock. Now wasn't the time to get heavy. "If I break the speed limit," I said, "we may just be in time to save your arm." What if that turned out to be true? There was blood seeping through the towel.

He wiped his eyes, and tried to smile. "Shit, Mum. I'm sorry about your mirror."

"Sam, you've really hurt yourself." I tried not to let my voice shake. "It's no good."

"It's just I thought ... I don't know ... Dad told me he wasn't going to the States this year. He told me that two weeks ago. He lied, Mum." He sighed, a brokenhearted sigh. "I guess he was pissed off at me. I smoked in front of Jackie and then I dinged the boat, but he coulda said ... shit, fuck it!" The anger was rising again.

"Calm down," I said.

"It's just Genevieve and Maggie. You know, it's not even the States. He *likes* doing things with them. He loves Genevieve because she's so damn smart and he loves Maggie because she looks like Jackie ..."

"Like *Jackie*?" I said.

"He's always saying they could be mother and daughter." Sam was triumphant, knowing this would defuse any anger I might have about the mirror. I tried to resist the thought that Maggie looked like Pouty Lips. Except she did a little. But she was mine, and Pouty Lips was the Wicked Stepmother. Even the Ex was mine, underneath it all.

"Darling," I said. "I think it's much truer and healthier if you blame your dad rather than blame yourself because he doesn't want to see you." This was a big turn around from my usual happy families scenario. It would have seemed like a cop out to me a few weeks ago. All his life, I'd been trying to get Sam to behave for his dad. But I'd been giving him the wrong message. The Ex needed to behave for Sam.

"How's that supposed to make me feel better?" said Sam. "It *proves* he doesn't like me."

I was negotiating peak hour traffic, trying to make it to the hospital before the blood soaking through the towel added to the substances already staining my upholstery. I felt sick inside at Sam's injury but on another level I was sure I was plumbing the mother lode of emotional truth. Sam had to get some perspective on how much his dad loved him or hated him. He had to stop blaming himself for the Ex's inadequacies. It was there, a clear and shining truth. This was a problem for the Ex. Sam's problem was that he saw it in a way that had made him punch the mirror and rip his hand open.

"He doesn't like *me*," I said, and felt the truth of it. "He used to, but he doesn't any more. And I wasted a whole lot of time worrying about it. But it doesn't make *me* any less. It just means he was a lousy husband. The way he treats you makes him a lousy father." It was the worst thing I'd ever said to any of the kids about the Ex. I'd kept up the mythology of him being a good and loving father even when he wasn't. He was fun, I'd reminded them, remembering bits of fun I'd had with him myself. He loved them. He'd even read their school reports. I glanced at Sam as we pulled into casualty.

"Actually," he said as he got out of the car, "I reckon he's a bit of a deadshit. And Jackie too. The girls like her, but I never did."

We were hours in casualty. "I punched a mirror," he told them jokingly. "I didn't like the look it was giving me." They joked with him as they picked out the splinters of glass, took X-rays, stitched and bandaged. Seeing the medicos laugh with him made me feel that Sam punching the mirror didn't automatically make him a self-destructive psychopath. We picked up pizzas on the way home and when we got there, he didn't play the mother fucker music or go into his room or smoke. We watched the *X-Files* and ate the pizzas, then chocolate biscuits and drank Coke.

He was drowsy from all the painkillers they'd given him and he dozed off on the couch. I did the motherly thing and put a blanket over him and then sat looking at him. He had such a sweet face. I thought about all the sadness there is in family life, all the disappointments. In the beginning, a child is hard work, but you think it's going to pay off. You're sure that deep down inside your children are wonderful. But then, they're just ordinary human beings. They hurt, you hurt. They disappoint you, you disappoint them. There are lots of times of clear, sweet happiness when you wouldn't want anything else, but then there's not.

I couldn't think about what I'd said to him about the Ex.

Tonight, with all Sam's pain and hurt, I'd felt some of that sweetness and closeness and truth, but I'd felt the other too, and it was all part of the same thing. "God only knows," as the Beach Boys say.

❀　　❀　　❀

Tookie came over before Christmas and brought champagne and news from the Federation. Tookie had decided it was to be a grand political battle of principle, way beyond me and the Twisted Sister. The Department was the evil empire, the Federation was the force for good. Twisted and I were just bits of paper. We drank the champagne at the kitchen table with Sao biscuits and packet cheese, gossip interspersed with the news of what she had begun to call my "case". She was convinced it would go to court. It was just a matter of finding some industrial law that had been breached.

"*I* see it as a test case," she said. "But it's taking them a while to get their head around it. They don't want to be seen as jeopardising the rights of permanent staff, but my argument is that the Department *used* you as a permanent, paid you casual wages, and then forced you out when it suited them."

"It wasn't the Department," I said. "It was the Twisted Sister."

"That only complicates it," said Tookie. There was a look around her mouth that told me that her mind had shifted to another plane. "It's a *policy* issue. It's *political*, not *personal*."

"But it was personal. She went out and got Miss Baker. She could have kept me on."

"But once she *got* Miss Baker, you had no rights."

"Twisted is such a bitch," I said. "Couldn't we charge her with harassment?"

"I know she's a bitch, but she was pretty upset about what you said to her. You had your reasons, but it sounds like a cat fight. It's got no substance, unless it's an *issue*. We have to define the issue before the legal people in the Federation will look at it. They'll want you to come in and have a chat at some point. Obviously, they'll support you, but it's much more powerful if *they* take action than if you take action with their nominal support."

"Tookie, I know this means a lot to you. And I'm all for teachers' rights, but . . ."

"You're not a political animal, Leah. I am. My dad organised the miners in Wollongong. It's in my blood. Look, this is important. You don't have to run this. But you happen to illustrate an important point. All you have to do is be there."

"Okay." I imagined myself in interminable meetings while people discussed what had happened. "But I'm more concerned about not having an income." I was living on dreams of my future retail career, which I wasn't quite ready to share with Tookie.

"You'll be all right. There are jobs out there. Miss Siskay seems to have spread a bit of gossip about you in the schools round here. But Jenny's made a couple of calls further out. The schools aren't close, but they're possible." She handed me a piece of paper, neatly set out with schools and names and addresses and phone numbers. "With Sam at this age, it's not like you can't travel a bit further."

"Maybe I'm burnt out," I said. "Maybe I've had teaching. Maybe I should do something else. I don't know." I folded the paper up carefully and respectfully, imagining how surprised she'd be when I had this retail thing in the bag.

"Fight this and then decide whether you're burnt out," said Tookie. "Don't go with your tail between your legs." Tookie picked up her champagne glass and we clinked. "Solidarity, sister," she said. "To the revolution!"

❀ ❀ ❀

"Would you like to come to dinner?" asked David. David from my birthday party. It took me a moment to remember. Rosanna's David, standing at my front door with a bunch of slightly sad flowers from a roadside stall. I had a moment of confusion, feeling like a teenager, and understanding that he was actually asking me out on a date. It was half past six in the evening and I'd already had a peanut butter sandwich and had been intending to have another one to finish off my evening meal. But a peanut butter sandwich wasn't going to stop me. It was years since a likeable bloke had asked me to dinner.

"I'd love to," I said. "Tonight?"

"Tonight," he said, and grinned and handed me the flowers.

"Come in," I said, not really sincerely, seeing as my washing was being sorted on the couch and I certainly didn't want him to see my greying underwear. "I'll just change out of these work clothes."

I managed to scoop the undies off the couch and chuck them behind the TV cabinet before he came in, and the room didn't look too bad, especially when Sam got up and shook hands nicely and behaved like a normal person while I went and put on a new shirt I'd got on special at work, and tarted myself up.

We drove into Glebe near the city and found an Indian restaurant, and I told him about Maggie being lost in India and he told me about doing drugs in India when he was young, which wasn't actually comforting, but made me realise there wasn't a hundred per cent mortality or a hundred per cent psychosis of the young who went to India.

He knew all about Indian food and we had a fantastic meal, while I fell for his blue eyes and wondered what on earth I could say to Sam if David wanted to come home with me. But I didn't come up with anything very good because we were laughing too much about my story of me going to work in pyjamas and his story of him saying something derogatory about the newspaper's proprietors while a proprietor's stooge was in the room, unbeknown to him − which was why he had ended up organising advertising on a *very* outer suburban newspaper and why I was unemployed. It seemed we had more in common than blue eyes and divorces. It was one of those fun evenings when you laugh a lot and nothing much happens because you know it's all going to happen later in bed.

Except it didn't. He paid for the meal, even though I offered. He explained he lived nearby and he suddenly felt tired, so if I didn't mind he'd put me in a taxi and send me home. I did say that was a shame, and he said it had been such good fun that we'd do it again. But the way he said that made it sound as if we'd been for a bushwalk, rather than having had a flirtatious evening. I thought sadly maybe it was flirtatious only for me, not for him.

Anyway, he hailed me a cab and gave the cabbie twenty dollars, and then kissed me on the cheek, and hugged me, but it was more like a consolation hug, like when you're sending your kid off to their gran's when you're intending to go somewhere really nice yourself. Still, I told myself to buck up, it least it was a date with a good meal thrown in.

❀   ❀   ❀

Katie Bless You came in the next day to boast about being overprepared for Christmas and to complain about Lucy undermining her vegetable garden with the hole she was working on next to the fence. The awful thing is that in any neighbourly dispute – "and let's do *stay* neighbourly, Leah dear" – I am usually in the wrong, and it's usually the fault of those nearest and dearest to me, such as Sam or Lucy.

"She's stubborn," I said. "She doesn't like to give up on a hole till it's finished. Then I can fill it in."

"Leah dear, she is only a dog. Surely you can stop her."

"She's smarter than you or me," I said, now stubborn myself, "and less co-operative. She's obedient, but she's not co-operative."

Katie Bless You wasn't going to play semantics. "Bless you, Leah," she said with a little laugh. "We've got to be able to control our dogs. Or we shouldn't have them. Jake is sometimes naughty, but I'm the one in control. Like with children."

44

I almost offered her Sam for a free trial period. Or Lucy. Because when it comes to the digging of holes, I can't control Lucy, and I don't believe Katie Bless You could either.

"I'll buy you replacement vegetables," I said, being positive in my search for resolution of this neighbourly dispute. "You just tell me what Lucy undermines every week, and I'll buy it for you." My mother always kept the neighbours at bay. Years ago, I decided to be different – warm, friendly and open was how I saw it – and foolishly, I let Katie Bless You into my life. If buying Katie's vegies was the price I had to pay for being different from my mother, so be it.

"Look." Katie Bless You was leaning forward with an earnest and open expression, which was one of her favourites. "It's a little vanity of mine to serve vegetables fresh from the garden. So having them bought really defeats that, doesn't it?"

I wanted to suggest she lie and just waltz into dinner, doing an imitation of vegies fresh from the garden. But I *knew* she wasn't up to lying. Or even worse, didn't understand its uses. This lack of understanding on Katie's part always put her ahead in the neighbourhood games. Besides, she had a wicked tongue for gossip, and I didn't want tales of my misdeeds spreading.

"I'll put bricks over the hole," I said. "But you'll have to give me a few days to dig the bricks out of the last hole she dug."

"You do it your way, Leah," said Katie, "but you know I've got Jake trained up so if I just say, 'Baaaad dog, baaaaad dog', he knows to stop what he's doing. He knows better than to mess with me."

"Me too," I said under my breath as I let her out the front door.

"It's so important to be able to talk these things through," she said, with the bless you smile. "We can always reach a solution, me and you."

I had a momentary impulse to chuck the bricks through her window. Some people make you feel that way.

❁　　❁　　❁

Genevieve and my mother and Taz and I went shopping for the Christmas dinner. It was an annual tradition that had started when Taz and I were kids and Dad had died and we were too little to be left on our own. It sounds cute, and it has its moments. It gives us a forum to put forward our opinions about money and our life choices. Also, it let Mum run on for a three-hour chatathon, without tying up the phone system.

I'm not going to say a lot about my mother, because I'm not one of those people who blame their crummy life on bad mothering. (Try substituting Pouty Lips.) What follows is a basic mother summary. My mother is an old-fashioned, thrifty woman and proud of it. She loves John Laws on 2UE and is proud of it. My mother is a talker. She never stops, she never listens. I'm not even sure any thought processes are involved. It's your classic stream of consciousness.

She knows everything. Life has dealt her some pretty hard blows. She's never been very motherly, more sharp and outspoken. I have the love for her that one has for one's mother, but she's not my sort of person, especially because she never lets up telling me the Ex left me because I got fat after I had Sam. "You were quite pretty before that," she adds. "You could have made something of yourself. Even with the mark you got in the HSC, you didn't have to go into teaching. Just because you liked it. When *I* left school..." This was the background noise to our shopping, along with the Christmassy arcade music.

"We can't pay eighty-eight dollars for a Christmas pudding," said Mum, grabbing the pudding Taz had picked up. "The 'Spread the Joy' charity puddings are only nine dollars ninety-nine and the money goes to a good cause." Mum loves good causes as long as they're on the right side of respectability. Although she doesn't say so directly, she feels her daughters have failed to live up to their upbringing. Our lives are too different from hers and we pay too much attention to what we're feeling, as opposed to what *she's* feeling – which was thrifty at this moment.

"We don't need pudding," said Genevieve. "Bad for the arteries." She has a modern moral agendum.

"Being bad to arteries is the spirit of Christmas," I said. "This one is twenty-five dollars. It's got brandy soaked fruit. It just hasn't got a tartan ribbon." It's not like you can eat the ribbon, I thought.

The stream of consciousness from Mum continued unabated, mainly about puddings of yesteryears and what her doctor said. (It's called a stream of consciousness, but I wonder if it hasn't been confused for a stream of unconsciousness – at least in Mum's case.)

"These are the best," said Taz, taking back the eighty-eight dollar pudding with the ribbon. "*I'll* buy it." She produced her credit card.

"That's right, treat me like a pensioner," said Mum, a thought intruding into the stream.

"You're behaving like a pensioner," said Taz.

"What's so wrong with pensioners all of a sudden?" asked Genevieve. Taz raised her eyebrows to indicate that everything was wrong with this particular pensioner.

"I think it's too expensive," I said.

"No-one has to contribute," said Taz. "I spend months paying Christmas off on my card, but I'm not complaining."

"You are," said Genevieve. "That's exactly what you're doing."

"I hope we're not going to have the duck from the Chinese place," said Mum. She defined herself as racially tolerant, but *their* food, whoever *they* may be, was always defective in a way chops and three vegs wasn't. "That pork you got that year . . ."

"Duck's very fatty," said Genevieve.

"Well so am I," I said.

"There's Boaz," said Genevieve, glancing over to the cheese counter. "That's my new bloke, Mum – the love of my life."

I had never heard the word "love" pass Genevieve's lips in relation to a man, so I turned and looked at Boaz. Tall, dark, good looking, ponytail. Not the usual doctor clone.

"He looks nice," I said doubtfully.

"He's divine," said Genevieve, the look of love in her eyes. "I'll just go over."

Taz didn't know the rules about Genevieve's blokes ("don't talk, don't stare, try to be invisible"), so she followed Genevieve in pursuit of the love object. "I'll check him out," Taz said. I watched the three of them talking, then Taz bounced back to us. "This is exciting," she said. "She's crazy about him. Not like Genevieve at all. Anyway, I said you wanted to meet him. But she wants to see if he likes a shirt she's chosen for him, so we're meeting them in the food hall in Queen Vic – after we've bought the pudding. We'll go to that Malay place." Taz seemed not to notice that she'd broken all the invisible boundaries of Genevieve's life.

"My goodness!" said Mum. "He's got a ponytail. On a man. Such a thing! They don't seem to know if they're boys or girls these days."

Even though I was alive and young during the sixties, I'm not sure about ponytails for blokes either. I worry such men will be too earnest about a good cause somewhere in the world, but I could hardly side with Mum.

"You can't judge by appearances," I said.

"Of course you can," she said. "Now let's get going. I need to sit down, my feet are killing me. I had those three bunions shaved, but I'm not sure that girl could really see what she was ..."

To the accompaniment of more information about our mother's feet, we bought the pudding, went to the food hall and found Genevieve and Boaz. There were no tables, so we all stood round, eating virtuous low fat ice creams bought by Genevieve, with Mum still talking feet, and Genevieve looking not at all like Genevieve, but staring lovingly at Boaz, and me trying to make conversation with Boaz without asking all those bad mother questions like "What's your name? Where do you live? What do you do? Have you got parents?"

He responded to me with general observations on the nature of Christmas shopping and the evils of consumerism, but it was hard going. Then Boaz said, "Well, I've gotta go," and then sotto voce to Genevieve,

"Can you lend me fifty?" at which Taz and I exchanged the bad men look. Genevieve gave him fifty and poor Mum became louder and more complaining, so we knew we had to find her a chair. We went to a furniture department somewhere up flights of escalators and she collapsed onto a couch, still talking, while the rest of us collapsed onto the matching chairs.

"Don't slouch, Leah," Mum said, always with an eye on my posture. "And Genevieve, see if you can get me a coffee, dear."

"They don't sell coffee here, Mum," explained Taz. "It's the furniture department."

"Well they should," said Mum. She was sitting up nicely with her feet neatly arranged, whereas the rest of us looked pretty deranged. That's the thing with Mum's generation — they've been well trained. "If they don't have coffee, we should work out what else we have to do. Christmas doesn't cook itself."

"God," said Taz. "Help me."

"The pork," said Mum. "We have to buy that."

"They sell it grainfed at DJs." Taz was persistent.

"I'll get it at Tom's," said Mum. "He has it on special before Christmas."

"Not Tom's, please!"

"Why have we got to have pork?" said Genevieve. "It's got that awful crackling stuff. Pure fat."

"Yum," I said.

"Would Modom like some help?" said a shop assistant, towering over us, clearly in non-assisting mode. She actually said "Modom" instead of "Madam".

"No dear, we're just having a rest," said Mum. "My feet are killing me. You know how awful it is Christmas shopping. We've been all over town, upstairs and down dale. We're exhausted."

"It is not permitted to *use* the chairs unless Modom is thinking of purchasing them," said the assistant in a very "move along" sort of voice.

"I am thinking," said Mum. She could be quick, I'll give her that. "This couch would go with my TV chair. Wouldn't it, Tania? Except it's the wrong colour."

"The wrong colour, Modom?" said the assistant.

Mum looked distractedly around. "That one's the right colour," she said, pointing at a green couch at the other end of the floor.

"Why don't you bring it over here?" said Taz, rallying to the call for solidarity.

"Modom, I'll have to call the manager."

"Maybe we should go," I said. I got the "letting the side down" look from Mum and Taz.

"Not till we've seen the manager," said Mum. She loved a fight. "Call the manager, pet," she added to the assistant.

The assistant retreated sullenly back to the cash register. Mum, chatting loudly, waved at her whenever she caught her eye.

"Tell me about Boaz?" I said to Genevieve, as if it wasn't a loaded question. "What does he do?"

"He's an artist, Mama," she said, as if a person as old as me could have no idea what an artist was. "He paints yellow circles."

"That's terrific," said Taz, which you can say if you're an aunt, even though she knows perfectly well there's no money in art.

The mother question here is: "Is there a good living in yellow circles?" but I'd been in the business too long to be trapped into asking that. Subtly, I approached it from a different angle.

"What sort of yellow circles?"

"Of course he doesn't make any money from it," snapped Genevieve. "It's a sort of exploration. By painting the same thing over and over he really gets to understand the form and the colour. It's not as if they're all the same," she added. I wondered exactly how different yellow circles could be.

"So you're ..."

"I'm not going to marry him," she said. "I'm in love with him."

"They're not mutually exclusive," I said, although I'd already decided against Boaz as a son-in-law. You see, I still have this ancient mother fantasy of my daughters' marriages, that one day, they'll float down the aisle in a meringue dress, I'll wipe a few tears, the Ex will gaze at me and we'll be ...

Fantasy – absolute and complete.

"Why do you like him?" I asked. "You've never liked anyone before, let alone *loved* anyone."

"I never knew about what fun low achievers were before," she said.

"Low achievers?" I said. "That's an awful thing to say."

"No, it's not," she said. "Because he is. 'Yellow circles,' I said to him, 'how hard can that be?' and he explained that it wasn't hard at all, which is why it isn't profitable, but it's good fun. And he knows lots of interesting wanky people just like him, whereas the only people I know – apart from family – are all high achievers." She said this without the slightest intimation that this might be insulting. "High achievers have no fun and aren't going to be impressed by anyone, whereas Boaz is a *lot* of fun and I impress the hell out of him."

"Genevieve!" I said.

"Don't give me the talk about those values you tried to instil. Please, Mum . . ."

"Well, I'm glad you're happy, even at the expense of someone else's self-esteem."

"No," she said. "His self-esteem is really high at the moment because he's hanging out with a doctor. The only down thing is that all his friends want prescriptions for drugs."

"God!"

"Which I don't give them." Genevieve got up. "I'm out of here," she said. "I'm on in casualty in an hour. Bye Nanna. Bye Auntie Taz." She kissed us all and ran off through the crowd, a beautiful red-haired nymph. We went back to DJs and bought the pork and the bon bons and then went to a bar with comfortable chairs and spent all the money we'd saved by economising. Mum relaxed and began to make outrageous demands in the name of charity to others. Taz and I gave each other the sisters in bondage look.

"I need some help," Mum said, as if she were offering us a particularly good deal. "I promised to take Mr Bonham to Mass on Christmas Day. Of course, I go every week, but if there are people who can only be bothered to go at Christmas, I can hardly judge them."

"He's the one with only one leg?" said Taz. She was immediately ready to defend us from demands on the part of Mr Bonham. "Don't *dare* ask him for Christmas dinner," she added. "That year he came and snored and dribbled, it was too awful."

"That was Mr Barker," said Mum archly, "who has now passed away." She looked at Taz as if the passing away was her fault. "Mr Bonham has only one leg, but *he* hasn't got dementia. And of course I'll take Mrs Andrews. Poor old thing. She's blind."

Mum didn't have a car. Taz wouldn't meet my gaze. I could see where this was leading. "Who else?"

"Mr Jeffries – his kidneys are going and he's just had half the skin burnt off his face."

"Professionally or accidentally?'

"Skin cancer, dear," said Mum, implying that none of her friends would be so careless as to burn themselves accidentally. "And there's Mrs McLauglin. She's had a stroke and her right arm doesn't work."

"I'll drive you all," I said, "but I'm not coming to Mass."

"Leah! It's only once a year."

"And the fate of your immortal soul," said Taz.

"Well you go," I said to Taz. "For *your* immortal soul."

"I'm cooking the pork. That's my sacred duty." She settled it with the older sister look.

"Well girls," said Mum. "Helping the elderly is very satisfying, as I have found. And it's never too soon to start."

"I just can't stand the way Mr Bonham takes his leg off and scratches his stump," said Taz.

"Dear, that was Mr *Barker*," said Mum. "You'd hardly know Mr Bonham only has one leg. He dances beautifully at the Club social. They're all spare parts people. I was thinking of starting up a club for them called the Spare Parts Club." My mother's help for the elderly dissociates her from any implication that she is old.

"Put them all together," I said, "then you might actually have one member, with the full complement of legs and arms and other bits."

I got the bus home and found Sam sleeping curled up on the couch. He had dyed his hair a snowy blond. Maybe that was his way of celebrating Christmas. I sat down and got out some copies of my CV, put them in envelopes and addressed them to the list of schools Tookie had given me. I knew I should have updated the CV and sent a begging letter, but it *was* an attempt to negotiate with reality, at least in passing. I went to bed and finished *Great Expectations* and felt a whole lot happier.

❀　　❀　　❀

I was dreaming of folding a blanket to go back into a too small plastic bag and trying to re-attach a label which said 38DD, and then realising the blanket was a giant bra, when I woke up to the phone ringing.

"Leah."

It was the Ex. I'd been trying extra hard to hate him, ever since I realised what a bad father he was to Sam, but his voice still aroused something in me, and I could feel myself getting warm and gooey, just when I should have been turning nasty.

"What time is it?"

I glanced at my alarm clock. "Two thirty."

"Good. I didn't want to wake you."

"Two thirty in the morning."

"Then I won't ring anyone else." He laughed. "I always get the time zones wrong."

"I've got to work in the morning," I said. I could feel steel in my heart.

"I just wanted to explain about Sam," he said. "You see it wasn't practical to bring him – not this time . . ."

"Listen, you don't have to explain *about* Sam, you have *to* explain *to* Sam. About this time – last time – next time . . ."

"You know what he's like . . ."

"Yeah, I live with him. Remember?"

"Leah." He sounded surprised at this little outburst, but he thought he could talk me round. "Come on. We agreed never to fight about the kids."

"I know, but I should have fought *for* him," I said. "I shouldn't have let you get away with it all these years. He's too old now for me to fight his battles. But maybe you should think about how he feels and why you make him feel like he's failed . . ."

"He's bloody difficult. That stunt with the boat . . . He doesn't seem to have learned how to behave. And he drives Jackie mad."

"*Poor* Jackie," I said.

"Leah. Sweetie, it's not like you . . ."

I hung up.

I hung up because I was angry but I knew if he got beyond the "Leah, sweetie" I would have been a goner. I hated him, but not enough. I'd always thought I shouldn't have got fat after Sam, that he had really wanted the video of the school concert and read their reports – whereas the truth was . . . I didn't know what the truth was. I'd slept with him when I was eighteen. I'd loved him, adored him, thought he could do no wrong.

I'd had no father so I thought I should be grateful that my kids had one. Now all my crazy thoughts and fantasies were swirling round with no place to land.

I had no job the next year. I still had Sam to support, myself to look after, the dog and the cat. As if reading my thoughts, Lucy jumped onto my bed and put her head on the other pillow. I didn't have the energy to make her get off. I had to bandage my blisters the next morning and put on the shoes that hurt and drag myself back into work, determined to become a buyer in a discount store.

Chapter 3

Jealousy, envy, greed and betrayal are the stuff of family relationships. In childhood, these things are played out spontaneously, with painful immediacy. In our twenties and thirties, family mythology develops, is embellished and twisted, taking shape as the cause of our woes, becoming the stuff of therapy and self-improvement. The immediacy fades.

In middle age, the mythology becomes a story, losing intensity, its old potency seeming childish and even embarrassing.

But underneath, the events of the past burn as intensely as ever, despite the illusion we have grown up. Leah and her family carry them in many ways − nostalgic laughter, polite dismissiveness, sharp words. This minimises the truth, giving it the patina of the past, as if it is irrelevant to life now.

Christmas is traditionally a disaster in our family. The disaster that began the tradition was my father's death − a Christmas Day disaster to remember. Except I don't remember it, being a babe in arms, a mere eighteen months old. The whole tragi-comic disaster has been related to me by Taz, who was five at the time, and an actual witness. My mother has never talked about it, except to give a sniff, which implies Taz's version of events is not correct.

I am the baby in all this. I am not to know. I hate not knowing. I have no picture of my father, or my parents' life together. The clues are missing. There is a wedding photo of my mother sitting on *her* mother's bed, but there is no picture of my father and mother on the happy day. "It's somewhere," Mum says enigmatically. "He is your father." And then talks about what John Laws said that morning, and what she said about what John Laws said, how she and John Laws are amicably conjoined in their opinions, and invariably right.

Taz's story about my father goes like this: after Christmas lunch, he decided to go for a walk – later revealed as a quest for alcohol – which apparently he found at a neighbour's place, as indicated by the shattered gin bottle found on his corpse, and the testimony of the neighbour.

My mother emphasises that my father wasn't a bad drunk. "He was happy, dear," she said. "But when he started, he couldn't really stop. And it was exhausting, because he wanted us all to be happy along with him." This sounds like a brave face, which is one of my mother's favourite faces. Like me, she's not crazy about reality.

On the fateful Christmas, my father (happily) took my sister out with him. He had a drink with a neighbour, and "borrowed" the bottle of gin. Then, with Taz, he wove his way back along the street and prepared to cross. By this time, he seemed to have lost his grasp of the fact that he had a small child in his care, so that

Taz lagged behind him, watching, she recalls, with fascination. He would bump into a front fence of a house, veer off and then bump into a tree on the edge of the nature strip, and bounce back towards another fence. Taz thought this was a joke or a dance. She wasn't quite sure which.

The joke took on a macabre aspect as he started across the street. Although we lived in a quiet suburban street, my father looked right and then left and then right again. He waited. Until he saw a car approaching. Then he struck out, dodging and weaving. The driver was evidently in much the same state as my father, and he too was dodging and weaving. Taz, sitting on the edge of the road, was giggling at our father, who got out his handkerchief and waved it at the driver, as if he was a bullfighter. The driver leaned out of the car and yelled "Happy Christmas" then accelerated. My father, with a sudden burst of speed, jumped into the path of the oncoming car, bounced against the front mudguard, up onto the bonnet, up onto the roof and then off onto the road.

Taz thought it was all a joke and applauded joyfully, laughed even, and didn't believe it when she was told her father was dead.

Mum had to go to work and bring up her children and pay off her house in a climate not helpful to single women. She did this remarkably well. She always used to say, "I could never marry again; not after your father." As a child, I fantasised that my mother had loved my father so much that she would be eternally his. I wanted her to possess a great romantic love. I tried to imagine it, but it was hard, because romance wasn't in my mother's character. Now, when she says, "Marriage! Not after your father," I see determination not to be seduced into that institution ever again.

Taz was left with the legacy of seeing her father's dance with death as a comic performance put on for her benefit; and that she failed to grasp its significance. "I worry," she says, "that I'll miss something again. *You* have to keep an eye on *Mum*. Make sure she's all right. I can't bear the responsibility. I'll *pay*." She says this every Christmas, wrestling with pork or pudding or both.

"What if *I* miss something and she dies?" I ask.

"Then we're even. One parent each."

Taz is no longer five years old and knows exactly what's going on, but I can't say that to her. So I take the responsibility for the aging of our mother, which consists of helping her look after other old people and not disagreeing with her neo-fascist views, because this would only increase her blood pressure and make me responsible for a stroke or her death from some other cause.

I feel a gap in my life at Christmas. I'd like more warmth, more happiness and less tension. "Margarine commercial again!" says Taz.

My mother had the authority of a mother, but not the instincts. We were taught not to dawdle, not to sniff, to keep our fingernails clean, our rooms tidy and do our homework. But there was no sweeping us up into the maternal bosom, no family jokes. Fun was when my mother decided the family needed an outing like going to the park or walking to the shop to buy biscuits. So we had secret fun, just Taz and me.

I overcompensated with my own children, teaching them how to have fun when I should have been teaching them survival skills. But now, at Christmas, family feeling and family fun have dissipated. There's none of the compensating excitement and hysteria of little children that I love so much. I long for meaning, love, rejoicing and hope – all those things that surge through you when you sing carols.

Nevertheless, I still look forward to Christmas, and even take pleasure in its traumas. We continue to repeat the old patterns, with new disasters. One year the kitchen caught fire. One year *I* caught fire trying to light the brandy and spent the day in the burns unit at the local hospital, which was packed with festive revellers. One year the new kitten got run over in front of the kids. "It's better than seeing your own father run over," Taz consoled the kids, and told them about the bizarre death of their grandfather, which didn't actually help them come to terms with the death of the kitten, or mortality in general.

We've also had theft (Genevieve's first boyfriend – age ten – stole all our Christmas presents and gave them to his family, but forgot to remove the gift tags); drugs (Maggie tried smoking one of the garden plants and had to have her stomach pumped); sex (Genevieve caught en flagrante aged sixteen); hail damage; raw pork; a pogo stick and a broken arm; suppurating blisters from much loved, but too small shoes and paper stuffed up Sam's nose by Maggie when he was a baby.

So I wasn't surprised, early on Christmas morning, to get a phone call from Mum's neighbour to tell me Mum had broken her leg and had been taken to hospital. "Bugger!" I yelled in the privacy of my car. "Stupid, bloody idiot woman!"

But by the time I got to the hospital Mum was busy doing her version of sweet, slightly dotty old lady for the assembled staff. I'm the only one able to detect the malice in her accident which was caused by pushing down the rubbish in her wheelie bin. To understand how this could happen, you have to realise that my mother is a small, rotund person who likes to keep her rubbish well down in the bin. She had performed the rubbish compacting so thoroughly that she had toppled head first into the bin, which proceeded to topple over. Trying to break its fall, she had broken her leg. I had to call all the people we had lined up for Mass, which was complicated by the fact that they had all turned their hearing aids off.

By the time I had made the calls, Mum was in plaster, ready for Christmas festivities and playing to the gallery. "Isn't she marvellous?" the staff murmured as she struggled out on crutches.

"It would break Tania's heart," Mum told the nurse who helped us to the car. "That's pronounced *Tania* as in *lasagne*, if I missed Christmas lunch."

Mum said she had no pain in the broken limb and even if she did, *we* certainly wouldn't hear about it, certainly not at Christmas. I could feel the tension in my back teeth. By the time we got to the apartment, Taz was immersed in a bad temper and was having words with the pork. Mum had not stopped talking about not talking about the pain in her leg. But Sam was happy, standing on the landing, smoking.

"Happy Christmas, Grandma."

"I broke my leg dear. Tussle with the wheelie bin."

"Geez, bet you gave the wheelie a going over."

"I'll be out later and join you for a fag, my sweet."

I settled Mum in the living room and went to see Taz.

"Pork trouble?" I asked.

"Mum trouble," she said. "I can't stand it. This broken leg."

"Well, you noticed. That's something."

"It's not the not noticing," she said. "That's just a joke. I just can't bear to see another parent die. And she's going to, I know."

"Nothing surer," I said. "But probably not today."

"This sort of thing is the start," said Taz. "*All* old people break their hips before they die."

"She's broken her leg, not her hip."

"It's going to send me crazy," said Taz.

"It's supposed to make you sad, not cross," I said.

"*You* don't understand," said Taz. She tipped the pork out of the roasting pan trying to get it into the frying pan. It slipped onto the floor. She picked it up, uncooked but horribly hot and ran it under the tap, while I ineffectually wiped the greasy bit on the floor.

"Go away!" she said, as if I were responsible for everything from our father's death to this latest tragedy. "I can't do anything with *you* here." I was the little sister, who couldn't understand the depth of Taz's tragedy, which was clearly being replayed in a porcine form. My tragedy was simply being the little sister with no tragedy, so I got a bottle of champagne out of the fridge and went in to keep Mum company in the living room. She had her plastered leg up and her crutches proudly displayed.

"Look at that face," she added as Taz, tearful and red faced, swept past. "She's saved it all for a rainy day."

"You save *money* for a rainy day, Mum."

"And misery," said Mum. "Misery loves bad weather."

It was actually hot, with a blue sky. Champagne was my defence against reality. I drained my glass quickly and felt a surprising Christmassy happiness.

"A job," said Mum. "Have you done anything about a job?"

"I'm going into retail," I said, although I hadn't found anything more about the training programs. I do procrastinate. The current idea is that you're supposed to face up to things straight away, but if you can hang out and avoid unpleasantness, they do actually go away. Well, sometimes. And it would be a ghastly world if everyone rushed round in an officious way and got things done the moment they needed to be attended to. I don't know what Stephen Hawking said about it in *A Brief History of Time*, because I've put off reading it, but I think time should be a little frayed round the edges.

"Don't be silly, you're a teacher," said Mum. "I read there's a shortage of teachers in maths, but a surplus of primary teachers. You'll miss getting your application in. Then you'll have to do another medical and what with your weight . . ."

"I don't want to teach, Mum. I'm going into retail."

"Taz says you're not fit for anything else," she said. My mother tried to soften her own opinions by attributing them to Taz.

"Who's that there with Sam?" I asked, to shift the attention away from the question of my future. Sam's hair had gone black at the roots and he now looked like a normal, evil teenager. It was Boaz, laughing with Sam in Taz's courtyard where they seemed to be sharing a joint. I don't want people thinking I'm soft on drugs. The truth was I didn't know what Sam was smoking. It was the way he and Boaz were passing it to one another and giggling that made me suspect it was dope. And in truth, I didn't think dope was any worse than alcohol. And I didn't want to make a scene on Christmas Day. Mum would have been horrified — she was generally in favour of hanging drug users, but she is convinced smoking is good for your health.

"The doctor told me," she often argued with Genevieve. "He said it would be a danger to give it up at my age."

"Then he ought to be struck off," said Genevieve, which cut no ice with Mum.

My mother looked fondly at Sam. "He's a lovely boy." The champagne was working and I felt a warm glow of approval creeping over me.

Then Genevieve arrived, kissed Boaz passionately, and kindly examined her grandmother's leg. She *was* different with Boaz around. More human.

Finally, lunch was declared ready. Taz and I ate the crackling while Genevieve clicked her tongue in disapproval and Sam ate the undercooked meat. Boaz, besides having the wispy ponytail, had the annoying habit of making moral pronouncements. He told us about all the antibiotics and hormones fed to pigs, while Genevieve looked at him adoringly and stupidly.

Mum muttered "greasy" not quite under her breath. After she'd had a bit to drink, she was legless. It's not a pleasant thing taking your mother to the toilet, Christmas Day or not, your older sister too pained to give moral support. We got into a terrible muddle with her underpants and the crutch (the wooden one, not the real thing) and then I annoyed her because I couldn't stop giggling. We had the crackers and the full catastrophe pudding, with brandy and flames and overheated conversation.

We exchanged presents no-one really wanted with false cries of delight. Except for Taz's presents which are always brilliant. She gave me a blue and white striped kitchen jug that conjured up yellow and white daisies without having to even buy the flowers. As well, I got another leather-bound Dickens to hide from Lucy; *Bleak House*, which is my favourite. She gave Sam an "8 Heads in a Duffelbag" video that is his absolute favourite, Genevieve a dress that she really liked, Mum a tin opener that looks old fashioned, but which she could actually work. The rest of us exchanged gifts to be recycled, or in Sam's case, sold. It was a good family Christmas.

The phone rang when I was in the loo. They were all drunk and laughing when I came back and Taz told me it was Maggie, who couldn't hang on because she had no money and nobody bothered to ask where I could phone her back, or where she was, or when she was coming home, and if she was sick with intestinal parasites, which I knew to be fearsome in India, or whether she had an incurable tropical disease.

"She's in love with a man called Lucas," said Mum as consolation.

"He's a Marxist revolutionary," said Taz.

"God, I didn't know such people still existed in the modern world," said Genevieve.

"Maybe they'll do something really cool and get jailed for life," said Sam.

"I hope he's not dark," said Mum. "An Injun."

At which I had a Christmas rage at everyone for being so smart about Maggie and me having been waiting for this call, and feeling hopeless about her and wondering if she'd ever come home and whether his name was really Lucas and why my daughters fell in love with unsuitable people. I noticed that Boaz and Sam were smoking out on the terrace again and Boaz was saying something about herbal alternatives to a rapt Sam. Taz poured me more champagne, which reconciled us.

Late in the afternoon, Rosanna turned up, very drunk, with David. They were hand in hand, and I knew he had never really pursued me because his heart was with her. That night he asked me out was probably a night when she was taunting him. I told myself, in an incredibly mature fashion, that he hadn't treated me badly and we'd had a nice evening, at least until the end when we'd never got to bed. I was just a little resentful that Rosanna, who was so good looking and full of brilliant ideas, had it all over me and always would. I still thought having a lie-in on a Sunday morning was one of the greatest ideas ever. *And* had passed the test of time.

David should have been embarrassed, but he detached himself from Rosanna and came and sat beside me and we had a long chat about families and Christmas. He'd seen his demented mother that morning and he'd felt he couldn't spend another Christmas sitting at her bedside when she didn't know whether he was her son or Father Christmas. It was all so desperately sad that he'd tracked down Rosanna and they'd had too much to drink and he was glad to see me, and I was lucky to have my children, bar Maggie, with me. I looked at the red-eyed Sam lounging out in the courtyard with Boaz and Genevieve in love and mushy.

David saw my leather-bound copy of *Bleak House*. It was his favourite Dickens too. We had other authors in common – Stephen King, Raymond Chandler and Peter Carey.

"We should have dinner again," he said.

"Maybe," I said. "I'm working really long days though, and I'll be doing a training course in the New Year." Really, I should have told him if he didn't want to sleep with me and if he did prefer me to Rosanna, he could forget it, because I had better things to do with my time. Like dipping into *Bleak House* and watching TV and eating Eat U Rite choc chip muffins all day.

But he was a lot better than the two romances (relationships? encounters? dalliances?) I'd had in the ten years since the Ex had divorced me. One had been an army major, with all that implies, and the other had been a deputy principal, with all that implies.

"Can I phone you?" he asked.

"Sure," I said, but in a very casual way. He wandered off and when I saw him with an arm round Rosanna again I thought it was possible I didn't understand mid-life dating mores. Maybe you went out with people and didn't sleep with them. Maybe there was no more lust or love or romance any more.

After David left, Rosanna saw Boaz out on the terrace and said, "Ohmigod. Boaz!"

"Do you know him?" Taz and I and Mum pounced for the lowdown on Boaz.

"He's a lovely guy," said Rosanna. "And a great shag." She looked at my mother sideways as a sort of apology at this crudity, but I could see Mum was actually trying to relate Boaz to the bird species of the Great Shag, her slang being anything but current.

"How do you know him?" asked Taz and I thought we'd get a blow by blow account of the great shag. What we got was worse.

"It was all a terrible misunderstanding," said Rosanna. "I was in a horrible, 'I want a rich husband' stage."

"He's not rich," I said, cutting to the chase.

"But I didn't know that, because *he's* looking for a rich wife," explained Rosanna. "So we're both trying to impress each other with how at ease we are in the world of wealth and power. We both spent a fortune. Then one night, we were at this fantastically expensive restaurant and I realised I was up to the limit on the Amex. I was sick of husband hunting anyway. I didn't want to marry him however rich he was, because he's thirty, absolute tops, and he paints these yellow circles which are a clever idea in the abstract, but not going anywhere. Which was why I thought he was rich – to be able to do something totally wanky like that. But it's why he's poor, actually. And he was at the same stage with me. And it all came out and we had a good laugh at us both being predatory and shallow."

"So who paid?" asked Mum, who lost the point of the story.

"Oh, we did a runner," said Rosanna. "Which was fun and so romantic that afterwards we ..."

But I cut her off. "I think I should warn Gen," I said, getting up.

"I don't think so," said Taz, pulling me back down.

"I'll have a chat to her," said Mum. "As the experienced older woman." Occasionally, Mum would pull the age card.

"Experienced at what?" said Taz, who still had shades of Christmas snitchiness about her.

"Life," said Mum, but a bit uncertainly. Taz, as her elder daughter, could intimidate her sometimes.

"I'll talk to her," said Rosanna.

"You tell her, Rosanna," said Mum. "Tell her sex is a terrible thing."

"I will," said Rosanna and winked.

❀   ❀   ❀

I went home and played the Beach Boys "Don't Worry Baby" a couple of times and then dropped in on neighbour Katie Bless You and her perfect family and got some bones for Lucy. Then I took Lucy over to Tookie's place. Lucy's like a perfect toddler – she gives enthusiastic kisses when she arrives and then goes straight to sleep. I gave Tookie a Christmas cake I wished I'd baked myself and listened to all the stuff she'd been doing on what had became my case, and her stern views on how capitalist Christmas is. We had cheap port and muscatels and it was calm and familiar. I went home and slept with Lucy next to me in preparation for the Boxing Day sale.

❀   ❀   ❀

"You'll be finishing after New Year," said the supervisor, "But you'll come back Thursday nights, won't you? We need you Thursday nights, Leah."

"I'd like to be full time," I said. "And do some training to become a..." but it trailed away because I'd forgotten what the new name for buyers was.

"What?" she said.

"I'd like to become full time and do some training courses," I said, but my confidence was ebbing.

"Leah," she said, "I'm sorry, but you're too old, dear. This job takes a lot of energy. It's the sort of thing you have to grow up with. I've got a bunch of kids starting training next week. They're seventeen and eighteen. You've got to start young."

I was so humiliated that I never wanted to go back, but seeing as Thursday night was my only source of income, I went into the change room intending to have a controlled cry, but had a short sulk instead because I realised I hadn't really wanted to be a merchandise co-ordinator. At the end of the night I told her I was going down the coast for two weeks with my son, secretly hoping I'd dream up a new career on my holiday.

Sam and I and his mate Filthy (derived from the perfectly good name Phillip) went down the south coast and stayed in a run-down caravan in a run-down caravan park. (Not at all like "Surfin' USA".) I always wish we could afford a tropical island because the south coast isn't quite hot enough for me and the caravan park is sufficiently down market to host a Bible convention, the members of which are always at you, promising fun in the marquee tonight and salvation by morning, and a little tract to put under your pillow while you sleep. We've been going there long enough that all my children have had at least one holiday where they've been saved, only to revert to type when we get back home. Mind you, being saved isn't that great in my book. It's not as if it made them any better helping with the washing up. Last year, Sam seemed to get in with the born again, everybody let's get stoned crowd, who had access to some ungodly drug.

There's a terrible loneliness being a single mum. At the start, you think the kids will be enough. I even thought I might be a better parent, because I'd devote all my time to the kids. But the fact is, they didn't want all my time. They got bored with me, although sometimes, out of kindness, they let me do motherly things like play Scrabble or go swimming. Eventually that was untenable, because they couldn't bear any of their friends to see them in the company of a mother (especially their own) and they just wanted my money.

At night, in van land, I lay on the narrow bed, and felt the hole in the doona cover where my toe always got caught. I felt the pillows I'd had for too many years and which had been on too many beach holidays. I felt the hardness of the bed, the slight clamminess you always get in a caravan, the remnants of sand, the sadness of lying here alone, as the little kids ran round with torches spotting possums and the Christians had riotous fun in the marquee. I remembered the first time the Ex and I had come here and we'd tucked the kids in and made love as quietly as we could but the caravan still rocked and the kids in the annexe all appeared at the door of the van and asked if it was an earthquake, and how later we made love trying not to move and giggling and kissing and just loving each other. And now, the girls were long gone and Sam and Filthy were down the beach with a fire and I was all tucked up with my life passing before my eyes.

The days on the beach were better. Hot sun, cold, clear water. I enjoyed the solitude.

And then there was teaching Sam to drive. It was supposed to be a bonding experience, but it turned out to be a non-event.

We got into the car, he turned it on, drew out onto the road and drove round as if he'd been doing it all his life.

"I'll teach you to park," I said.

"Watch me!" He drew up alongside another car, moved my car carefully back, turned quickly and slid in beautifully against the curve, straightened up, and turned and smiled at me. "Okay!"

"How do you know how to drive?" I said. "I mean, that was amazing."

"I watched you. I watched Dad."

"But you *criticise* me all the time," I said.

"That's how I learned," said Sam, "your mistakes."

"I've never had an accident," I said.

"Not as such," he replied.

I pulled myself together. "Well darling, I'm sure you'll be an excellent driver." But we'd lost the moment. I sounded like a kindergarten teacher, then I remembered that I wasn't.

"I *am* an excellent driver," he said, grinning at me.

❀　　❀　　❀

Tookie kept on my case. The week after I was back from the coast, she was on the phone.

"Leah, there's a job out past Campbelltown – very big new school. I think the infants alone is about four hundred and they need someone first term."

"It'd take me an hour and a half to get there."

"It's better than sitting at home all day."

"I can't."

"Leah."

"Don't lecture me . . ."

"I don't lecture you," she said, "but I will point out you've got no savings, a mortgage and a child to support."

"Now you've cheered me up . . ."

"It's got nothing to do with cheering you up or not. Those are facts."

"Shut up, shut up." I didn't exactly say that, but I tried to convey it with my silence.

"Leah?"

"I'm not going back to teaching."

"It would look much better for this action the Federation may be running if you were teaching."

"It's got nothing to do with the bloody Federation. This is *my* life."

"Except you're not doing anything. School starts in two and a half weeks."

"I know."

"I'll come round Friday. Have a cup of coffee with you. Try to talk some sense. Is that okay?" She was using the voice she uses on recalcitrant six year olds.

I sent the CV off to the school at Campbelltown, with a good letter. I knew I should ring. I knew I should follow up, but I just couldn't.

❊   ❊   ❊

I forgot about Friday coffee with Tookie, because Sport and Rec rang me up to take some of the "learn to swim" classes at the local pool, which I do every year. I took the job because I like it and because it stopped me thinking about a real job. Swimming teaching goes like this: they schedule it for the rainy part of January. You get a class of six kids who, with wet hair and goggles, all look remarkably similar.

There's usually a prowling mother who works in child development and hovers during the whole lesson giving me pointers on understanding her child's vulnerabilities and insecurities. Getting the kid to swim seems the last thing on her mind. Then there's the child from the large family whose siblings are off to other classes and whose mother is going off to cappuccino land with the fatal words, "You don't mind keeping an eye on them if I'm late, do you?" There's always one child who is blue with cold and phobic about water who says with potent dread, "What does 'sink like a stone' actually mean, miss?" Then there are over-confident kids who jump straight in and sink like a stone, and need to be retrieved coughing and spluttering.

When the hovering mother goes away, I give full rein to my primitive emotions. I use a mixture of threats, bribes, competitive urges and other forms of harassment. At the end of the two weeks, most of them were swimming and feeling good about it. I was feeling good about it too, because I'd done a fine job with all of them, and had really given them something.

Whereas I was sunburnt and waterlogged, and was still nursing bitterness about my dismissal from Grevillea and the knowledge that Twisted would block me getting another job. I needed to find something else, which felt like a great yawning pit, so I avoided it and immersed myself in the back to school sales, praying something would turn up.

❀   ❀   ❀

I avoided my sister and my mother and Tookie and Katie Bless You. There had been no phone call from David. I came home tired with sore feet to find the house was as much a disgrace as I'd left it that morning, which I explained to Sam, after I'd opened the curtains and turned off the TV.

"I washed my clothes the other day," he protested.

"And you left them in the washer. You're like a baby, Sam. They were practically growing mould by the time I found them."

76

"You told me not to use the dryer."

"We have a clothes line. I'm so sick of this. I go out to work every day. I come home I expect the place to be halfway decent but it's worse than when I left. You're just a bludger. You won't do anything to help yourself. You won't help me. What do you think it's like living with you?"

"Well, I think it's okay."

"Well it's not. You're supposed to pay for the petrol. And it was nearly empty this morning."

"That wasn't me!"

"And there's a scrape on the side."

"That was you, Mum! That car had scrapes before I started driving it. Now every single one you blame on me! But you know, you did them and you wouldn't even notice."

This was actually true, so being on shaky ground, I let it go. "Well what constructive thing have you done these holidays? Just one thing?"

"I've given up smoking and you haven't even noticed. Boaz helped me."

"Boaz helped you stop smoking," I said. "I suppose you just smoke dope with him now."

"Not much. But sometimes. Gen says it's better than fags as long as I don't smoke too much and get psychotic. Don't you think it's good I've given up smoking?"

But I was on a roll now. I didn't care. "You can't smoke if you're in bed fifteen hours a day so I don't think it's all that great an achievement. And what have you done about your schoolwork, looking at your books, organising your room? You're hopeless Sam, totally hopeless."

Silence. Passive-aggressive body language.

"Sam! I'm out there slaving for you. *I'm* trying to help you."

"I don't want you to."

"I'm your mother. I put the food on our table, the roof over our heads. While you lie in bed. And I can't rely on you ..."

"Mum." Sam looked at me. Straight. Serious. "I'm sorry. I'm no good at that stuff. You know that."

"I certainly do know it. You're throwing away everything I've ever done for you."

"Mum, I'm seventeen. It's not like I'm an axe murderer."

"Fantastic! Congratulations!"

"Look, I've given up smoking. That may not seem much to you. But Boaz said ..."

"Boaz!"

"He's a really cool guy."

"Yeah, he paints yellow circles and uses women. And don't you tell Genevieve I said that."

"Why not?!" yelled Sam. "You have all these rules about what you can say, and I'm supposed to be nice about people like Dad, but you're allowed to go off your brain at me. You tell me, don't criticise your sisters but then *you* pour shit on a really good person like Boaz. I saw you act so nice to Boaz at Christmas. One day Dad's a good guy, the next he's evil. You're a fucking hypocrite, Mum. A bloody hypocrite."

And then he stormed out and I tried to repress all the terrible things I'd said to him about him being totally hopeless and the fear he'd tell Genevieve what I said about Boaz. And I tried to suppress my disappointment with him and my fury and my upset that I'd yelled at him and the fact that shameful scenes like this littered my relationships with all my children, but I told myself all mothers do it and if the Ex had stayed it would be different, except it had been the same when he was here, but maybe I would have grown out of my temper and short fuse.

No wonder David had never called again.

❈   ❈   ❈

The next morning school started. I woke round six o'clock and tried to find the piece of paper Tookie had given me with all the schools I'd sent my CV off to. Some of them had sent acknowledgments, but no-one had rung up or said they were interested. That wasn't how it worked. I should have rung them. I should have lobbied and got other people to call. I found the piece of paper, all crumpled and smudged, but you can't ring at six so I went back to bed. I lay there, watching the eggshell blue sky get bluer, and saw Jack the cat climbing up the cotoneaster outside my window and look in at me as if he'd never seen me before. I felt like a stranger in my own life too. I lay there as I heard Sam in the kitchen and out the door, without even saying goodbye, because we still weren't speaking.

I got up at nine and began making calls, but it was no good because all the jobs were gone. I didn't want to teach anyway, I told myself. In teaching, I'd been crushed, used and abused. Finally, I realised I had better think about this problem known as my life.

Chapter 4

The optimist's theory of middle age is that the addition of years has been enriching – in the scope of possibilities, in the depth of perception, in the development of one's sense of the world and oneself. Imagine Leah's distress when she discovers this airy optimism is a deception. Not only have her options decreased, but she fears that her ability to cope, her flexibility, her very sense that life is wonderful, are sadly diminished.

The reality that I was no longer a teacher hit me that first day of the new term. The memories of first days kept running through my head – the new kindies, their tearful mothers, the rows of fresh faces, the new uniforms, the anxious ones, the tense ones, the out of control ones, the ones who slotted in as if school was their place in life. Whereas I was back home, out of the shower, getting dressed, trying not to fall into the unemployed lifestyle. That's not meant to sound derogatory. I have nothing against watching Oprah Winfrey, and if any poor devils are entitled to a lifestyle, it has to be the unemployed. But I was going to be out of the house by lunch, making Oprah watching impossible.

The *Telegraph* had a supplement on "getting your first job". There was an article about the man who looked after the polar bears at the zoo, which I didn't think was quite me, along with a woman in human resources whose photo made her look totally inhuman. There were articles about bright young things called Chelsea and Felicity and I thought, with the name Leah, I didn't do too badly in the name stakes. At least Mum hadn't called me Lynette and frozen me in time forever.

But the jobs I was familiar with from my youth – like bus conductresses, clerks and shop girls – seemed to have gone, and although there were still secretaries and receptionists, youth was at a premium. The jobs in education were all for deputy heads or Maths teachers in the western third of the state. No cosy primary jobs at all.

I took fate in my hands with the "More Beautiful in ten minutes at home! Economical too!" kit. The purpose of "More Beautiful in ten" was to dye my hair red and my eyebrows brown, which took a lot longer than ten minutes. There was a splodge of dye that wouldn't come off under my ear, but it was generally an improvement, especially after a blow dry and a bit of gel which gave it a spiky look – the hair, not the eyebrows. I rang the bank and found out how much money was in my account. Enough to feed us for a week or two. Nor had the Mastercard quite run dry.

I rang the local employment centre (actually an unemployment centre) and was assigned to a case worker. She couldn't see me for two weeks owing to staff shortages ("Employ me! employ me!"), but she said she'd send me the forms so I could claim benefits. Unfortunately, there was nothing she could recommend over the phone as a job, she'd try and help as soon as she had a minute, but it was really up to me. This was a new policy initiative – the government didn't like unemployed people sitting on their bums and watching Oprah. She said there might be something extra I could claim for Sam, to educate him. Though I didn't know if that was possible, I kept my mouth shut and thought it would at least buy us a couple of takeaway pizzas every week.

I got off the phone and did a quick circuit of the house with the Spray and Wipe, stacked the dishes and felt a "Sound of Music" cheerfulness, which took me whirling out of the house, into the car, up to the mall to get a looking-for-a-job outfit. Underwear first because that was on sale and secondly because I still nursed a hope that David might be interested. Then, a very depressing look at the clothes which were either tiny garments or very matronly or made my red hair look very flaming red and very dyed. I bought a cheap, highly flammable, faux silk, grey shirt and some fake pearls and cheapish new pants. I knew the trouser fabric all too well as the sort that gets little balls on it where your legs rub together. Finally, I got a cheap pair of shoes. The credit on the card was reduced to a sad level.

But I was still full of the "can do" confidence. There was a notice pinned up saying "Work available. Ask at counter" at the Home Bakke Breadde Shoppe. I asked, but the job was only Saturday and Wednesday afternoons and the man thought I was asking for one of my children, and I wondered why all the jobs were for children. I got another copy of the *Telegraph* and a red pen, and went to a coffee shop and ordered a capp and a piece of cheesecake. I had a hollow feeling in my stomach, either due to the job situation or no breakfast. But when I marked things with my red pen, it went through to the other side so the whole paper was a mess of red marks that meant nothing. I felt petulant because I had wanted ice cream with my cheesecake which they hadn't given me. But when you're size sixteen, it's embarrassing to kick up a fuss about not getting your ice cream.

There was a story in the paper about a poor old man eating dog food and I tried to remember how many tins we had left and how long it would last Lucy, Sam and me. I thought Lucy and Sam could have it and I'd get thin. Maybe that's what they call negative thinking.

I decided to make a list, using the paper serviette and the runny red pen.

Schools – phone. I didn't want to teach, but I had to be practical. But there wasn't much chance anyway. In addition to her other qualities, Twisted could organise a hate campaign effectively. Not everyone would believe her, but it would be easier not to employ me. Part of my brain said to keep ringing schools however far away they were and eventually I would find a job, even if it was on the other side of the mountains. I had a moment of imaginary heroism, seeing myself driving through mountain fog and sleet every day. But something, apart from procrastination, had been at work. I used to think teaching was a great job, but nobody else did. It was as if teaching had sucked my soul in and then spat it out. I crossed out school phoning.

Instead, *Get new skills* went down on the serviette. The Ex had sent Sam a computer last year to help him with his schoolwork. Sam is not a person who is interested in computers, or in schoolwork for that matter. In fact, just as the computer arrived he'd failed computer science for the third time and had finally dropped the subject. So the machine just sat there, out of its box, the cords still tied up in neat bundles. I knew where the on/off switch was, I had learned some of the literacy programs at school with the help of my more computer literate six year olds. Surely I could master other programs. Except what other programs?

That led me to the number three item which was *Ring Taz*. There's an odd process which goes on when I call Taz. It's called big sister/little sister. As big sister she has stock phrases.

"If you look at this in perspective ..."

"Taking a rational view ..."

"There are a couple of ways to approach this ..."

"If we can just look at the issues ..."

This is totally infuriating.

On my part are silences, theatrical protests, teethgrinding, a sense of deep despair or unassailable optimism, wild flights of fancy and sweeping generalisations. She finds this infuriating.

So why did I phone Taz? Because really and truly, I did not know what to do. Because under all the "can do" and the "she'll be right" was a horrible panic. At this point, I was tempted to order more cheesecake. There had to be something else I could do besides teaching and eating, someone else I could be. Being stuck with Leah Jarrett, forty-five years old, unemployed infants' teacher, single mum, size sixteen, felt too horrible.

"I'll take you to lunch," I told Taz. "Because I'm hoping you'll give me some free advice."

"I'm sure I will," she said with a laugh. "We'll go to that sushi place just along from my building."

"Okay," I said meekly. I like sushi, but it's not a food for depressed persons. When you're depressed and have sushi, you feel as if you need a real meal afterwards – something in the line of choc chip muffins.

I rushed home and changed into my new clothes to impress Taz with how hard I was trying, and then thought I should also be supermum and make Sam Eat U Rite choc chip muffins for when he came home after school. But I didn't, because he scorned such maternal indulgences, and anyway I was really making them for myself as comfort food after the sensible and rational advice Taz was going to give me. "Stop," I told myself, "I'm not falling for that any more."

No muffins and I was on the bus to town, not wanting to be late, pumping up my "can do, will do" attitude, trying not to panic, trying to imagine what I might do for a job, then having fantasies of how wonderful it might be. Sam might do his homework, we might be rich, he could be nice to me and become a responsible citizen (or even just a rung below that). Maggie might finally phone me and I could talk to Genevieve sensibly about Boaz and not falling for men with ponytails and poor job prospects.

The thing about Taz is she is impressive in a very definable sort of way. She started work as a receptionist and now she's a company secretary. It's only a mid-sized company, so she doesn't get paid a fortune, but it's a good income nonetheless. She works long hours and she takes it seriously in a way I never could. She's always fiddling about with reports on weekends and checking cash flows and telling me she's legally responsible if things aren't done properly, which tends to make kindergarten teaching sound fun.

I got to the sushi bar before her which seemed like good karma. I sat nursing that tea that looks as if the chef has heated up the water from the fish tank, but is very soothing once you dismiss that piece of imagery. As Taz was coming along the street, I saw her check her hair in a shop window, the same place I'd checked my hair. I checked my hair because I knew she'd check my hair. But she checked her hair to set me an example of how checked hair should look. And I knew already that my gelled-up coif had fallen a little. And my new clothes didn't even look so new. I swear the trousers were rubbing already, making those little pills of acrylic.

That was the superficial part of the sister experience, but it is important to mention, because it set the tone for what followed.

"What do you *want* to do?" asked Taz.

"I want enough money to live comfortably," I said. "More than teaching but I'm not greedy. And I don't want to work at night or on weekends or any of that stuff. I'd still like plenty of TV time and not be too tired to read in bed at night." It sounded realistic to me.

Taz looked at me as if I were mad. "Yes, but what do you actually want to *do*? What are your *ambitions*?"

"I don't know," I said, although secretly I thought TV time and reading passed muster as ambitions. I had never had any burning aspirations.

Taz looked cross. "Leah, this is serious."

"I know," I said and blurted out the whole story of looking in the paper and buying the new clothes and dyeing my hair and eyebrows and not wanting to go back to teaching.

"If you look at this in perspective," said Taz, "you can

see it's a real problem. You are forty-five, and you've never done anything except teach."

"And work at Target," I said, expecting her to dismiss this, but she didn't.

"That's good actually," she said. "Dealing with the public..." I didn't explain it was only the public's rejects I dealt with, picking up their dirty socks so to speak, not the public as such.

"If we can just look at the issues," she said. "First, I guess you need something fairly quickly." I thought she meant in the sushi line, so I called the waiter and we ordered, but she explained she meant in the job line. I was not as focused on this problem as she was.

"I do need something quickly," I said when I'd eaten a few delicious prawns and downed my miso soup. "I don't have much in the way of savings." When we were children, Taz had always saved her money in a large pink pig money box, whereas I always spent mine on iceblocks. It had pretty much stayed that way.

"The first thing is to look at your skills," she said. She produced a clipboard and a pen.

"I can make the kids laugh," I said.

"That's a sense of humour," she said sternly. "It's a personality characteristic, not a skill." The thing is Taz has a good sense of humour, but sometimes, she gets dead serious and then absolutely *everything* is serious. "Skills are tools you have learned to use in the workplace to perform your job in a way you couldn't if you didn't have that tool." She looked at me expectantly. I was tempted to argue sense of humour as a skill, but I didn't.

"I can get up in front of people and keep their attention," I said.

"Children," she said with a slight note of dismissiveness.

"They're harder," I said.

She thought for a moment. "I guess you're right," she said. I swear she wrote "crowd control".

"I can explain things so that the kids understand them," I said. "I know how to break things down into steps and then teach each step, and adjust to kids learning at different rates." She looked slightly impressed and then began writing it down. I was on a roll. "I can make mistakes, admit them and move on. I'm standing up in front of the class, something goes wrong, and it isn't like it floors me. And," I said, thinking of the crowd control, "I can pick out the trouble makers and get them motivated. And I perform," I said. "I can adapt myself to perform what's needed. I'm also very quick at making shifts. *You* mightn't believe it, but I'm also very organised in my program. I have the kids for a year and I have a really clear picture where they should be by the end of the year. And that's an overall view but then I also have a micro view of each kid and where he or she can get to and I really bust my guts so they make it. Against, I might say, the opposition of parents sometimes, or the school."

"This is excellent Leah." Taz was scribbling crazily.

"Taking a rational view . . ." I was right into Taz's way of thinking now. "I can see I'm into problem solving . . ." As in how to stop Jenny Ford, precocious gymnast, climbing on top of the cupboard.

"Creative thinking." I'd picked up enough of the way Taz thought from her parties where I met all those high powered people.

"Multi tasking." Tying shoelaces and teaching reading at the same time.

"Event management." I'd organised the school athletics carnival for three years.

"Prioritising." Getting through parent–teacher nights, my priority being to get out of there in one piece.

"Sectionising." I didn't really have a clue what this meant or if I'd ever heard anyone say it, but it sounded like the sort of word Taz would use. But Taz snapped her folder shut.

"Great," she said. "I'll get Paula in HR to write it up, and we'll organise a CV for you. Now, if you're interested, I've developed a career path." She produced a piece of paper from her bag. With Taz, everything needs to be written down. She started creating a flow chart with bullet points down the side, stars all over the place and references at the bottom.

"You're in a good market position," she said, "Women with skills." She pointed to the chart. "Except your skills are general, so you need specific office computer skills to enhance the general skills." She pointed to another part of the chart marked *skills enhancement*. "You can work with tutorial programs to do that – there's a spreadsheet program, a basic typing program, a Word tutorial and some very basic accounting software. That's so when you go for an interview, you'll be able to tell them you can enter data, even if you can't use the programs very effectively." She pulled a box of computer disks out of her bag and handed them to me.

"What interview?" I said. She was way ahead of me.

"Spend a few weeks studying and practising these programs," she said. "Then," she pointed at the chart, "then you can apply for temping work. See the agencies listed here? You register with them. From there, you can start to think about office management. Don't do personal assistant. You aren't suited. You're too combative. [I felt like hitting her when she said that.] From office management, you might get into sales. Or perhaps something in marketing. I'll have a better idea when I've talked to Paula about your profile." She smiled at me. "Don't worry, I'll do your personality test. I can guess what you'd answer."

This didn't sound right, but I was looking in amazement at the figures along the side of the page. "I start at $22,000 a year, but I finish up at $90,000? How long does that take? I love the ninety, but I can't really afford twenty-two, you know."

"That depends on you," said Taz. "How hard you try."

I gathered up the tutorial disks and the piece of paper. "Thanks," I said. "That's really great." And I felt more grateful because it was great. I gave her a hug and then twirled round to show her my new clothes. "I am trying. See, I bought executive clothes."

But she looked at me dismissively. "You're going to have to get a proper wardrobe," she said, and opened her bag again. She handed me a cheque. "I'm lending you two thousand dollars. But I want it back by July because I'm going to Bali." Once, like about thirty years ago, Taz had lent me money and I'd forgotten to pay it back. And even though she has continued to lend me money, which I always pay back, she has continued to treat me as if I am a bad payer. She's the only person I could borrow money from, besides the evil Mastercard, but it always came with a bucketload of moral superiority, whereas Mastercard just charge you bucketloads of interest. I didn't even try to work out how I could possibly repay two grand by July, even if I got a job.

"And please," she said. "Get your hair coloured professionally. You have no idea how bad those home dyes look in the sun."

❋ ❋ ❋

You might think that lunch with Taz was better than sitting home watching Oprah. It was but it was ghastly too. Why? Because it was humiliating and demeaning. And true. I had a look in the bus window and the hair dye looked ghastly, and the false silk shirt looked like a housewife-teacher blouse rather than an executive blouse. And my handbag was scratched, and my shoes were scuffed at the heel and even though they were supposed to be comfortable, they weren't, the way cheap shoes never are. When you're a single parent, you learn to do a good job of stretching your money, but eventually, it gets to you.

I still felt hungry and was ruminating on Eat U Rite choc chip muffins when I got home, but I told myself that it was this sort of attitude which had seen me end up size sixteen. Another part of my head was saying it was Sam's first day back at school and maybe he needed mother love (AKA muffins) to encourage him to embrace the challenge of his final year of "education". Come on, Leah, I told myself, he's not seven years old. And I was going to be an executive, not a mother. In time, I wouldn't even have muffins in my head.

This train of thought stopped when I turned the corner and was catapulted back into reality. A police car was parked on the nature strip outside our house, with its blue light flashing. A woman, obviously very angry, and Sam, were standing by it. Sam, looking very hangdog and very like the child of a single parent with his shirt hanging out, was attached to a policeman who had him by the collar.

Silent prayer. Please God, don't let it be drug dealing or car theft, but just a high-spirited boyish prank (which probably is drug dealing or car theft these days).

When I puffed up and said, "I'm his mother, what's he done?" to the policeman, the very angry woman started screaming at me that he'd tried to kill her and she wanted him arrested. She then started yelling at the policeman about how hopeless the police service was and how the country was teeming with young thugs running loose. Sam raised his eyebrows and looked at me to say it was okay, he hadn't tried to kill the woman, so I tried to give him the look that said it *might* be okay, but how did he give this woman the impression he had tried to kill her? All this was hard to convey in significant glances.

And then she turned around, and I saw this ghastly red bloody thing on her neck where she was holding her hand. I screamed, from sheer terror, until I put things together, that even if she did have a gaping wound in her neck, she was still upright, walking and talking very crossly, even if the stuff coming out of her neck looked very scary. I turned to the policeman, who suddenly did seem very young and incompetent.

"Why don't you call an ambulance?"

"It's only a persimmon, ma'am." I looked again and I saw that it was only a persimmon. One of the overripe persimmons from our tree near the side fence – which allowed me to piece together the scenario pretty quickly – Sam and Filthy had been sitting on the fence and had idly decided that chucking ripe persimmons was a fun idea. They'd hit this woman and Filthy had taken off.

"It's evidence," the woman said, clutching the persimmon more closely to her neck.

"You can let it go, ma'am," said the policeman. "It's not really evidence and it's staining your coat."

"I'll pay to get your coat cleaned," I volunteered.

She started yelling at me. "What about my car? It's all over the seat. It's all over my shirt. What about nervous shock? I'm driving down here and I'm turning this corner and this thing comes in the window and I put my hand up and there's all this blood . . ."

"Persimmon," said the young copper.

"Well, I know that now," she said, "but I thought I'd been shot. I want him charged."

"You can't charge people with throwing a persimmon," said the copper. "He just needs a boot up the arse." He looked at me and actually winked and I suddenly realised the woman was as angry with the policeman as she was with Sam.

"He'll apologise," I said to her. "He'll pay. I'm sorry." And I was sorry, but I was glad it wasn't drugs or car stealing. And she was an awful woman and there wasn't that much persimmon juice on her jacket or her car. She kept ranting, so I made Sam say "sorry" very profusely, and I also got into the sorry saying until he nudged me to let me know I was overdoing it. The policeman explained about the good kick up the arse again, but was adamant he wasn't going to use police resources to charge dumb-arse kids with fruit chucking.

We backed into the house, where Sam realised it would be politic to say sorry to me. Then he told me it was really Filthy. I said I didn't care, because Sam should have stopped him because they were our persimmons, which ended up in a stupid argument about mateship and property. I was glad I hadn't made him the Eat U Rite choc chip muffins and I didn't really care how good or bad his day was because all the power and the glory and hope had suddenly drained out of mine. I thought nostalgically back to the holidays when he slept fifteen hours a day and was less prone to trouble.

I didn't do the arse kicking recommended by the young policeman, but I told Sam he was grounded and he had to do his homework and he couldn't watch TV, or ever have anything approaching a good time till I said so. I sat out on the back verandah with a cup of tea and Lucy's head on my lap and we talked quietly about the hole she was digging along Katie Bless You's fence, and how I'd like to bring our house up to neighbourhood standard.

And I was sitting there and thinking of Sam, and what to make for dinner, and I thought that one thing about teaching little children was that you stayed hopeful about life. You believed things did get better and would be all right. And while that wasn't actually true of life in general, it got into your consciousness. And I talked to Lucy about building a nice little sandstone terrace with a pergola and how she could stop digging and I'd come home from my flash new job and life would be great.

And at that moment Jack the cat dropped out of the sky and dug his claws into my neck, which was a message from him to me to feed him.

Then my mother called and gave me advice on getting a job, which seemed to consist of wearing gloves and crossing my legs nicely. Plus advice on how to lose weight. I was sad I couldn't tell her about Sam and the persimmons. I always felt I had to defend myself and the kids against the high standards she'd passed on to me in theory, but not in practice, which she felt was my fault, not hers. She was probably right, but I still managed to feel glad I didn't have to live the grey constricted days of my childhood any more, even if I was unemployed and Sam wasn't perfect.

❀ ❀ ❀

The Ex called late that night. Well, it seemed late but that was because I'd gone to bed early because watching the *X-Files* without Sam seemed like a particularly desolate and lonely thing to do and I was reading the lovely *Bleak House* again. Then I got up and caught Sam taping the *X-Files*, which seemed to go against the spirit of the agreement not to watch TV and we had a general argument about responsibility, especially focused on the fact that he had spent his non TV time dying his hair navy blue. I asked him if he'd rung KFC to get his job back to pay for the woman's cleaning, pointing out I was barely in a position to support him, let alone pay for his misdeeds. And then we had one of those strange conversations which make you wonder whether adolescent children live in a parallel universe.

"You haven't got a job?" he said. "I mean serious?"

"I haven't had a job since the end of last term."

"You coulda told me." Hurt tone.

"I did."

"You didn't, Mum. I woulda noticed something like that."

"I did."

"I don't think so. Anyway, do you want me to leave school and go to work full time?"

"Yes," I said.

"Seriously?"

Then I heard him on the phone to KFC saying he needed his job back because his mother was unemployed but he didn't want to work Saturday nights because that was "party night" and he had only given up his long-term devotion to KFC because he'd stopped smoking and he thought the KFC income would inevitably jump out of his pocket and buy cigarettes. I thought that he wasn't so bad and all he needed really was to get in touch with the conscious world. Or a good kick up the arse.

Then when the Ex called I forgot all about Sam because the Ex dropped a bombshell which sent my head flying in all different directions.

"I'm thinking of coming back to Sydney," he said. "I thought I'd let you know."

The cool ex-wife at this point would have said something very cool like, "Oh yes," but I wasn't the cool ex-wife. I bombarded him with questions.

"I think the business prospects are better in Sydney," he said.

I was puzzled. "For Queensland property development?"

"I'm thinking of doing something else." He sounded gloomy.

"Like what?"

"I thought I might do an MBA."

I tried to get my head around why a man with a prosperous business in commercial property development in Queensland would want to go back to university.

"An MBA isn't exactly a business prospect," I said.

"Well, short term," he said. "Anyway, it's only an idea. You know this life I've been leading gets pretty meaningless sometimes." There was sadness in his voice, but pompousness too, as if he knew something about the meaninglessness of life that I hadn't yet fathomed. "I'd like to see you too, Leah."

"What about seeing Sam?"

"Yeah, Sam too. I've been feeling bad about Sam since Christmas. I mean maybe that's one of the reasons for coming. You know, if I'm just around, it's not such an artificial situation, so there's less tension. I could take him to some sports events."

The way he said "sports events" sounded really phoney, which it was, because the Ex hated sport.

"He's not into sport."

"Yeah well, movies."

I didn't tell him that Sam would not want to risk being seen in the company of his parent in public. The Ex was better off being in another state if he wanted to go out with Sam. "You can try," I said.

"There are a lot of things we never sorted out, Leah. A lot of the big issues. And I think that whatever happens, we should. And we can, because we've stayed good friends."

"Suddenly very warm and fuzzy."

"Don't be like that. Come on."

"Okay. Maybe we should talk." But when I got off the phone, I had an odd feeling. I'd been hanging on all these years, imagining the happy family we'd once had, imagining that if he'd give me a chance, I could talk him into coming back, imagining he had really loved me all this time and Pouty Lips was the wicked witch who had stolen him. But now, I just felt resentful. I wasn't sure I wanted him to talk about all the things we never resolved. I couldn't even remember what they were, apart from him breaking the marriage vows, and I was actually a little less outraged about that now. Life's experiences had touched me. Divorce happens, I knew that. Even mine. Apart from controlled crying on anniversaries, I was used to it in an odd sort of way.

And then the romance intruded – reconciliation, growing old together, taking Sam to the football together (wish!). It took Jack biting my feet to bring me back to reality.

❀   ❀   ❀

Tookie popped round the next morning on her way to school and I felt an awful nostalgia, seeing her big bag, and with her clutching a pile of worn readers and her school cardie, and the schoolie look, which no-one in their senses would want, but made me feel full of longing. I must have looked ghastly because her face was full of compassion.

"Leah," she said. "Do what you want about a job. I've been too hard on you. This has all been such a terrible stress."

I thought she said mess, which was more like it, but when she explained she'd said stress, I began to feel as if my life was falling apart. "Oh Tookie," was all I could say. And she smiled her wonderful smile and patted me on the shoulder and I realised I didn't appreciate her enough, until she groped in her bag and produced a great big file.

"I want you to read that," she said, "and make corrections. It's a statement of what happened when you left. I promised them I'd get it in this week." My appreciation dropped about fifty per cent.

"You promised *them*?"

"The legal department of the Federation."

I handed it back to her. "Tookie, you know I can't read and correct things unless somebody holds a gun to my head. I'm sure you've written it right. I'll take your word."

"I would like to have it checked."

"I know you would," I said. "I'm not ungrateful, but I can't, not this week." Then I hugged her. "You're a wonderful friend and I really miss school because of you." And the funny thing was that when I was hugging her, I realised she smelled like an old teacher. Now don't ask me what an old teacher smells like, but it's something like school lunches and craft paste and photocopy ink mixed up. And when I smelled it, I didn't miss school any more, but I couldn't tell Tookie because she had tears in her eye and I had the feeling that me and this case meant far too much to her.

After Tookie left, I went and banked Taz's cheque. Then I went to an expensive, upmarket hairdresser who inflicted the sort of harrowing humiliation that only people in the beauty industry are trained to perform. Which is at about the same level as the secret police inflict in the less desirable South American dictatorships.

The fellow who did it looked like a smartly coifed Latino policeman and he immediately started the interrogation.

"You dye your hair at home?"

"Yes." Low and apologetic.

Then he left me for an hour with cold purple sludge on my hair before he ripped my head back and rinsed my hair with boiling water. Then he sprayed chemicals into my eyes.

Deep sigh. "It's very damaged."

"I guess it is." I knew a plea of poverty wouldn't cut with him.

"Remember, what we're doing is different from your usual style." He said "style" in a sarcastic way. "Big women need big hair to balance them. We don't want you looking like a little pinhead person, do we?"

I felt a surge of rebellion. Maybe I did want to be a pinhead.

"You really need a subtle colour at your age."

After hours of this, he made a snap judgment that I was sufficiently worn down by the pain and humiliation and was at a stage where he could get lots of money out of me. As I paid up, in the mirror next to the cash register I could see my face, red from sitting under their dryer. I had what looked like a small pink tinged animal curled up on my head. Anyway, it came to the price of six takeaway pizzas, which Sam and I could have enjoyed, had I stuck to the old home dyed red hair regime.

"Weren't you going to do my hair red?"

"It's mulberry, madam. We don't do red."

But I remembered Taz's lecture and pressed on to a boutique where they were extremely kind to me, which they should have been, given what they were charging. And then, joy! I bought myself some good, expensive, comfortable shoes. And then I added it up and realised it was a large amount of money, and I should keep what I had left for pizzas (or dog food).

Then I went home and, true confessions, watched Oprah, and thought it wasn't such a bad program or even such a bad way to spend my life. Everyone was very open and honest and Oprah was pretty kind – much kinder than the beauty parlour people. Then I remembered I had to pay

Taz back and I got out the computer and joined up the plugs and wires and got it going and even started work on one of the programs. I felt enthused when I did because it was not as baffling as I expected. Even where it was baffling, you only had to keep at it and it eventually became clear. It was a nice feeling, learning something new and hard.

Then Sam came home and didn't notice the small pink animal on top of my head, now considerably less sleek. But he did make me a cup of tea and said he didn't mind me being unemployed and showed vague interest in our future together. So that night, we watched the tape of the *X-Files* I'd banned the previous evening, and I went to bed with dreams of aliens and deadly viruses from the *X-Files* all mixed up with the accounting program I had been learning. At one point a large yellow dog invaded the accounting program, but when I woke up, I saw it was Lucy with her head on the other pillow. I spoke sharply to her, but she snored, pretending not to hear me.

"My darling Mama," said Genevieve. "Aunt Taz says you still haven't got a job." She sat at the kitchen table, in a sort of glorious disarray of red hair, blue shirt and a pair of paisley harem pants. "Sam told Boaz he had to go back to work at KFC because you were so poor."

"He had to go back because he owes a woman money to get persimmon stains out of her car upholstery."

"They're a bastard to get out. But they've got a very high vitamin C content, although *I* think they taste disgusting. I don't think Sam's very well adjusted, Mum."

Genevieve does that to me. Since she's got her medical degree she thinks it's fine to point out glaring deficiencies in the way I live my life or the way I've brought up my children (excluding her) and tell me the vitamin content of various foods. Pizza, she insists, has no nutritional value, which hardly explains how Sam is the big strapping boy he is, although maybe it explains why he needs to sleep fifteen hours a day.

"He's lovely," I said. "All boys are difficult at that age."

"Boaz thinks he's disturbed."

"How would Boaz know?"

"He's done psychology. He almost got a degree." She sounded almost impressed, which was odd from someone who actually had a medical degree.

"I thought he was an artist."

"He is. But he still knows other stuff. He's very deep, Mum."

"Did Rosanna tell you about her experience with the very deep Boaz?"

Genevieve rolled her eyes. "Mum! The way you and Taz interpreted that. I mean Rosanna's out there preying on young men, but no-one gives her a hard time. And just because Boaz is interested in money, that isn't why he's interested in me."

"He might be. That's all we're saying." I gave her the older woman "experienced in life" look and she gave me the "you're an old hag" look.

"The world's changed, you know," she said.

"Not much," I said. "It still goes round the sun and is inhabited by idiots."

She ignored that. "Did you hear about Dad and Jackie?" she asked. Which is the name she uses for Pouty.

"He told me they're thinking of coming to Sydney. Some mad stuff about doing an MBA."

"And *she* is going to get the lot," said Genevieve. "He's going to be left with nothing."

"You mean they're splitting up?" The penny finally dropped.

"I think so," said Genevieve. "There goes my inheritance! *She's* going to get every last cent. *He'll* lose everything!"

"Well, *I* know how that feels."

"You've never got over it, have you?"

"I have."

"It's awful having *two* parents going through a mid-life crisis," said Genevieve. "You're getting out of teaching, he's going back to uni. The wicked stepmother is taking all the money – again!"

"It's not a joke," I said. "It's people's lives."

"It *is* a joke, Mum. You'd go mad if it wasn't a joke." Genevieve sat back with her arms folded. That's Genevieve trying to be sympathetic. "Mum, really ..."

"It's just if it had lasted with your father and Pouty." I tried to explain how I felt. "She came in and wrecked our lives. If it's over with him and her, what's the point? It's all carnage and destruction."

Genevieve got up and put on the kettle, a sympathetic gesture she'd learned from her grandmother – "If you don't know what to do, give them tea, dear" – and I thought for a moment she might hug me, but she leaned back against the fridge.

"You take life too seriously," she said. "Things come and go. Forever's not forever. It's just as long as it's good. Anyway, maybe they're not splitting up. It's an educated guess on my part. She was as sweet as pie when I was talking to her the other day."

She could marry Boaz for all I cared.

That night, just when I thought I couldn't stand any more excitement, David phoned me. "I've got seats to a concert Monday night," he said, "and I was wondering if you'd like to come. It's mainly Bach, so if you like Bach ..."

The truth was I didn't know much about Bach to like or dislike him. My musical education started with Elvis Presley, then the Phil Spector Wall of Sound, especially the Ronettes, then the Beach Boys to whom I was still faithful. I then progressed through the Beatles and the Stones and stopped with Cyndi Lauper and Blondie, whose sun-twisted tapes still play on the old tape deck in my car though nowhere else. I've concentrated on the Wall of Sound and the Beach Boys. I'd got interested in them when Taz and Rosanna started buying their stuff in their early teens. Rosanna was an expert on cool, so I thought they must be cool. I guess it was my first betrayal when she and Taz moved on and began to despise them. I stuck with them, because I loved them so much. But Bach was neither here nor there.

"You know what worries me?" I said.

"What?" he said.

"I think you already asked someone else. Maybe Rosanna. Then, most likely, she dropped out at the last moment and you thought of the person least likely to have something on Monday night, so you asked me."

"No, actually, that's not true," he said. "It's worse than that, worse than you could ever imagine. The truth is, I was going to take Danni Minogue, but some old flame of hers came into town unexpectedly, so she didn't want to be seen out with me. So I phoned every other single woman in my little black book and they all refused me. So I went through the brown book, and they refused me. Then I found your phone number on a piece of paper sticking to the sole of my shoe, so I tried you. You still want to go?"

I laughed.

"Leah, I *want* to take you out, really," he said.

"I don't know about Bach. I mean apart from the name . . ."

"A beginning." But *he* sounded doubtful then.

"And I really don't know why you're asking me," I said. "You know the last date was fun, but it wasn't exactly sizzling."

"You want sizzle?"

"I want sizzle," I said.

"Can we talk about that?"

"Well, I just said it." Bach I didn't know and David I didn't know either. "So we are talking about it, aren't we?"

"I appreciate your honesty," he said, which is a sure sign of a person not appreciating your honesty. "But can we talk about it later, at supper? After the concert?"

"I wouldn't want to put any pressure on you," I said.

"Leah, I really like you," he said. "I find you very attractive. I want to go out with you. But I just need to talk to you about this – you know, before it goes any further."

"This is the sort of talk I give my kids before their first date," I said. "The only thing you haven't said is that we shouldn't take drugs before Bach."

"Well, that too," he said, and laughed, and I liked him again. A good laugh and blue eyes go a long way with me.

❀   ❀   ❀

Next morning, I was messing about with my accountancy program. I had a concept called a cash flow that I was working on, and another called a bottom line. I knew about the cheque writing program and scheduled payments and credit card break-up. I was going to start learning about different tax categories when Maggie rang. Maggie is my middle child, my wanderer. I'm never sure where I am with Maggie, but we've often been at odds. I remember when she first started crawling, she crawled away from me, whereas the other two crawled to me (with Sam it was affection, Genevieve exploitation). When Maggie was twelve, she decided to go to another high school from the one I'd chosen for her and went and enrolled herself – it was that sort of high school. When she got good marks in her final exams, she said to me firmly, "I'm not going to university, Mum. You need to get your head round that." And then went to Western Australia and then to South America. I sometimes feel I don't quite know her all that well. Or not the way you should know your daughter.

So when she rang, I was careful not to be effusive or too motherly.

"I'm fine, Mum. Bit sick of India at times."

"So, you're moving on?" (Not "coming home" which would have been provocatively motherly.)

"Oh no," she said. "Only some of the time. I get pissed off, but I've got loads more to see."

"Are you well?"

"I'm fine," she said. "It's okay, you know, if you're careful with the food and water. It's really fun, it's so different."

"Darling, where exactly are you?"

"I'm in Bombay, but I'm moving on next week. I thought I might come home in a few months – for a while, anyway."

"Fantastic. I miss you Maggie. I want to sit down and have a good talk to you and find out what you've been doing."

"Me too, Mum." She sounded sad.

"Are you okay?"

"I guess. I just broke up with an English fellow. Lucas. I was crazy about him, but he wasn't so crazy about me."

"I know the feeling."

"Have you been going out with someone?" Since the divorce, Maggie had always wanted me to get married again.

"I meant with Dad, darling."

"Ancient history."

"Is it definitely over with this fellow?"

"Yeah, for sure." The phone started making noises about cutting out. "But Mum, I wanted to tell you ... oh shit ... I haven't got any more coins ... I'm pregn ..."

And that was it.

Chapter 5

A good mother. How quickly the phrase unravels in middle age. The failure of good mothering in middle age is more public, more humiliating and less controllable than the petty setbacks of tiny tots. As Leah begins to forge a new life for herself, she is sabotaged by the failure of her motherhood. The promise that "they'll be off your hands" turns out to be another of life's cruel tricks.

On the long dark nights of the soul, shared with the Labrador, this calls into being Leah's very reason for existence. Instead of the production of children being a justification for her life, it turns out to be a stain on her character.

Maggie, Maggie, Maggie.

"Hey Mum, what's up?"

Sam was running late for school. This has happened every school day for the last ten years, but he is still surprised that he is about to miss the bus, breakfast, hasn't had time to finish his homework or feed the dog. And, if I'm in a bad mood, reminded that he hasn't tidied his room, done his laundry, mown the lawn.

"Mum." He put his hand on my shoulder. "What's wrong?"

"Maggie's pregnant," I cried. "She just phoned from India. But I don't know where she is, or whose baby it is. Just that's she pregnant."

"A cousin," he said, looking at me puzzled. "That'd be cool. I mean lots of girls have babies now. Lots. Don't stress out. It'd be great to have a baby in the family. And we've never had a cousin."

"You'd be an uncle," I said, "not a cousin."

"But the baby would be a cousin," he said.

"It wouldn't be," I said. "It'd be a niece or a nephew."

"We'd be *cousins*," he said, "but don't stress, Mum. Can I have the car today?"

"You didn't replace the petrol."

"Yeah, but can I have the car?"

"No."

He kissed me forgivingly, but then he stopped at the door. "You know you put a ding in the back bumper." And then he was off. I wanted to run after him and tell him not to tell all the kids at school about Maggie's baby (or the ding in the back bumper), but it didn't really matter, because none of them seemed coherent enough to tell their mothers and what did it matter anyway except as a bit of gossip? I had Maggie's photo stuck on the fridge. You look at Maggie and you know this is a strong person. But however strong, an unmarried twenty year old having a baby wasn't a good idea in my books, especially if it was my daughter and especially if she was lost in India.

I needed to talk. Mum was out of the question. Apart from the fact she doesn't listen, she's still convinced that her grand-daughters are nice girls and nice girls don't get pregnant. She's convinced single women get pregnant to get the pension. She's a great believer in the deserving poor, of whom she is one, even though she'd be horrified if anyone ever said so. I rang Taz and sobbed my heart out.

"It's not knowing where she is."

"It's not knowing how to get in touch."

"She's too young."

"I feel like I've failed."

"I can't bear telling Mum."

Taz was sensible, practical and mature. She was sympathetic without being gushy. If *she'd* been Maggie's mother this would never have happened.

"Leah," she said, "you're a wonderful mother. You've given your life for those kids. It's not your fault she's pregnant. And I know you're worried, but she knows how to look after herself and you've taught her that." Lucy was outside dragging herself along on her bum. Maybe my house was infested with intestinal parasites. India was full of intestinal parasites too.

I *knew* it was because I'd given her condoms when she was fifteen. I did that because I *knew* she was sleeping with her boyfriend. Sexual permission. Too young. I'd thought so at the time, but we weren't into mother-daughter talks at that stage of our relationship and it was pretty clear she was deeply into sex.

How would she cope now? What would she do? She was tough but being a single parent is harder than you imagined. My daughter having a baby shouldn't be like this. I wanted her married to a nice sympathetic man with a regular wage. I'd do a spot of babysitting, give some fabulous advice. The grandchild would be beautiful. Everyone would be blissfully happy. Life isn't like that. But why can't it be? Just once?

Women have reserves of energy for a crisis like this. All the mothering hormones switch on and flow powerfully through the system. But someone should find a way to switch them off, because they're no use when your child is in India. They're not even much use when the child is no longer a child. They flood the body, unused, toxic, affecting the intellect and inducing hysteria. They produce mood swings from reality black to pretty picture bliss. Maybe Maggie will be really happy and go to uni with her baby in a backpack. She'll do well and meet a nice man who will love the baby. The baby will be the flower girl at their wedding, I'll be the Matron of Honour in that dark blue silk number that never fitted me again after I had Sam. The Ex will be there and we'll fall into each other's arms and laugh about his silly passion for Miss Pouty Lips, who is not looking a patch on me in some ugly green number. She'll slowly disappear like the Cheshire cat. And Sam will be there and be scooped up by some friend of Genevieve's who wants a house husband, but isn't too particular. And Genevieve will become like Aunt Taz and be the wise and beautiful (and vain) aunt. Yellow circles will have disappeared from her life. And Mum will have dementia and will not notice the baby is illegitimate.

That's the thing about being a romantic. You turn everything round in your head and create a fantasy. You do it because reality is so unforgiving and so persistently real.

It was probably for this reason that I found myself in bed with David about eleven o'clock that night.

❀　　❀　　❀

I liked the concert. Boom, boom, boom. A lot of percussion, although when I told David it was almost as

111

good as the percussion band I'd worked with at Grevillea Public he gave me a strange look.

"We'll have to go to more concerts," he said. "So you can tell the difference."

I felt shy, being on a date. I wanted to tell him I did have some musical knowledge, about much later and more popular composers and performers, but I didn't feel very sure of myself. I also wanted to ask him why we were on a date, why we had only had one date, why he had asked me rather than someone else, what he expected of me, who did he think I was? And of course, who was he?

My mother had told me when I first went out never ever to let a boy touch my breasts and certainly never let him do anything else. At which point, I told her it was the seventies and to get real. She told me a slut is a slut, whatever decade it happens to be.

The trouble was I could never resist a dare and I liked my breasts being touched. I liked the attention and I liked the sensation. But it was complicated by the knowledge that "he might only be using you", a phrase that should have been out of date by the seventies but was still powerful in Catholic girls' schools. Sometimes I wondered if I was "using" him. No, I was too insecure about my wrong shape and the shame of my red hair. That's what I wasted my youth on – anxiety. Maybe I fell for the Ex because he took the uncertainty out of things. "I love you. We'll get married. Buy a house. Have kids." It was only when we began to do those things that it began to unravel.

"Did you find a job?" David asked me over supper. If you're a single mother, Pizza Hut is your definition of upmarket. If you're a teacher, it's the pub or the club. So to be sitting in a cute little late night Spanish bar eating tapas was something that was taking up a whole lot of my attention. I love tapas. It is the perfect food. Perched on a high stool. Rich red wine. Crisp sardines. Tiny broiled potatoes strong with garlic. I should do it every night. Did I find a job?

"Not yet," I said. The sardines were so strong they got rid of my "what to do on a date in the new millennium" anxiety.

He leaned over and stroked my shoulder, which was nice, but a bit precarious on those high stools. I was unable to respond because my mouth was full. "You are an amazingly calm person," he said. "You're not at all worried about this job thing, are you?"

I was about to say I was, except I'd just had a big swig of red wine, and I didn't feel worried any more. A date, a concert and food I liked more than cheesecake. Or maybe it was the underlying panic about Maggie that made it impossible to panic about the job.

"I'm training myself on a computer," I said. "My sister thinks if I learn a few programs I'll be able to get into office work and get ahead in life. Doing something helps absorb the panic. And I'm quite good at it."

"Do you *want* to get into office work?" he asked.

We were into conversation now, but after he had stroked my shoulder, I hoped we might get back to kissing like we had on the last date. Or even sex. Because the thing is that sleeping with a Labrador is the refuge of the desperate. For a long time after the Ex left, I just wanted a warm body next to mine, usually one of the kids wanting comfort in the night. Except I wanted someone to comfort me, which is where the sympathetic nature of a Labrador comes into play. They are not judgmental dogs and have genuinely kind natures. I had three kids to bring up, and sex seemed like a luxury – like eating at a decent restaurant or having really nice underwear or lovely matching sheets.

And I had bad taste in men. The Ex obviously, because he left me. I had fallen in love once since him because the man looked a little like the Ex. He was an army major. In the beginning, he was good manic fun and he liked the kids and he'd taken us out in the bush and showed us how to walk on the leaf litter and leave no tracks. Then he showed me how I could detect if my phone was being bugged. I left it at that. Besides, he wasn't all that interested in having sex, being pre-occupied, perhaps, with leaving no traces.

But the feeling I had about David was new. Maybe it was because my feeling about the Ex was changing, or even disappearing.

There was still Rosanna.

"Rosanna," he said. "She's not my type."

"Despite being musical and beautiful?"

"Yes, despite that."

I leaned over and kissed him, a nice, long wet kiss.

But he started talking again. "What sort of office work are you after?" he asked. I could tell he was asking because he didn't know how to negotiate this any more than I did. "What do you *want* to do?" Which is a real first date question.

"I can't even imagine what it would be like to work in an office." I had another sip of wine. "Except going up in a lift. And the office being carpeted. That's only because schools mostly aren't. But I'm not ambitious. It's not like I've seen somewhere I want to be and I'm determined to get there. Nothing like that."

"I'm not ambitious either," he said. "People think it's ghastly that the proprietors have sent me out to the outer suburbs to run the advertising, but I quite like it. I'm working my way down the company ladder. One day, I know, I'll get to the bottom." I laughed and he moved closer. I was drunk, and full of desire.

"We've had a very odd relationship," I said. "Not actually a relationship. More like a couple of near misses. You've chatted me up on a number of widely separated occasions. Last date, you even kissed me. Then when I saw you again, you're back with Rosanna, but with sweet talk about dinner. Now there's tonight. I liked that boom boom music we went to. A little like Phil Spector's Wall of Sound, except the Wall of Sound is more complicated. Phil had at least two pianos at every recording. He was inspired by Wagner, which isn't so politically correct I believe, but it's not as if I know about Wagner. I love this bar and tapas is my favourite food, but I think I really want to go to bed without any more stuffing around."

We did. (It would have been ghastly if he'd said, "Thank you but no thank you," after my brave declaration.) We went back to his flat, kissing and smooching, up the stairs of an old dark building, where the stairwell smelled musty, and there was a horrible little tiled landing outside his flat, with a window of frosted glass.

"Welcome to Cockroach Towers," he said, and I could tell he was ashamed and it *was* awful and pokey and dank with cockroaches running round with a sense of great ease and familiarity. I was, I'm ashamed to say, very used to cockroaches. Every time Katie Bless You carries out one of her periodical reigns of terror against the insect world, my house is invaded by cockroaches. Gen won't allow me to spray them except with the mildest of sprays which seem to put them on a high, encouraging brazen and fearless behaviour. Sam took to spraying them, but he used my gold spray paint I used for Year 1 stencil Christmas cards, so now we have the occasional gold cockroach and areas of gold cockroach stencil on the kitchen floor.

Which is a way of saying I didn't care about David's cockroaches and so we just fell into the double bed. And it was better than childbirth and better than sleeping next to the Labrador, or the kids, and better than the boom boom concert. And I'd worn my best underwear which looked great in the dim lighting of his flat, even though I hadn't handwashed it in warm water and pure soap flakes and all the rest you're supposed to do. I didn't feel bad about my less than perfect body because I just didn't, and anyway, he was slightly paunchy and less than perfect in the way middle-aged men are. In fact, he had little breasts with grey curly hair all over them, and even though it's something you'd never think was sexy, it was. I found his sense of relaxation and my sense of not having to hold my stomach in very erotic.

And when we made love, I had the feeling he was enjoying himself and I had the feeling that maybe I'd lost that convent girl sense of how awful sex was supposed to be. I felt I could really get into this sex business, better than with the Ex and I had before we were married. I had an orgasm that made me see stars and I felt as if I was riding a great wave. I had sensations in parts of my body I hadn't felt for years. I smooched him and he smooched me, and that hadn't happened with a grown man for years.

Then there was the afterglow that I'd read about so many times, but had never really felt like I felt now. And then we chatted, lying in bed, drinking the bottle of wine we'd brought from the tapas bar.

"You may think this is a terrible place," he said, "but it used to leak, right over the bed."

"It doesn't any more?"

He got up, naked, and traced a small plastic pipe coming through the louvres, down across the wall behind us and then disappearing out the window.

"My *ex*-wife said I was a lousy handyman, but *I* fixed that so it didn't leak. Waterproof glues and everything." He lay back down and I laughed.

"Does it drain into the flat downstairs?" I asked.

"Straight into their kettle," he said, and we both giggled and chortled about other household repairs we had made, my most impressive being tying a window sash cord to the TV aerial so the window couldn't slam down on my hand.

"SBS is pretty bad reception though," I said. "If I want to watch the French news or anything."

"Have you had many affairs?" he asked when we'd stopped laughing. "You know, since your divorce. If you don't mind me asking."

Two. But I didn't say so. "Almost none," I said, which was true, because the two were of very short duration. The army major ran a very long campaign to win me back after I rejected him, but that's because he was mad, and I could have only lain in the leaf litter two or three times at most. The other wasn't nice enough for all the hassle involved. It was with a deputy principal, having sex in the school sick bay on the narrow, vinyl-covered stretcher with the first aid chart pinned above my head, and all the guilt about *his* wife and *my* Catholicism. "I can feel all my desire coming back though," I said. "It feels as if I've been hugely repressed, like I need this." And he laughed and kissed me and held me.

"Have you had many affairs?" I said, "you know, since *your* divorce?"

"Too many," he said.

"How many is too many?"

"Well, I haven't actually counted," he said, "but I can't remember without counting. So it's that many."

"That depends on how good you are at counting and remembering. Give me a ball park figure."

"About ten," he said.

I was thinking ten in a year somehow cheapened my little sojourn with him, or at the very least reduced the future possibilities.

"My God!" I sat up. "We didn't use any protection. Why didn't you use a condom at least?" Okay, I was forty-five, but there was no sign of the hot flushes yet.

"I've had a vasectomy," he said. "And no diseases." And kissed my thigh. "The vasectomy was a first wife thing. Anyway, why should it be my responsibility?"

"Because this is the new millennium. I've heard that it's the men who are going to get pregnant and breastfeed this next thousand years."

"Maybe that's why I had the vasectomy," he said, and pulled me down next to him. "I have something I want to tell you."

That's always bad news. Because the next line is always worse – *I'm going to leave you; I've found another woman; I've started taking cocaine; I'm pregnant; I've been fired; the police are on their way; the dog's dead.*

"About, you know, so many affairs . . . you see, since my divorce, I've been a bit of a, I've become, I'm not sure . . ."

118

"What?"

"Well, the technical term is that I've become a sex addict ... you know, sex addicted ..."

I laughed. Halfway between deep, sexy throaty which would have been very classy, and a schoolgirl giggle.

"Sex addict?" I squeaked. And then got myself into teacher mode. "Define. Explain." That's a phrase I used a lot the year I taught Year 6.

"It's like any other addiction," he said sadly. "You get obsessed to the point where your desire for sex interferes with the relationships. The sex becomes the most important thing in your life. It's like being thirteen, never having grown up."

"I thought all men were supposed to be like that," I said, which was a bit sharp.

"Leah ..." he said. A plea not to be flip or sarcastic.

"Okay ..."

"Look, it's a terrible term. I only use it because I went to a couple of anonymous meetings – you know, like Alcoholics Anonymous."

"Tell me," I said, trying to look serious.

"Well, they're called SLAA – Sex and Love Addicts Anonymous. And you have to stand up and say, 'Hi, my name's David and I'm a sex and love addict.' My doctor told me I should go because I was depressed. It was that or drugs, which I'm not keen on. And I was looking for new directions, some guidance on how to live my life. So I went a couple of times. And they were quite good, until the fourth one I went to, when I was the only person there, you know, so there was really nothing to say."

"When there was something to say ...?"

"There were a lot of blokes. And they were obsessed by one woman, or by chasing women, or conquering women. It's not lust – it's more desperation. Maybe that's what lust is. For me, it was a combination of loneliness, and sadness my marriage was over, and all those years gone by. I was pretty empty. And when I met you, I really liked you . . ."

"But you were attracted to Rosanna," I said, thinking how quickly he'd dropped me that first night. When they had started to sing "happy birthday". To me. And he'd put his arm around Rosanna. "Is Rosanna sex addiction?"

"Leah, please. Hear me out."

"Okay." But I was beginning to feel all the feminist wisdom of the staff room coming back to me. Men couldn't really be trusted. The wisdom of the convent school. All men were after one thing. Which he had just admitted. Sex addiction. New name for male behaviour. Or maybe not. I did like him, apart from this latest twist in the evening of passion.

"Rosanna's like me. Except she doesn't see it. Yes, she's attractive, but she's a pain in the bum. And she promotes being a free spirit, because she's scared that she can't make any relationship work."

"You're not just saying that to make me happy?" I said. "I mean it's awful dumping on friends to make yourself feel better." Then I kissed him because I felt so grateful that someone else in the world thought Rosanna's pursuit of men wasn't necessarily healthy. Even though she was otherwise a nice person, and very good looking.

"Look, she's a really nice person, and she's smart, but it's hard to get to the real Rosanna," he said. "But when I met you, it felt real straight away."

"So you decided to sleep with Rosanna and leave me dangling. Because I was so real."

"I knew a relationship with you would require more. With Rosanna, it doesn't matter, because I knew it would end and she wouldn't care."

"Whereas with me it will end and I will care?"

"Well, wouldn't you?"

"If we ended it right now, I'd be out of it with just a few scratches and bruises. If we continue, you being a sex addict and all, I'm not sure."

"Sex addict's the wrong term," he said. "I think that's why I only went to four meetings. It over-dramatised it. It was more running after women, to make myself feel better. After my divorce, I felt shot to pieces."

"I know about that," I said, but what he said made the evening feel like someone giving you an ice cream and then licking off the top half before you get any. Something along those lines. And the lovely red wine was swirling through my veins and I knew that if I delved into this sex addict business that I'd feel even worse and I was going for an interview with an agency in the morning, and Sam had to get to school and I hadn't fed the dog or the cat, and I really had to get home, so I pulled on my clothes and got my purse and said I'd love to hear the sex addiction bit, but I really had to go and thank you for having me at Cockroach Towers, or thank you for ravishing me and I was off into the night.

❀   ❀   ❀

I was out the door the next morning before Sam was even awake, just a backward "Wake *up* Sam," before I left, down Waratah Street to the bus stop, onto the first bus, hanging on with all the other commuters, off at Town Hall, through the arcade, cappuccino in a polystyrene cup, very city girl feel to it, up to the Office People Agency on the twentieth floor. Where I had a handbag tizz, thinking I'd lost my keys, down to the nineteenth floor, went to the loo, drink of water, up to the twentieth floor again. Remembered the advice of my mother when I applied for my first job in a dress shop. "The worst thing they can do is reject you completely. They can't hurt you." I had never understood what she thinks hurt is.

I'd spent all those hours, learning those programs, headed for the job of my dreams, which should have a salary of at least sixty thousand. A fun job. Where I didn't have to stand up all day. Where I didn't have to talk loudly to reach the people at the back of the room. And imagine having a job that people *thought* was a really great job. I'd do better at Taz's parties. I'd been near the bottom of the heap too long.

I was clutching the resumé Taz had done for me, and the problem was, I didn't really match it. It was very professional and slick and impressive, whereas I was a novice and I knew they'd know. But it was also the resume that got me in the door of the Office People Agency and I knew how Taz had fussed and worried over it, so I was grateful.

I was over-confident and under-confident all at once.

The Office People did this every morning. They gave me a battery of tests – personality, intelligence, as well as testing me on various computer programs. I thought I did pretty well with the exception of one on the phone system which I didn't have a clue about.

I then sat down with a blonde perfect woman. The thing

about later life job applications is that the people employing you are not just better qualified, but they're younger as well. She did this thirty times a day, so even though she was nice, it was a little mechanical.

"You score well on intelligence." I couldn't tell whether she thought intelligence was good or bad. "You didn't have a clue about the phone, but you should be able to learn that pretty fast. You were extremely good on a basic level with the programs we tested you on." She put down the bundle of papers. "Why are you doing this?"

"I need a job," I said.

"I presume," she said, looking at my resume, "that you've been retrenched."

"Yes." I like the retrenched word. It sounded better than leaving after a cat fight.

"Have you thought of retraining?"

"I can't afford to."

"You wouldn't be much worse off on social service than on the sort of starting salary anyone could offer you. And there are training programs available free of charge. The wages you could attract with this sort of work are very low." She was sympathetic.

"I'd prefer to work." I tried not to sound desperate. "Do on the job training."

"That would be incidental really, at receptionist level. Being a receptionist can be pretty invisible in terms of people wanting to train you."

"Are you telling me it's going to be hard for you to place me?"

"Look," she said. "We deal with the big corporates and the firms that serve them. They want a look, they want a product. For someone with your office skills, they want a decorative nineteen year old. For someone with your maturity, they want much higher level skills and experience."

Maturity, decorative nineteen year olds, skills and experience. This was going nowhere.

"What would you advise me?" I asked.

"You could probably do a bookkeeping course. Or a degree in accountancy. Answer ads. Small to medium size. Family businesses, even retail. If you're lucky, you'll find somewhere which is growing and you'll learn to do everything from billing to preparing the accounts. Do that for a while, then come and see us." She extended her hand and smiled her smile and I swear I saw pity in her eyes.

❀ ❀ ❀

I rang Taz and tried to be brave. I think Taz had expected me to fail, but she was kind. "That's good advice about suburban and family businesses," she said. "I'm sure you'll find something. Maybe a bookkeeping course, although then it would be a while before you got a job." I was thinking about her two thousand dollars and I wondered if she was too. And while I was pleased that my computer skills were so impressive, they didn't quite feel like a career path. They didn't make me burn with desire. I felt dismissed by Taz, but it made me feel better about not being able to pay her money back in time. It was as if I'd explained it to her, and we had squared off over the two thousand dollars, even though we hadn't.

At home, I took off my good clothes and hung them up, and got on the phone to a litany of "looking for someone younger", "need more experience", "we'll call you back".

I changed the resumé Taz had done for me and made it simpler, more modest. I wrote letters. I folded them neatly, put them in envelopes, took them down to the post box with Lucy. Then I came back home and took all the snails out of our mailbox. I looked round. I was sick of living in a house that was never right. I got out the secateurs and cut the roses down to size. Lucy stood beside me, pathetically, silently begging me not to fill in her latest hole, but I did, although I knew she'd dig it up again. I mowed the lawn and put the clippings up the back. I pulled out weeds. The garden was still a bit scrappy, but it looked better. "Informal" is the magazine term. Then I went inside and scrubbed the kitchen table and soaked my sheets in something that softened, disinfected and deodorised, and then re-odorised with a soft rose perfume.

Because under all the desperation, I could feel a new me emerging, that had something to do with my experience with David the previous night, which left me wondering if I had caught sex addiction from him, because the truth was, I felt more sexual and more physical than I had for years. I kept getting flashbacks of tingles and excitement that made me feel as if maybe I had wasted my life with children, earning money and longing for the Ex.

Luckily, just as this was beginning to get to me, Sam came home from school and declared that the entire world sucked, and banged his door. Then Tookie arrived and even if I looked a wreck, the house and garden looked okay for once. Not that Tookie would notice. She told me all the Twisted Sister gossip and what a terrible time the poor Miss Baker was having because she'd ceased to be the golden girl and had become "the one who could do no right", a dangerous radical when it came to teaching children to read.

Which simply meant she'd said something Twisted disagreed with, or looked the wrong way one morning. And Tookie said it was a pity I wasn't there because I had always taken the young ones under my wing and taught them how to deal with the terrorist children and with Twisted and her foot soldiers, forgetting the very reason Miss Baker was there was because I wasn't.

Then she explained my "case" to me. Now she'd written it all down, it was actually a case. Under the guidance of the Federation, I would sue the Department for unfair dismissal, loss of income, mental distress and general thuggery. The Federation had managed to get Twisted onside to claim she *had* to dismiss me because she wasn't supposed to have long-term casuals, except she had had to have me because I was the best qualified kindergarten teacher she had ever had. Which was a bit at odds with the fact that one of my complaints was that although the Department had employed me as a virtual permanent while paying me casual wages, they had denied me extra training because I was a casual. This wasn't quite true. It had been Twisted who never sent me on training courses, simply being as nasty as she could.

But I was expected to get on the stand and swear by Almighty God to these reconstructed events which, Tookie assured me, were actually true.

It all made me feel extremely nostalgic, hearing about the new classes and who was teaching what and the new library program and the kids who'd grown a foot in the holidays and those that were as much trouble as they'd always been and those who'd somehow reformed over the holidays and would it last? I felt sad, but then I felt stabs of my new life of posting resumés and scrubbing the table and the sex addiction I had caught from David. I promised Tookie I would go into the Federation and talk to the man on my case. I gave her a big hug. It was odd, because it was different not being work mates, but we were still friends, although I wondered what we would have in common if I ever actually got another job and she ever stopped fighting on behalf of my lost cause.

❀   ❀   ❀

I more or less gave up on David when I didn't hear from him the following week. And when he did call I felt myself blushing, trying not to let Sam overhear.

"How are you?" he asked.

"Pretty good." My mother always said nice girls should be polite and perky.

"Sorry I haven't rung," he said. "I've been flat out."

"The suburbs have been busy, have they?"

"I resigned," he said. "That night after I saw you, I realised I really hated working out there. And I'm sick of living poor. Cockroach Towers and all. You gave me my spirit back."

"That's great," I said. "I haven't got a job, but I feel ready for one. I've got these programs under my belt. And it's been nice learning something instead of teaching it."

"Leah," he said. "Something's come up."

I hate that phrase. It always means the man of your dreams is going off with another woman, has been posted to Iceland, or has contracted a dreaded disease.

"I've got a freelance assignment in Italy," he said, "covering the election and doing some travel stuff."

"Fantastic," I said, trying to feel enthusiastic. "Do you speak Italian?"

"It's my one accomplishment," he said. I felt crushed somehow. We did community language Italian at school.

Buongiorno was about as far as I'd ever got. I cursed myself for not paying more attention.

"I'm sorry," he said. "I would have liked to see more of you."

"Me too," I said.

"I hope you'll still be around when I get back."

"You could write," I said.

"I'm hopeless, Leah," he said. "I'd love to but..." He hesitated. "I could e-mail."

I felt that sinking feeling. No Italian, no e-mail. "I'm not set up for e-mail," I said.

"Well, I'll see you when I get back."

And that was it. I knew Sam would be no earthly use to me, so I went and lay down on the couch. Lucy came, smudged my cheek with her nose, and then lay in sympathy next to me until *Seinfeld* came on.

❋   ❋   ❋

Genevieve and Boaz came over that night so I had to order an extra pizza. I knew pizzas weren't the basis of a truly excellent diet, but cooking for Sam was soul destroying ("Chops? Pasta?" he'd say as if I was trying to poison him), so I gave in and got us pizza.

"Heavens," Katie Bless You had said when she saw all the pizza boxes in our recycling bin. "Pizza's so easy to make, and it's so much cheaper and nicer and I'll give you my recipe." Which of course involved rising dough and pounding tomatoes, which is nice in theory, except Sam hates food that doesn't come out of a cardboard box.

"Pizza?" said Genevieve, as if I was trying to poison *her*. "Boaz is vegetarian."

"It's vegetarian pizza," I said firmly.

Boaz was chatty throughout the meal, as if he knew he was on trial with me. He even asked me questions about my life that children never ask, such as what I was doing and what my plans were and what I cared about. Sam and Genevieve tolerated this with undisguised boredom, and after dinner Sam and Boaz went out into the garden and I craned my neck to see if they were smoking dope again, which I didn't want them to do, especially with Katie Bless You likely to see.

"Have you heard from Maggie again?" Genevieve asked. Genevieve and I had had long talks about the pregnancy, mainly along the lines that I was worried sick and that she thought obstetrics was a bad specialty to go into, however much she might like to do something for her sister.

"No," I said.

"I think you ought to find her, Mum."

"You can't find people in India. Well, you can find people, but not a person. It's too big. And disorganised."

"Dad thought he might go."

"Go where?"

"To India. To find her. And maybe himself at the same time." She giggled.

"Really? Your father's going to India? He can't stand curry."

"Or Indian music. That's why I think he's cracked, Mum. I mean I really think he's going round the twist. But anyway, he makes it all sound rational and thinks he'll find Maggie plus he's got some ashram he wants to study at. It's one where you get reincarnated without having to die. You just have to pay big bucks."

"Is he really splitting up with Jackie?"

"Well, I can't see her going to India. Maybe though. She always got on well with Maggie."

Another dagger in the heart. I tried to be mature and not to care about the Ex and Pouty Lips. I put on the kettle. "Will Boaz have a coffee?"

"Oh no, he's very pure. All herbal, his lot are."

"Well, he's not so pure about smoking dope with Sam."

"He only did that on Christmas Day to keep Sam company. You know he really likes Sam. He's got a mission to get Sam on track."

"On track to what? Yellow circles?"

"I wish you'd be nicer about Boaz, Mum. He's so interesting, he's funny and he's got a really good heart. You're always saying I've got no heart, so you ought to be glad I've got a boyfriend with one. Anyway, we're moving in together." She said it quickly, the way she did when she was a little girl, when she'd make life changing decisions and announce them as if they didn't count. ("I got that Rotary scholarship to go to Japan. So I won't be here for Christmas." That sort of thing.)

"Gen!"

"Mum!"

"Where are you going to live?"

"I'm buying a house. In Randwick. Close to the hospital." Again, she was quick and low key, as if all this was nothing.

I felt a stab of jealousy mixed with pleasure. When the Ex and I had bought our first house, we'd had to scrimp and save and buy a rundown little cottage in the least trendy suburb you could imagine. Later, when we bought a better house, when the Ex had gone into real estate, I was busy bearing children, earning no money. That house hadn't felt like mine at all. And then it was Banksia Close, bought for me, last prize in the marriage stakes. Genevieve was doing a whole lot better, but it seemed too easy. But she'd always been good (read mean) with money, like Taz. I was jealous, but pleased for her.

"How wonderful! What's it like?"

She was cool. "Ugly liver brick, but kinda cute in a repressed sort of way. It's got three bedrooms, polished floors, nice little courtyard. One bedroom for my study, one for a studio for Boaz, one bedroom for us. It's only a semi, but it's got good light, Boaz says."

"So he'll be paying you rent?"

"Mum, we're just sharing. But I'm paying the mortgage because it's my house."

"So he's getting free accommodation?"

"It's none of your business. I don't know why you're so hung up on money."

At that point Boaz and Sam came in and I knew Boaz had just heard me casting aspersions on his character. But what was worse was the way Genevieve looked at him, devoted and adoring. When I see that sort of adoration, it sends shivers down my spine and makes me think of the Ex and me in better days but I was also reminded of what it all led to and what a trap it was to base your life on adoration and romance. But what's the alternative? If you ever thought about marriage in a cool and rational frame of mind, you'd never do it. You need adoration and stupidity for the survival of the species.

Evidently Boaz knew this and he put his arms round Genevieve and hugged her.

"You'll be pleased to know," he said to me over her shoulder, "I sold a yellow circle yesterday. Not for very much money, but the guy who bought it is really interested in my stuff. He thinks I should go blue, but I think that would be selling out to commercial interest, just to do it because he wants it." He looked down at Genevieve and smiled. "If I go blue, it's on *my* terms, isn't it, baby?"

And she looked up at him, even more adoring.

"Did you hear that, Mum?" said Sam. "Boaz selling a picture? Cool, isn't it?"

"Yes darling, and now he's going into his Blue Period, just like Picasso," I said.

"On my terms," Boaz said, but uncertainly.

"You know I'm worried about you and Genevieve," I said.

"What's the exact nature of your worry?" he said.

"I worry about you using her. I can see you really like her, but it seems to me not very healthy that you depend on her financially."

"Mum!"

"Well, you don't have to worry about that, Mrs J." Boaz smiled at me.

"Don't patronise me Boaz," I said.

"Mum!"

"Boaz knows what I think, so isn't it better we talk about it?" I said to Genevieve.

"Finally!" said Sam.

"What do you mean *finally*?"

"You're always crapping on about stuff," said Sam, "and you never say it to anyone's face."

"That's diplomacy," I said.

"No it's not," said Genevieve. "It's bloody carping bitchiness. I won't have it, Mum. This is my business and you're not interfering. We're not talking about it." She picked up her bag and took Boaz's hand. He gave me an "I win" smile which annoyed me no end and then Genevieve was off with one of her famous door slams, and I was left with Sam.

"A fat lot of good that did," I said, "saying what I think."

"You stuffed it!" he said. "Getting all aggro like that." Then he went into his room and played the mother fucker music really loud.

I calmed myself by reading *Bleak House* while Lucy looked soulfully at me, aware of my distress. Then the phone rang.

"It's David."

"Hi."

"Leah. I guess I sounded dismissive, about not writing to you when I go away. And I know it's a bit strange, being a journalist, but the thing is, my personal letters always sound stilted. But I do want to see you when I come back, and I hope you want to see me. I don't want you to be put off by me having had quite a few relationships, because really, they were just friendships mostly, or one-night stands. It's different with you and me."

"I hope so," I said.

And I did, I really did.

Chapter 6

The guides for the middle years advocate realistic comfort with our bodies. They offer encouragement, pointing out that confidence and maturity are better than youth and beauty. But this is mere cover for the reality that the middle aged are in mourning for their lost youth, all the more so because they didn't appreciate it when they had it.

Death by sex is part of the painful slide into middle age. No sudden cut, but a slow fade. A painful diminution of the erotic life force.

There are sharp and painful reminders, sudden and unexpected flashbacks — old photos of lost youth, meeting old friends, sudden memories. These awaken a slumbering sense of what might have been, what could have been. The longing! If only there had been an endowment of confidence and maturity back then! Because now, a cruel trick, confidence, comfort and maturity, even if they exist, count for little against the waste of the past — the beauty, the energy, the life!

I trotted along next to Tookie up towards the Federation's office. I had told her my story of the supporting parent benefit, takeaway pizza and the humiliation by the employment agency, all of which convinced her that I had no other option but to return to teaching. For her, there was no life after teaching because teaching and life were pretty much the one thing. But I still wanted to experiment with another life, to know I *could* do something else.

"Now remember, Miss Siskay isn't the enemy."

"You've turned to the dark side, Tookie."

She stopped in the foyer of the building and looked at me the same way my mother used to look at me when she took me to the dentist when I was a child. A "don't embarrass me" look. An "act your age" look. A "this is important in a way you can't understand" look.

"She's devoted her life to teaching," she said. "That's got to count for something."

"Yeah, well L Ron Hubbard devoted his life to scientology," I said. "Devoting your life doesn't put you on the stairway to heaven. Kylie Minogue is devoting hers to singing in that girly voice." As I launched into this, I realised it wasn't such a fantastic argument. L Ron and Kylie both had barrowloads more money than me, and were thinner. Or was L Ron dead? I'd lost touch with the scientologists since they stopped working the local mall.

"Leah, this is a political argument about the way the Department uses casual teachers – of which you are one. It is not personal. Please!"

I was supposed to be quiet at this point, but being quiet is not my strong point whether I'm going to the dentist or into a political debate.

"I know Twisted has stopped being the Wicked Witch, but how come she's the Good Fairy now? She can't be *helping* the Federation, can she? The way she used to lecture us about strikes."

"Well, she is," said Tookie. She pressed the button for the lift. It arrived, opened and then closed, but we ignored it.

"You'd better tell me."

"She's in trouble with the Department herself. There's a dispute over the school budget. She fudged the numbers of kids to keep the staff levels up."

"I remember her telling all those mums their darlings were ready to start school aged four and a half. And then we had to try and teach the poor loves. That was wicked."

"It's worse." Tookie leaned towards me and lowered her voice. "She enrolled two of those kids who came for a day. But it was a set-up. They were never going to start, but they got her the numbers for an extra teacher. Which the Department got wind of, through some disgruntled parent. So she's going along with the Federation on this casual teacher thing. She needs *their* support, or at least a diversionary tactic because she's also used casuals where she should have employed permanents — and that breached the guidelines as far as the Department was concerned."

"My heart bleeds."

"Leah, you know *you* weren't all that easy." She said it kindly, but something told me she'd rehearsed this.

"What do you mean?"

"Look, you undermined her wherever you could. You made fun of her. You never took her seriously."

"That seems fair enough."

"She's only a person. Okay, she's not too smart and she's old-fashioned and a bit of a tyrant ..."

"Listen to you!" I said. "You know she's an old cow — stubborn and stupid and ..."

"Which is probably true of a hell of a lot of other heads and deputies – to say nothing of teachers. Or people in general."

"Are you saying I'm a lousy teacher?"

"You're terrific," said Tookie, "but you wouldn't be easy to have on staff. If you disagree with people, you don't hold back."

"You're complaining because I express my opinions. I thought you were a revolutionary."

"It's the way you do it . . ." She was looking at me pleadingly now. "I was scared of really explaining the strategy the union is using in your case. I was scared of how you'd react. But there are a dozen ways to skin a cat."

I had a sudden vision of Jack skinned, which didn't make me feel at all good. "What *are* you trying to tell me?" I asked.

"Look, you're a terrific teacher. And Twisted *is* difficult. But she told you about losing your job in public because she was *scared* of you. She hasn't got the brains to know how to deal with things. But that's all past – this is the best strategy for you to get your job back."

Twisted had been hurt by what I said, but that was what I intended. And the fact was, she had cruelled my chances of getting a job in any other school by spreading malicious gossip. She'd wrecked my teaching career, paltry as it was. It wasn't as if other worlds were opening up. Despite all my slavery to Sam's computer and not watching Humphrey Bear and Oprah (when I could resist), the wild, wide dream of doing something else had narrowed to something resembling a rat maze. Sympathetic people on the end of the phone – "Sorry – no experience, someone younger, better computer skills".

At best, I might end up in a crummy local office shuffling papers for some old codger going broke. Or patronised by a young hot shot who'd call me "Mum". So being burnt out and disillusioned about teaching was neither here nor there.

"Okay," I said, pressing the lift button. "Let's do it."

Unions have become career territory. People in the union movement have decided that they have to act like they're running a corporation, so the flannel shirt and jeans look doesn't work. Tookie didn't know it, but ideological inspiration wasn't fashionable any more either. Tookie reverentially introduced me to a man in an imitation Armani suit called Jason, who was on the way, via the union, to a seat in parliament. Jason felt he had to explain the facts of life to me, as he saw them.

"This case is a mixture," he said as we sat down in his office, "of political pressure and human rights."

"And me getting my job back?" I smiled.

"Well, we *hope* that would be the result of course," he said, "and improved conditions for casuals."

"I'd hope we could drag Miss Siskay over the coals a couple of times," I said. Tookie kicked me on the ankle.

"We can't," he said. He leaned across the desk and looked at me intently. "She's key," he said. "Absolutely key." Tookie stared at me sternly.

"You know she's effectively stopped me getting another job?"

"That's another issue," he said.

"Not for me," I said.

"You haven't got a hope in hell of getting back into teaching unless you co-operate with this strategy we're proposing," he said.

"What do you need from me?"

He looked up and began talking as if he were reading a shopping list. "We need a sense of your dedication, your passion for teaching, your unswerving devotion to the profession, your absolute love of it, your acceptance of the unfairness of your position. That is, until the final straw – losing your job at Grevillea – purely because of Departmental regulations – the straw that broke the camel's back." Maybe he did have an ideology after all.

"Okay," I said. "Always wanted to be a teacher. Went to teacher's college. Started off at country school. In love with the job. Moved to the city. Gave my life for teaching. Brilliant career only interrupted by bringing three fine Australians into the world – that's the sort of stuff you want?"

"Exactly." He allowed himself a smile.

"And Siskay agrees and weeps crocodile tears because she had to fire me because of the regulation on casuals. *You* explain why it took her ten years. But she is sorry and wishes she could hang on to teachers of my calibre."

"Pretty much." He had a note of doubt in his voice. "We don't want to put words in your mouth," he added. "We just want to present it in a way the judge will warm to our case. We want public sympathy and awareness too."

"Is this a big case?" I asked.

"Pretty big," he said.

"Why me?"

"Because you've been at that school long enough, so you *were* de facto permanent. Because ... you've had ... well, years of experience. So you *should* be valued. Because Miss Took told me you'd be a good spokesperson for our case." He rubbed his hands together.

"So why haven't I got a job now?" I asked. "I mean, won't people ask that? Surely you wouldn't want to mention Miss Siskay's vendetta against me . . ."

"No," he interrupted, "we wouldn't."

"So what's the story?"

"Look, Leah, this is a very important point so let me explain it. You've been in this job a long time. But as a casual teacher you're aware of the precariousness of your position. You know as a casual you're at the bottom of the heap and you'd have to start at the bottom again. I would guess you were heartbroken at not being able to keep the job you had. I would guess you were pretty much disillusioned with teaching." He stared bleakly at the pebbled ceiling again and then swung forward on the swivel chair. "We can't have a *problem*, you know."

"You don't want any loose cannons, no flying shrapnel?"

"Exactly. What's worrying me in your case is still your attitude to Miss Siskay."

"I loathe her."

He smiled at me. "Look, she's not my favourite Martian either, but we'll make sure you don't cross swords. The thing is to remember we're not fighting *her*. We're fighting for *you*."

"A great and noble cause?"

"I certainly hope so." A cat got the cream smile, an animal smile, a political smile, but quite a nice smile nevertheless. Jason had ambition, but maybe a little bit of heart too, and he was right about us poor downtrodden teachers. Furthermore, this might give me a chance of getting a good job in teaching, which didn't exactly thrill me because I *was* disillusioned. But in view of the lack of other employment of any sort, this seemed to offer at least some sort of useful way to support myself (and son, and grandchild). And there was Tookie, pink faced and bright eyed, with a good and dear heart. She thought it would help the union, fight the good fight, but also she'd gone in to bat for me.

I suppose at that point all my years of teaching came back, all the camaraderie, represented by Tookie sitting next to me. The Irish in me. My sheer bloody mindedness. The memory of the unfairness of it all. Even if this wasn't exactly shaping up as a fair fight from my side of the fence, even if part of me really wanted to leave teaching behind.

I gave him *my* cat got the cream smile. "Okay," I said. "I'll do it."

❋　　❋　　❋

With the case a way off I turned my attention to matters closer to home – namely Maggie (who wasn't in fact close to home and hadn't called) and my employment situation. All the resumés I'd sent out, the phone calls I'd made, amounted to nothing. Sometimes in the middle of the night I read my book on intestinal parasites to divert my mind, but then of course, I had Maggie pregnant, with intestinal parasites imported from India.

The bright spot was David. He didn't write, but he was keen. I knew that. It felt like a possibility in my life.

The Ex rang with pompous pronouncements. He was winding up his business; he had no intention of splitting from Pouty Lips; he had never said he was coming back to Sydney; he was interested in "higher things", whatever they were; and he was going to India to find Maggie, if I could please find out where she was.

"So it's up to me," I said. "As usual."

"Don't be like that, Leah."

Genevieve and Boaz moved into Genevieve's gorgeous new house. It's a terrible thing to be jealous of your own children, but I was sick with jealousy over this beautiful little house. It was like a house I'd always wanted but never had. It was tranquil and sunny, painted pale yellow with rugs on the polished floors and big lilies growing in the courtyard. I was angry too, because Boaz had hung his yellow circles everywhere, although I was rather taken by one called the floral circle, which was actually an incredibly detailed yellow circle made up of very finely drawn daffodils. Which made me think why couldn't he get a job (drawing daffodils?), except I didn't seem able to.

"Leah *is* looking for a job," my mother announced to the Spare Parts Club, who I now took to bowls each week. This weekly outing with my mother and her friends was like an out of body, out of mind experience. I was a chief topic of my mother's monologue. She interpreted my life for them, explaining my difficulties and extolling my virtues, which she never actually acknowledged to me directly before.

"That's good," said Taz. "There's a guilt chink in the old dragon after all."

I drove, made sandwiches and chatted to Mr Bonham, who, despite taking off his leg and scratching his stump when my mother wasn't around, turned out to have a wicked sense of humour and a wry appreciation for my mother.

"She's a fine woman," he said one day as we sat on the club verandah. "But she thinks I'm beneath her."

I took this to mean he wanted some sort of sexual dalliance. "Where's there's life there's hope," I said.

"I'm losing both pretty damn fast," he said.

Losing life and hope. I was and I wasn't. I was kept informed of what was going on in my case by Tookie and the Federation, but I wasn't too interested in the minor procedural details that had everybody else so excited. I got into the garden, and it began to look halfway decent. I even got cuttings from Katie Bless You. I made far too many Eat U Rite chocolate muffins, but they sustained Sam, who swore he was studying like mad and still not smoking. His hair was bright yellow now. I prayed he wasn't manufacturing amphetamines under his bed.

I used my new computer skills to draw up a household budget and cash flow. It was apparent that even cancelling all takeaway pizza from here to eternity, even living on cans of Pal dog food, I wouldn't be able to pay Taz by July, whether I got a job or not. My life fell into a routine. I practised on the computer every morning for a couple of hours, then watched Oprah and saw the dregs of life and felt a warm sympathy towards them, although generally not quite as much as Oprah herself felt. I started reading Dickens chronologically, and was distressed to find that Lucy had chewed at the leather-bound copy of *Great Expectations* that Taz had given me last birthday. I'd have to get it replaced, because Taz checked on the things she gave me. I put all the leather-bound volumes on a high shelf and began a paperback Stephen King.

I began a part-time travel course in the guise of re-training, but it was all about airline schedules when I really wanted tropical island experiences.

David sent me a short letter from Italy, which read a little like a newspaper article. I began to wonder about the nature of love and romance once you've turned forty-five.

I dreamed and thought far too much about David. It seemed like I had a talent for creating warm-blooded fantasies out of nothing.

Then, one day he rang, just as I walked in the door. He was back in town.

"Well," I said. "Hullo."

"I wrote," he said, "didn't you get it?"

"It sounded like something I could read in the newspaper," I said. "Not like you."

"I can't write like me," he said. "I'm a journalist when I write. But I thought about you."

Did he think about me like a journalist, or in the throes of passion?

"I've just got back. And now, the same bugger who sent me to Coventry has put me in charge of court rounds and I'll be doing travel features too. A hack for all seasons."

"Is that good?" I asked.

"It's great. Right mixture of responsibility and irresponsibility."

"I thought you lacked ambition." I felt betrayed by this resurgence of his.

"I'm not ambitious. I didn't mind that stint on the local paper because I was in such a bad space after the marriage ended. But Italy made me feel I could really do things."

"What about the sex addiction?" I asked.

"Sex addiction?"

"You went to those meetings. You chased women."

"Cured," he said. "Except for you."

"Very flattering," I said. "But really?"

"Leah, you know what a divorce is like. It sends you crazy. That was just part of it. I wouldn't guarantee my emotional stability now, but it has improved. I want to see you."

144

I felt excited and terrified and hopeful. I took a deep breath.

"Why don't we go up to the vineyards on the weekend?" he asked. "I've got a freebie. At a semi luxury resort."

"I was planning pizza Saturday night," I said. "I'd be reluctant to let that go for *semi* luxury."

"Saddle of lamb basted in olive oil with rosemary and dill," he read. "A spa bath and indoor swimming pool. But then it's got an asterisk with 'summer only'. But not next to the lamb."

"Sounds better than supreme with extra pineapple."

"Leah," he said. "You know I take this relationship with you seriously."

Women are supposed to be good at this stuff, but what I really wanted to ask was why he had only sent me one strange letter from Italy even though he was a journalist; whether I was a consolation prize for some other woman, and if he was still sleeping with Rosanna.

"Well," I said, "then pick me up round about eight on Saturday. That way we'll get a nice early start." It's a wonder I didn't offer to pack a picnic lunch and fruit for the journey.

Then I had to deal with the delicate matter of telling my seventeen-year-old son I was going away for a weekend of debauchery while at the same time making sufficiently threatening noises to prevent any of his debauchery occurring while I was absent.

"Sam," I said tentatively when he came home. "I'm just thinking I might actually go away for the weekend – you know, with a friend."

"Okay." He disappeared into his room and turned on his devil worship music, which meant of course that I didn't have to explain that I, his mother, was embarking on a sexual liaison. When Genevieve called, however, I did tell her.

"Mum!" she said. "Who is this guy? What does he do? Where did you meet him?"

These of course were exactly the questions I was never allowed to ask her. I stumbled through the answers like a guilty teenager. Only with Taz did I regain my sense of balance.

"Dave's a nice man," she said. "He can be a bit uncouth, but he's a journalist, so that's to be expected. He only speaks Italian because his mother's Italian. But have a good time. You need a good time."

"My life's not *that* bad," I said.

"I didn't mean that," said Taz. "But you put all that energy into the kids and you haven't got a job. What could be better than a weekend away in the vineyards?"

"With a nice man," I reminded her. "And sex thrown in."

"Well," she said, "I suppose he is a nice man."

"But it's the sex too," I said. "You know, I used to think I just missed the Ex. My great love affair. But now, I think I've missed out on all those years and years of sex."

"I intend *never* to have sex again," said Taz. "I'd like a man to go places with and flirt with a bit, but I'm fully over sex. It's so overrated. It's really quite grotty. Not very hygienic. People just pretend they like it, Leah. It's like swimming at the beach." She said this in a very lofty way, putting me in my place, as a person pretending they like sex and beaches. It was hard to give a sensible answer.

"Do you know," I asked, "if he still sees Rosanna?"

"He talks to her on the phone, but she's over him – as a lover."

"Are you sure?"

"Absolutely. She told me. He's not her type anyway. She likes people who are interested in ideas. But she did say he was a nice sort of fellow." This of course made me feel as if I was going to spend my weekend with a someone one step up from a Labrador (which *was* a step up for me). I went to sleep (with the Labrador) with fantasies of witty conversations with David, sensational sex, fantastic sophistication, and a passionate declaration of love from him. Wish!

❋　❋　❋

There I was on the motorway, with David, chatting and laughing, dreaming of passion, when my mind flipped a switch to panic mode. Jump out of the car panic. Fake appendix attack, straight to hospital panic. From being chatty and amusing, I became silent and pale, sweaty and withdrawn.

He didn't notice. He put on a tape, Bach or similar, and hummed along. It's odd the way people don't notice. I understand those women who shoplift their way through menopause because it seems that the only time people do notice madness is when you try and steal their things. The attention of a security guard is better than having no-one at all. At times I've even felt that with Katie Bless You. At least she *notices*.

I suddenly realised that although I had been saving my good underwear for an occasion like this, this morning, I had put on the daggy greys, as if it had been any other morning. I'd bought the smart stuff to become corporate woman from the inside out, a strategy that was enjoying so little success that I had taken to wearing the daggy greys on a daily basis, saving the beautiful new underwear for my future (now receding) great romantic liaison in semi luxury. Now, all would be revealed when I undressed tonight.

This was magnified by the longstanding shame that comes with being slack enough to wash underwear with school shirts and dirty sheets in cold water with cheap soap powder, something that Katie Bless You, my nemesis, would never do. Katie Bless You has told me she even washes the tea towels separately. "It just seems nicer, Leah."

So I sat there in grey, wrinkled underclothes, sweaty and in pain from clenching my hands together so tightly, trying to get perspective, trying to remember (and convince myself) that human relationships don't rest on the state of one's underwear. Surely I could find a gracious, flirtatious, sexy way to tell him that though my flimsies didn't look good, they were clean, or at least as clean as anything washed with school shirts can be.

And piling on top of this was the fact that I didn't speak Italian, had never been to Italy, and was an expert on the wrong sort of music. He was cultivated enough to hang round with Taz and Rosanna without being related, whereas I knew in my heart I wouldn't stand a chance.

And this gap between us would widen as David had risen out of the ranks of the underemployed towards some journalistic glory, whereas my only hope of rising lay in a court case, being held to help the cause of casual teachers in general, rather than for my specific benefit.

The vineyards. What did I know about wine except a good bottle usually cost more than a cheap one? My idea of a classy wine is Mateus Rose. I knew I liked that sweet red Spanish wine I'd had with David, but I had no idea what it was called. I knew my mother never paid more than fifteen dollars for a bottle of sherry, so I figured you'd have to pay more than that to get a good sherry. But these scraps of information weren't going to get me through the weekend of wine-tasting, with grey underwear, no Bach to speak of, a cheery *buongiorno* and no job. We were hopelessly mismatched.

David put his hand on my knee. "You're quiet," he said.

I wished I was at home cooking and simultaneously eating Eat U Rite chocolate muffins (a very calming activity). "It's just the scenery's so beautiful," I said as we flashed past a service station.

"Hmm," he said.

I'd recovered a little by the time we got to the three and a half star luxury accommodation. But going round the vineyards was joyless – not serious drinking or even serious tasting, unless you knew something to begin with and could murmur, "Um yes," knowingly. Driving from property to property, getting an anxious spiel from every winemaker, predictable snacks and instructions on how to taste and spit, or not spit, seemed to keep us moving and out of touch with each other. I drank too much during our tasting tour and ate too many of the snacks. We would have been better off lying on our beds, reading, and sharing a bottle of sweet red Spanish wine.

Back at the three and a half stars, I had a shower, a quick cry, put on fresh grey underwear and then changed for dinner.

"Is anything wrong?" he asked me over dinner.

By then, I knew it wasn't my grey underwear or my lack of Italian or a job: the way you know it's not missing the bus in the morning when a second class kid is still distraught at playlunch time; the way you know it's deeper than getting a spelling word wrong; or not being able to read something; or getting the drawing of your dog the wrong colour. But like those kids, I didn't know what it was or what it could be, and I certainly wasn't in any mood to tell him about my grey underwear, which in less stressful circumstances would have been a funny story, but at that moment was too painful, and too close to my heart, both literally and figuratively.

"Not really."

And then he got black and depressed and talked a lot about Bach, which is hardly exciting when you've barely met Bach and aren't on speaking terms, but he went on and on and on, and I drank a whole lot more and by the time we got back to the room, I was too drunk to care about my grey underwear, except I was savvy enough to take it off in the bathroom, and then hide it in my bag.

When we made love, there was none of the fresh excitement of the last time and I had that terrible feeling I'd blown it and I was on the edge of tears all the time, and on the edge of apologising, but too drunk to do it in a coherent and meaningful way.

In the morning we didn't make love, but the chat over breakfast was bright until he said that maybe we'd go straight home and not do any more wine tasting as he'd just remembered he had a feature to write that somebody else had been going to write, but hadn't.

And all the time on the way back, I wanted to explain, but it seemed too trivial and too stupid and I'd only come out of it looking pretty much as silly and trivial as it all was. But I looked at him and thought what a kind, clear face he had. Even if it was a bit tight round the mouth.

As I got out of the car, I made a little speech about it being good but I wasn't quite myself and I hope he wouldn't hold that against me and the "thank you for having me" which my mother had imprinted on my brain and he got out of the car and kissed me and said something about the long haul, which went straight out of my head, so by the time I was in the door I couldn't remember if he said we were in it for the long haul or we weren't. Sam was playing devil worship music and Taz was out when I rang and Genevieve said, "Oh yeah. How was it?" in such a bored way that I had to gush "Fabulous".

Later that night I saw Lucy dragging her bottom along the floor and I realised I hadn't been vigilant enough in the worming schedule so I rushed out and bought worm tablets for the dog and Combantrim for Sam and me, in case we'd caught them, and then had a huge row with Sam because he refused to have the Combantrim. I looked up parasites in the medical dictionary to prove to him he must be infested, but he'd gone out. I couldn't stop reading about the parasites that invade your brain or are forty metres long, or both. When Sam came home, I was armed with this information and I asked him again nicely and casually, out of consideration of the parasites eating away his nerve tissues, and got another horrible refusal.

When I was lying in bed lonely, so lonely that when Lucy Labrador's head appeared by magic on the pillow, I had no heart to resist, even though I couldn't be sure all her parasites would be dead by now. However I did get up and put an old towel under her, for which she gave me an extremely baleful look. And then I sat in the dark thinking I couldn't face another day of answering ads and practising my computer skills without much prospect of being able to use them. I thought maybe I'd just have a day off with Humphrey B Bear and Oprah.

Then I had a sudden, brilliant idea for getting the Combantrim into Sam and I went into the kitchen and poured out his dose in a medicine glass and then crept into his room. Exactly like when he was four I lifted his head up and said, "Hey Sammy, take this," and poured it down his throat and went back to bed feeling I was smarter than the average mother, which felt good but didn't quite dissolve all my self doubt and fear in other areas.

❋ ❋ ❋

I woke early. Too early, and with a terrible feeling of being wrenched away from the life I was supposed to have had. The Ex and me young and happy and in love. Life wasn't like that, but what was cruel was that almost none of it was like that. There were just flashes – us laughing on the beach; us dancing round the kitchen of our first house; drunk on the lawn and looking at the stars; out in a scary thunder storm; with the beautiful baby Genevieve. Flashes imprinted on my brain, tantalising proof of another universe.

The phone rang. The Labrador startled and started barking. I answered the phone irritably, which was fair enough because it was 5.30 in the morning. Then halfway through the sharp "Who is it?" I thought it might be Maggie and I softened my tone. But it was the Ex.

"I had the most terrible dream about you," he said. Very strange, but this was exactly the sort of thing he did back in my dreamtime days of romance with him when we had matching dreams. "And I'm ringing to check you're okay."

"Was it about me running away with a man and all my underwear being grey?" I asked, hoping there would be some psychic connection between us, forgetting how cross I was with him for his failure to parent Sam.

"No," he said, "it was about Maggie being in India. And I dreamt I took you to help me look for her and you were in some sort of danger in this strange temple."

"That *was* a dream," I said. "And Maggie *isn't* lost. She just hasn't phoned home, which is irritating but predictable." I sounded just like my older sister, which impressed me so much I went on. "There's nothing we can do about Maggie, but you could think of doing something with Sam next holidays."

"You and I could go to India and look for her."

"Genevieve told me you and Jackie are splitting up," I said. "Is that right?"

"I'd never leave her," he said.

"You said that about me in front of some priest about twenty-five years ago. Swore to it as far as I remember . . ."

"Leah . . ."

"Leah what? You did swear to it. Why should it be any different with *her*? You screw up my life, so why not hers as well?"

"There's a lot more to relationships than standing in front of someone promising to love, honour and obey . . ."

"I don't remember that *you* promised to obey *me*."

"You know what I mean."

"Not really. First you're moving back here and you think you might take Sam to the football and do an MBA and sort out things with me. Now we're going to India in search of our lost daughter."

"It's a very spiritual place. I've become really interested in spiritual things, Leah. We should talk, you know. I think I could help you. You've got a lot of anger."

Which was certainly right at that moment.

"You know a simple apology and a holiday in the tropics would probably do," I said. "When you left, you never even told me. You were supposedly going to look at a business proposition in Queensland, and I was dimly wondering why you had to take all your clothes."

"Leah, there was a lot more to it. And we *were* looking at a business and we bought it. It *was* a business trip. As you know."

"But you never came back, is that it?" He'd always maintained this idiocy, that it had just "happened", that it was "meant to be". I'd let it slide until I got the divorce papers and then he'd slid out of it with the "let's be friends for the sake of the kids, and haven't we always been friends, Leah?" I'd fallen for it. And it had been similar the day before with David, falling for my own nonsense, not being brave enough to declare myself a person with grey underwear.

Maybe I wasn't brave enough to declare myself to the world. Maybe it was just the way my mother always said to me, "Why are *you* moping? *You've* got nothing to complain about." Whereas Taz who had seen our own father carried off in front of her eyes never moped, although she got a bit tight round the mouth, but was brave and noble and kept her underwear in excellent condition. I lacked courage and moral fibre.

Sam came into the kitchen and said, "I had the weirdest dream."

To which I replied, "Dreams don't mean a lot."

"But I've got the worst taste in my mouth. In this dream someone was trying to poison me."

"Well," I said. "There were only the two of us here last night. And your own mother would hardly try to poison you. Would I, darling?"

Chapter 7

Energy and power in the young are the product of natural vitality. In middle age, they are more often the product of obsession and an attempt to regain lost youth.

But even obsession is better than lethargy. The terror of middle-aged emptiness can fuel passion and action, create the possibility of movement in a stagnant life. As Leah discovers, mindless activity may lead to new places.

I think Katie Bless You has a roster to ask me for a "cuppa" on a regular basis, as a neighbourly thing. I can't complain because it was through this neighbourly act that I became acquainted with Eat U Rite choc chip muffins, which are low in fat and low in sugar. Never mind that they have a slightly metallic taste, a bit like eating tailings from a tin mine; their low calorific properties have probably contained me at a neat size sixteen, as well as being a food that Sam, Lucy and I all enjoy.

"No, no, no," Katie says cheerfully to Lucy as we arrive. "Big puppies stay outside at my house." Which implies Katie's unpleasant terrier is a superior animal. Lucy does not dignify this idiocy with the disdain it deserves, but leans against her door, crying for pieces of Eat U Rites, which at home I toss to her and she catches. *She* cannot comprehend the smell of warm Eat U Rites and Katie Bless You's meanness.

I get nervous in this bright blue kitchen with its shining surfaces and no sign of domestic chaos. I am even more nervous when Geraldine, aged eighteen, rushes in from uni, kisses her mother on the cheek, says, "Hi Mum, how was your day?", gets a cheery reply and then goes off to put her dirty laundry in the machine or some such unnatural act. This is not a normal household.

"You're looking very down, Leah," says Katie.

"I haven't got a job," I say, "which takes the shine off life." I leave out the other stuff.

"You should do *voluntary* work! I've taken to going to the Gum Nut Homes on a Thursday. The 'Friend in need' program. You should see the *looks* on their faces."

"I *can* imagine," I say.

"*They're* thrilled," says Katie and I remind myself she is a person with feelings and an occasional understanding of sarcasm.

When I was a child, my mother was always lecturing me and Taz about not hurting people's feelings by making pointed jokes. "It may seem clever dear, but it's not kind."

"But it's funny," we'd protest, which cut no ice with my mother at all, who regarded funny as pretty far down on the level of social skills she was cultivating in her daughters, who seemed to regard everything, especially their mother, as very funny.

"I'm going to be blunt." Katie said and picked up the yappy and horrible Jake, who was tormenting poor Lucy from behind the safety of the security screen, and petted the horrid creature as if it was he who was the tormented one. Lucy had her lip curled, but only in self-defence. Katie Bless You patted Jake and then put him down.

"Puppies on the floor in this house, Jake," she said. I knew this was a broadside at Lounge Lizard Lucy's bad habits. "Now, Leah, *you* need to do something to lift your morale," she said. "You've done everything for those children, and nothing for yourself for years and years." My opinion of Katie Bless You shot up for a moment. "I understand why you don't do voluntary work – you've given so much to others – your children, all those other little ones at the school."

She was nuts. "I did get paid," I said. Little Jake was looking at me pleadingly. He knew I was his one chance for an Eat U Rite. Even Jake knew Katie was nuts.

"Of course you did," she said. "Quite rightly too. I suggest a walking program," she went on. "Nothing strenuous." She raised her hands to ward off my protests and smiled her sunny smile. "Why, bless you, there's that nature reserve the council's done at the end of Waratah Street. It's a nice brisk walk and it's so pretty when you get there. You could take the dear dog. Get out, commune with nature, I'll guarantee you've never done that, have you?" She says guarantee instead of bet because she doesn't believe in gambling. But she did have a point. I hadn't been to the new Waratah Street Reserve, although, if I had been teaching, I would certainly have taken my class down there, never mind the communing with nature.

Katie might have a font of wisdom in her pea-sized brain. Jake might be a nice dog. I picked up the last Eat U Rite on the plate (I had eaten two, Katie one) and tossed it to Jake. If it had been Lucy, she would have caught it neatly, gulped it down and licked up the crumbs. Jake stared at it as if a meteor had dropped out of the sky. Katie stared at me, as if I'd gone crazy.

"Lovely cuppa," I said, getting up and making for the door. "Really wonderful. And the walking idea. I'll get going on that." At least I hadn't chucked a cream sponge. Lucy gave me her "never trust terriers" look, but I walked back to my house with a spring in my step. I liked this walking idea.

Lucy was still depressed because she hadn't got a muffin and Jake had (and hadn't taken it), but I explained to her that we were swearing off muffins, even Eat U Rite choc chips. Maybe I would get a job soon. Maybe the Federation would get my job back, which I didn't want, but that was better than nothing. Maybe I'd get thin and beautiful. Maybe I'd regain my lost youth. Lucy nudged my hand with her wet nose. Bless you, Katie Bless You.

❀　❀　❀

Early next morning, I set off with Lucy down to the Waratah Reserve. Sam, in whom I had confided, had wondered why I felt I had to go early. "Other people go early, Mum," he said, "because they work. I don't even know why you bother to get up."

"Like you," I said. "Zest for life!"

It was a wonderful misty morning, which improved the look of the suburb of Grevillea no end, softening the graffiti, obscuring the stray pieces of rubbish, casting the dry gardens into a romantic fuzz. Lucy, unused to any exercise apart from her digging projects, trotted along beside me, carefully smelling all the things dogs smell. I had fantasies of how much weight I might lose if I did this every day, maybe twice a day, maybe walking over the other side of the railway line as well. I puffed up Waratah Street, which was the posh end of Grevillea (brick houses instead of fibro, trees instead of shrubs), feeling my calves taut, imagining my thighs, long and smooth. Well, smooth at least.

A path led down to the Waratah Reserve, with the usual noticeboards exulting the councillors responsible for its conversion from a rubbish tip to something of ecological significance. A piece of wood in the shape of a duck gave me the information that ducks had now returned to their rightful place in the suburb of Grevillea. There was another wooden block in a dog shape, saying "Please keep your dog leashed and respectful of the wildlife population in our reserve", but I'd already let Lucy free and I was sure she wouldn't know wildlife if it was right under her nose.

I wandered among the trees, discovered a little fernery, stared at the reflections in the water, admired the dew on the grass and smelled the beautiful lemony morning smell and thought this wasn't a bad way to become a better person with smooth thighs, presuming the varicose veins would disappear with all this wandering around. I began to think of other methods of self-improvement, like watching the news instead of *Seinfeld*, or reading a newspaper and then impressing David with my extraordinary knowledge of current affairs. Except I noticed that being informed about the news was largely a matter of opinion with Katie Bless You advocating hanging and compulsory courses to make people bring their children up properly, whereas my sister and her friends were dead against hanging and not in favour of children at all. *Seinfeld* probably tells you more about life than any of them.

"Hey, Mrs J! What *are* you doing here?"

"I'm walking," I said. One of the problems with teaching, especially infants, is that you bond with about sixty parents every year who are thereafter convinced of your deep interest in their offspring. "How's Emily?" I dredged the name up. And then his name. Jeff Smith. Three years ago. Transfer to a private school. Gifted and talented parents. And rich. He'd been on school council. Got on the wrong side of Twisted by not agreeing with her absolutely and totally. Good all out brawl one P&C meeting. My heart warmed at the memory, although I suspected he was bolshie rather than bright.

"Emily's terrific," he said, "but of course *you* always knew what a smart little kid she was."

He was *still* a gifted and talented parent. "Well yes," I said. Emily had been a pleasure, despite her pushy father.

"You still down at the school?"

"No," I said. "I crossed swords with Miss Siskay."

"She *was* the bitch from hell. We had Emily assessed and she refused to accept the assessment. *She* claimed a seven year old couldn't be that bright." His eyes blazed. "That's why we pulled her out. She didn't fire *you*, did she?"

"She did. The Federation are looking at it. But I was just a casual."

"You working somewhere else?"

"I'm looking for a job. She put the word out about me so I couldn't get another teaching job. I've been re-training for office work. But it's a bit hard at my age."

"I hated the cow." He paused. "You know, I might have

something. I've been looking for someone. You got computer skills? Could you run an accounting program?"

"MYOB," I said. "I'm pretty good, although I haven't had hands on experience." My heart was beating fast. He was one of those people who love doing other people favours, not out of goodness, but so he can boast to everyone else about it. But I didn't care. I could see he thought I was a worthy recipient of his help, one of the few who had recognised his child's genius. I wasn't going to change his mind.

Then there was a sudden bark, a scuffle, and a lot of quacking.

"Bloody hell!" he spluttered. "I can't believe people who let their dogs go down here. You know I'm on council. We got a grant from the government and we got the environment people in here. They got the wildlife back, and then people don't follow the rules. I got them to run the reserve right up behind our house." He winked at me. "One of the advantages of being on council."

I could feel Lucy's lead in my trackie pocket. This man had just said something about a job. I had a vision of Lucy, smeared with blood, fresh from the kill, wagging her tail at me. Except Lucy couldn't kill anything. She was full of energy, but it was mindless, hole-digging energy. But there *was* a lot of scuffling about down the creek in the mist.

"I'll have to go," I said. "I've got to get my youngest off to school. HSC, you know."

"I've got to get going too," he said. There were more sounds, further down the creek which was fortunately shrouded in mist. "Bloody disgrace," he muttered. "Look, nice seeing you. And if you want standard office work, it's pretty dull, but I could do with someone. Give you a bit of a start." He extended his hand and I shook it, not quite able to juggle the conflicting emotions coming from a real live job offer and the awful barking and snuffling and quacking noises. "You really got Emily going." I tried to remember any specific acts of kindness to Emily, but I think I just taught her to read like all the other little tykes. Never mind, if it meant a job.

"That'd be wonderful," I said. "Maybe you could give me your phone number?" More barking from Lucy down the gully. Sounds of desperate struggle. Dog versus job. If she appeared, I'd ignore her. Pretend I'd never met her.

He smiled. "Haven't got a pen on me. But I'm only up in Waratah Street. Number forty-four. Pop over tonight. Round six." He was serious. Lucy in the bushes coming closer. "I've got to be off! I jog." He smiled. "You know, the doc told me that gear about the pulse rate. See ya, Mrs J." I hated being called Mrs J. It smelled of patronage. Still, a job. Stay away Lucy. He jogged up the path, just in time to miss Lucy coming through the bushes, a duck in her mouth. The duck was making very faint, but horrible noises.

"Put it down," I hissed. I could see him further up the path, my employment salvation, the light at the end of my dole payment tunnel. It wouldn't take much to make him turn round and catch me aiding and abetting a duck killing. He was the sort to turn round for a last cheery wave. I prayed and said Hail Marys. He disappeared. I looked at Lucy, the now totally limp duck hanging out of her smiley mouth. I should say, on completely independent moral grounds I didn't approve of Lucy's behaviour. Or of mine, in having her off the lead. But I didn't think it should cost me a chance of a job. "Put it down. Drop!" I remembered

162

the command from puppy school, but clearly she didn't. Jeff Smith must be back on the street now, the rate he was going. "Put it down!" I said louder and more fiercely. Lucy isn't exactly obedient, but nor is she defiant. But now, there was something important at stake (for her, and for me) and she actually growled at me (but without opening her mouth and letting go of the duck). The duck still had an eye open. It was dead, but I swear the eye looked pleadingly at me. The way home was past Jeff Smith's house on Waratah Street. Lucy was incriminating in her very being, let alone carrying the bloody duck. I attached her leash.

"Now *drop* the duck." She stood there, duck in mouth.

"Drop it." Another growl as I tried to prise her jaws open. She seemed to have lockjaw. She looked at me as if this was the one thing she'd done in life. It was hers and hers alone. She didn't care about the park notices or the fact I had to walk past Jeff Smith's house.

I could run past the house. Number forty-four. Best house there. Nice lawn. A hedge. Even if they were looking, they wouldn't see Lucy. There would be other people on the street though. It wasn't a good look, the dead duck look. It'd get around, become gossip. So I took my jacket off and explained to her what I was going to do.

"You can keep the duck," I said. "I understand the duck is important to you, even though it is *not* a good thing that you've killed it. But you don't know that. So, I have to make it look like you haven't done it." She stopped growling. "I'm not taking the duck away," I said, and I swear the duck looked at me again with its beady eye, even though it was dead. I put my jacket under Lucy's jaw, bunched it over her head, then tied the arms over the top of her head and firmly under her chin. She whined. "I know you can't see," I said, "but that's your fault." I was about to remind her Labradors have a fine reputation as guide dogs, but I realised this was actually a reversal of the situation. "I'll help you. Just follow me."

It looked odd, but it didn't look like she had a duck unless you knew. Maybe I could say she'd been attacked by a duck.

I pulled on the leash and she followed, a little uncertain, but obviously still intent on the duck. We moved stealthily into Waratah Street, Lucy obediently at my heels, with just an occasional squeak from the jacket (Lucy, not the duck). I was right. Number forty-four had a hedge. I'd just flash by. They wouldn't be looking. I'd be fine. I hadn't jogged for years, but I'd do it now.

Bugger. He was in the front yard. Picking up his paper. Wouldn't see me. Bugger. His eyes met mine. I jogged faster. Breathless. I'd probably have a heart attack any second. "Getting that pulse rate up," I squeaked. "Hope I don't die!" I raised my hand, tightening Lucy's lead. She yelped, muffled by feathers. I ignored it. Big smile. He couldn't see her anyway behind the hedge. Jogged on. He looked bemused, but retreated back into the house. Reached the corner. Slowed down, round the corner and bumped into Katie Bless You.

"Oh, Leah. How wonderful. You've been jogging. But what happened to poor doggie?"

"Car hit her," I said. "Nothing serious, just a cut. Got to get to the vet. See you."

"Oh I'm sorry, bless you, you poor dear."

I summoned up one last tiny reserve of energy and picked up speed to break away from her, vowing never, ever to run again.

I was just back into the kitchen, recovering from the jogging and duck horror, having locked Lucy and the duck remains in the laundry, and waiting for Sam to wake up, when Katie Bless You stuck her head in through my kitchen door.

"Is the dog all right, Leah? Dear, what a fright for you."

"She's doing as well as can be expected," I said, like a police person. "It was only a superficial wound."

"I bumped into Mr Smith. He said he'd seen you down at the reserve."

Oh shit, oh shit, oh shit. "Yes. I was looking for Lucy," I said in an extremely calm manner. "She'd got out."

"Because he thought there was a dog down there messing round with the ducks. He was the one on council who lobbied for the money for it to be made into a reserve and for the wildlife to be brought back. Their house backs on to it, which was why it was awful having it as an old tip. He thinks it's doubled their value."

"I heard those other dogs," I said, "tormenting the poor ducks when I was looking for Lucy."

"Well, as long as she's okay," said Katie with a Bless You smile. "You know he comes to our prayer meetings at church sometimes. He told us there are dreadful things going on at council. We pray for them. I think he's really a good man at heart." I could see she was settling in for a long chat about Jeff Smith, the local council and God, except at that moment, Jack ran through the kitchen with a mouthful of duck feathers.

"Has he got a bird?" shrieked Katie.

"He sometimes catches the Indian mynahs," I said. "Not natives. Never natives. Katie, thanks for coming in.

I'll have to get moving now." I got up just as Sam came into the kitchen.

"Hey," he said. "There's blood all over the laundry and the dog's got a . . ."

I pushed him out of the kitchen and with a smile shut the door in Katie's face. "Sam," I said. "You must never ever let this get out. Lucy caught a duck, but there's a man who might offer me a job, but he won't if he knows that Lucy killed a duck. Katie saw it, except she thinks it was a car accident because the dog was all wrapped up in my jacket. But if she did know, she might tell him, so you keep your mouth shut."

He laughed. "Are you going nuts, Mum? And why is she in the laundry? That wasn't such a good idea. The washing looks like Charles Manson got to it."

"Because I didn't want anyone to see the duck." I was getting stressed. "And most of that's your laundry that I washed but you were too lazy to put in your room."

"Blood-stained clothing . . . cool."

"Sam, it's not cool. Don't speak about it."

"Not even amongst ourselves." He lowered his voice to a conspiratorial whisper.

"That'd be a relief."

"And if I tell anyone outside our compound, I must then kill them. Right! Or sacrifice a duck."

"The important thing is we keep to the story that Lucy got hit by a car and got a superficial wound that bled a lot."

"Which made her shed feathers?" He grinned.

"No! Sam! This is serious!"

"The truth, Mum. The truth is so simple!"

❀　❀　❀

It was hideous the way it played through my mind. I had trouble getting my story straight and believable, no matter how many times I ran it through my head. I had told Jeff Smith nothing, but Katie may have told him that I was running my dog wrapped up in a jacket because it had just been hit by a car. So why hadn't I told him that I was looking for my dog? Well, because I was obviously upset at the dog having escaped, and while I knew it would never hurt wildlife – no, I would leave that bit out. Someone had told me there was a dog fitting Lucy's description down in the reserve. So why hadn't I asked Jeff if he'd seen it? Because I knew my dog always ran away to a friend of Sam's on the other side of the park. And who was that? Well Filthy of course. For once I blessed Filthy.

But then, how did I get back to the Smiths' place so fast? Because Filthy was coming to meet me with Lucy because *he'd* found her after she'd been hit. Perfect! He'd seen some other awful dog (a spotted dog! Genius!) attacking ducks! No, don't get too elaborate. That's what I'd learned at the Convent School – if you're going to lie, keep it simple. By this time, Sam had gone to school. My head was in a whirl, going over the story. It was believable if extraordinary. Would I tell Jeff, straight out? Just in case Katie had said something? Only if he asked. Keep it simple.

And the laundry was still covered with blood and feathers. Deep breath. And I'd have to keep Lucy in all day, so Katie wouldn't see she wasn't injured – unless I could do a number on her with red texta. No, keep it simple. Deep breath. And where was that bloody cat getting the feathers? Deep breath. I rushed outside, but Jack had gone. Deep breath. What had happened to the simplicity of the smooth taut thighs? Because for a short while, before I met

Jeff, I'd enjoyed the walk and especially the thigh idea. Too exhausting to think about. A cup of tea and an Eat U Rite choc chip muffin. Taut thighs. Half to Lucy. Turn on *Humphrey B Bear*, the soothing bear.

❀　　❀　　❀

I rang the school at recess. It's unusual for a principal to answer, but just my luck, Twisted was on the other end of the line.

"It's Leah Jarrett," I said, remembering what Jason at the Federation had said. "How's the reading program going? With the talented Miss Baker?"

"You know, Leah, you can have all the *qualifications* in the world, but if you can't teach, you can't teach. You and *I* know that."

I imagined poor Miss Baker was probably standing in her office at this point. Twisted often put on these phone performances for the benefit of some hapless staff member trapped in her office. I was merely an incidental player.

"Well, you have to train people, don't you?" I said. "That's what being a principal is all about, isn't it?" I couldn't resist this little dig.

"We do miss you, Mrs Jarrett," she had the hide to say. "What can I help you with?"

"I need a word with Miss Took."

"I'll switch it through to the staff room. Nice to talk to you."

Somehow, the buzz of the staff room, the babble of voices, perhaps even hearing Twisted, suddenly made me feel nostalgic.

"Miss Took speaking."

"Tookie, it's me, Leah. I'm on the verge of a job, but I need some info."

"Oh Leah, how wonderful. What school?"

"No, no, no, not teaching. With that man Jeff Smith. Do you remember he had that little one, Emily, the year we were team teaching? Nice kid, but he was a pain."

"Leah, you're losing me."

"Well, he's offered me a job. But I just need to know what he does."

"I think they were in business."

"I know that. What sort of business?"

"Just a moment, I'll ask."

Diane, the school gossip on the line. "He ran a fishing shop – not selling fish, fishing gear, you know, hooks and things. In fact, that's what it's called – Hook Line and Sinker. You know, Robinson Road. It's got a big blow-up stingray out the front. And he's on council. He went for the family vote, whereas my Don lost out on picking up the garbage on time. No, Leah, further on than the chemist. Fancy him offering you a job. He was a live wire, wasn't he? We miss you, Leah. Got to dash. Bell's going."

But could I sell fishing gear? I'd never been fishing. I didn't even like the idea of it. It was cruel. Worse than killing ducks. Deep breath.

❋ ❋ ❋

"There was a duck killed down there this morning," Jeff Smith said to his wife as he handed me a glass of wine. It was one of those big living rooms with black leather sofas and glass tables, but not much else. A cut above mine, but nothing like Taz's and Rosanna's place. Expensive, but nondescript. Probably it was designed by Jeff, who clearly like the sound of his own voice echoing round the room and the idea of himself reclining grandly on his leather lounge. "Really, the coppers should be down there patrolling the area instead of stuck up in the station sitting on their bums."

"Prison," I muttered, thinking of the bits of duck shoved safely in my wheelie bin.

"Well, a fine perhaps." Susie, Jeff's mild wife, passed me a bowl of peanuts. She had a slightly ironic look, as if she didn't quite believe she was married to Jeff Smith. "There was that time you went duck shooting, after all, Jeffery." Emily, who hadn't really suffered by being so gifted and talented, sat beside me, colouring in a rather good picture of ducks.

"That was a long time ago," he said. "And it was mainly pigs. But those wild ducks out in the bush are a pest. They have to be culled. And Emily, shouldn't you be practising your violin?"

"She wanted to be here with Mrs Jarrett," said Susie. "She'll do practice straight after dinner." I detected a conspiracy between mother and daughter.

"Kids." I smiled, wondering when he was going to get round to the job. "Someone must have seen the dog that did it. There's always people jogging through in the morning."

"Yes, but the mist," I said. "You mentioned this morning you might have some work ..."

"Katie Stenmark told me your dog was injured down there."

"My son Sam, he's got a friend up in Wattle Street. The dog had wandered up there, and had been hit by a car. He was bringing her back."

"You didn't say anything about it," he said, "when I met you there."

"Well," I said, remembering I had made an agreement with myself not to change my story, except I wasn't sure any more which version of the story I was actually sticking to. It had all begun to get a bit hazy under the influence of the alcohol, which I wasn't used to at this time of day. "I was just going to get her then. She was hit by a car while Sam's friend was bringing her back."

"Weird time of day to return a dog," said Jeff.

"He had to go to school." The job better be good, I thought. All this lying – it was in my nature, a nun had once said, but surely not this much, or with this complexity.

Susie glanced at me and I had the distinct feeling she knew that my story wasn't quite the full truth. But perhaps she knew people had to lie to Jeff, for whatever reasons.

"You go off and do your homework, Em," he said. "I have to talk to Mrs J." He waited till she got to the door. "If I'd had her opportunities," he added as Emily departed. He assumed I agreed with him, which was made worse by the fact that I did, out of desperation for a job. It was only the thought of getting off the dole and repaying Taz that was keeping me here.

"I'll go and give Emily a hand," said Susie.

"I don't think you should be helping her," he said. "Bad practice, wouldn't you say, Mrs J?"

"Sometimes they need company," I said. "It's a bit unnatural working on your own." I smiled brightly, knowing this wasn't the right attitude.

"She'll spoil Emily," he said. "Make her a wimp."

"You can't spoil a child like Emily," I said. The wine was helping now. "She's so bright. And very sweet." A full suck-up.

"Well, I worry." Then he brightened. "You'll have to give me all the latest educational ideas when you come to work for me." By which he meant he'd give me all his. But at least he said "work".

"So what *is* this job?" I asked.

"Well, you know my shop?"

"The Hook Line and Sinker," I said as if I went shopping there every week. "Sam goes there."

He took the bait, so to speak. Obviously, everything he did and who he was were very important to him. And he wanted to share his importance around. "I want you to be my office manager," he said. "I think you'd be up to the responsibility. I've got all these young blokes working for me. And Laura. She's from my first marriage. Hopeless. Totally different from Em. Nice kid, but you know . . ."

Office manager. My heart pounded. This was a career, not just a job. The oppression of my months of unemployment began to lift. "As office manager," I asked, "what would be my duties?"

"Well, we got this computer system. Laura can't get the accounts onto it properly. It's like a bloody mad woman's breakfast. And then the ordering. The young fellows, they just order what they want, do what they like. I need a system."

"What program are you using?"

"MYOB. But no-one is using it properly. Laura's still doing the invoices manually."

"It shouldn't be hard to sort that out." Even though I'd just been practising and not using it in a real life situation,

I felt confident. "I can give you reconciliation, a cash flow, write the cheques on it." I felt a warm glow.

"It's a great business," he said, "but it's all over the place. I've got a million other things on the boil. You know, through council. I'm getting into residential development. Got a block of townhouses going up in Bluegum Terrace. I'm moving into property. Not that I'm letting the shop go – I mean it's a great little bread and butter enterprise. I'll tell you the problem. Here's an example. We had this rod on order. Two grand. It's sitting in the back of the shop. Guy comes in to collect it. No-one can find it. We order it again. Then we find the other one. Guy's got the shits. Gone elsewhere. So now I got these two rods sitting there. Someone will buy them. That's not the problem. It's a great business. But there's a pissed off customer out there and a system that isn't working. Laura can't control the boys or the computer system."

"So you want me to?"

"Exactly. I mean that's the other thing. There's probably a lot of thieving going on."

"I'll do your organising, but I'm not a security guard," I said. "That's another problem altogether."

"If I know what's going out and what's coming in and what's in stock, I'll have an idea if things are being thieved."

"So what's the salary level?"

"I thought starting money ... thirty grand would be pretty generous."

Not bad, I thought. If the job worked, it would be great experience. I had a feeling I could do it.

"I think you should up it to $35,000 in six months," I said, "if it works out."

"Look Mrs J, we're a suburban shop," he said.

"But you told me it's already profitable. And if I make the system more efficient, it will increase your profitability." Suddenly, I felt reckless. All those months of unemployment catching up with me. "It's a very responsible position," I said.

"But it's not like you're experienced."

I shrugged my shoulders and stood up. "Well, get someone experienced," I said. "Because I can see this job is going to keep me awake at nights. This job is going to drive me crazy. This job is bigger than both of us." I hoped it wasn't true, but he liked this sort of talk.

"You're hired, Mrs J," he said, and slapped me on the back. "You're well and truly hired."

❀   ❀   ❀

To celebrate, I ordered takeaway pizza with extra pepperoni when I got home. I didn't care if Jeff was a madman. I didn't care that I didn't like him. I didn't care that I knew nothing about fishing. I had a job. More than a job. I was an office manager. It would impress people. It impressed me. I could support myself. I was out of teaching. I could pay back my sister. I got on the phone.

"You're crazy," said Taz.

"And Tania said you'd never get a job," said my mother.

"Mum, you can finally hold your head up in front of Boaz," said Genevieve.

"What does she mean by that?" I asked Sam.

"She hates the way you slag off at him for not working," said Sam, "when *you* haven't even got a job. And could I have one of those Razor scooters for my birthday?"

"Maybe," I said.

The pizzas arrived and we sat down at the kitchen table, Lucy waiting expectantly for the leftovers. I opened a bottle of champagne and poured a glass for me and a glass for Sam.

"This is cool, Mum," said Sam. "Champagne every night now?"

"And oysters, and caviar. No more pizza."

"I like pizza!"

"I know. Look, Sam. About Boaz. I know you think I'm mean, but I just think people should pay their own way."

"Why? I mean that's what you've got to ask. Why shouldn't Gen support him if she wants to? He does good stuff like his painting and he helped me heaps giving up smoking. He makes her happy. What's so bad about that?"

"Because," I said, trying to think, "it's unfair to Gen." I tried to be even-handed. "And to Boaz. People with money have power. So they always have it. So the relationship is unbalanced."

"Yeah," said Sam. "That's why *we* don't get along. You have all the power."

"You have a wonderful fund of passive resistance," I said, "when it comes to sharing the work."

"That," he said, "is a mother–son thing. Resistance is necessary for me to develop maturity and responsibility." He finished his pizza and took his plate over to the sink. But left it there. Unrinsed, unstacked. I decided to ignore it. A person with bright orange hair obviously had limited maturity. I picked up the remaining slice of pizza and tossed it to Lucy, who caught it neatly and devoured it in one gulp, looking up expectantly for more leftovers.

"I was going to have that for lunch tomorrow," Sam said.

"Well, you can't," I said. "And rinse your plate."

"I know I can't," he said. "Unless I strangle the dog and reach down her throat and pull the pizza out." And with that he lunged at the dog, wrestled her to the floor and started trying to prise open her jaws, yelling, "Give me my pizza, you bitch! Give me my goddamn pizza!" Which was a game the dog entered into by barking loudly, growling and seizing him in her jaws.

All part of the grim fun of family life until I looked up and saw David, standing at the back door, with a bunch of sad daffodils, grinning inanely.

"Hi," I said.

Sam let the dog go, and said, "G'day, how are ya?" in a bluff sort of masculine way, and then left the kitchen. I picked up the pizza box and put it in the recycling bin next to the door and took David's daffs and chatted as I put them in water, and we sat and talked. I knew he knew things were okay with me, and I knew things were okay with him, but somehow we felt too raw to discuss it. I felt I could hold my head up now I had a job. Having a job gave me a nice warm feeling inside, whereas before there'd been a horrible hole and only Oprah to help.

"Leah," he said. "Were you insulted? Taking you somewhere that was a freebie? And only three and a half stars."

"I think freebies are great," I said.

"I got myself into a funk, thinking I'd insulted you. Because you seemed in a bit of a funk."

"I was in a funk because I'd worn my oldest underwear instead of new and sexy stuff I had especially for the occasion."

"God," he said. "I'm not a lingerie sort of bloke. I never even noticed."

So we went out for coffee and had more of a good time, and went to bed up in Cockroach Towers, and had the best time, and I came home very, very late indeed, but somehow, I felt good enough to get up and go for a taut thigh walk, although not with Lucy, and nowhere near the duck reserve.

Chapter 8

For the young, life is like climbing a steep slope. It doesn't feel as hard as it should, because it is full of promise, full of the future; and the climbers are young. It feels fast and racy, but in reality, the young life is slow.

The young get married, have a baby, buy a house, get a new car, have an affair and only a year has gone by.

In middle age, we reach the summit. Finally, there's the chance to stretch, look around, admire achievement, lament failure. That contemplative moment is not as wonderful as it should be because failure is more prominent than success. But even more importantly, it has all passed. This brings a sense of uncertainty, unease, and then, a tiny stumble, which catapults us off the summit, down the slippery slope. Jobs of increasing irrelevance, the death of parents, retirement, a grandchild, dementia, we're done. It's over in a flash!

They say you have to want taut thighs for yourself – it's no use wanting them for anybody else. And it's true. I felt enormous contentment at wanting the thighs for myself because they (potentially) felt like an extension of who I *really* was. I enjoyed myself with David and I wanted how I looked (slightly daggy) to line up a little more with how I felt (deeply erotic). While I knew the two would never marry completely, taut thighs were worth a try.

So I decided to walk to my new job. Never mind that I had spent the previous day digging my new rose bed, much to the delight of Lucy and Katie Bless You with her head over the fence. Never mind that this was further than I had ever walked in my life. Or that I would be exhausted by the time I got there. And disheartened by the knowledge that I had to walk home again at the end of the day. The thighs felt distinctly possible.

In the end, taut thighs and walking were a mere footnote to my day. On the way, I had dreams of what my new job would be like. I imagined my office. I imagined my managing. I imagined my computer skills. It all looked good in my head, but in reality, a woman in a fishing shop is something else altogether. A woman in a fishing shop is not a sex object, or a token woman – she doesn't actually exist. I stood there, waiting for someone to take notice. Nobody did. As I looked around, I realised Hook Line and Sinker was a masculine shrine, a gadget lover's paradise, sleek and expensive, serious and boyish at the same time.

In theory, the Hook Line and Sinker variety of masculinity seemed quite appealing, except I was being ignored. There was something elemental in it, concentrated, instinctive, like a dog digging a hole without reason (or catching a duck).

Being Monday morning, the shop was hardly packed, but there were two men engaged in deep conversation about breaking strain and "how she floated" and whether to use "muddies" or "yer live frog". Two younger men were unpacking a crate. I didn't know if they were staff or customers, but it didn't matter. I was as relevant as a piece of dust on the floor. Jeff was nowhere to be seen, so I walked up and down, idly fingering fishing rods, wondering how I would break into this magic circle.

"You're Mrs Jarrett," said a female voice. "I'm Laura. Jeff's my dad." She assailed one of the men. "Mike, couldn't one of you guys have paid this lady some attention? You know you're supposed to look after people in the shop." Mike ignored her. "Well, where's Dad?" she said.

"He's in the carpark, checking the parking for the weekend."

She went to the back of the shop. "Dad! Mrs Jarrett's here."

Jeff came in, looking distracted. "Oh, hello Mrs J. You're starting today?"

"Today's the day," I said.

"I said next week," he said, although he'd written down the date for me. He looked annoyed. "You know, there were more dogs down at the reserve last week. That environment fellow we've got on the payroll says duck numbers are dropping – they've been scared away, or destroyed. Someone saw a pack of dogs going out that top exit. Katie Stenmark tells me your dog is a fair size."

This fed into my deepest fears of being on the unemployment scrap heap forever. "She's fat," I said. "Not Katie, the dog. And placid. Nearly eleven years old. Past it, not that she would have ever been into it."

"You keep the dog locked up, don't you?"

"Of course," I said, recalling the loose catch on the gate. "And she's not a pack dog."

"All dogs are pack animals," he said.

"How's Emily getting on at school?" I asked.

"Damn fancy private school. You pay a fortune and they don't lift a finger."

I could have launched into my defence of the public school system, and explained how at the very least they would have neglected Emily's amazing talents for free, but I stopped myself. "Where would you like me to start?" I asked. "You know, doing the office management." This sentence trailed away, making me sound as if I didn't know what office managing was.

"I was going to give you a management plan." He looked at his watch. "But I haven't had time to set it out in detail. So, Laura can show you around and introduce you to the boys. I've got a meeting up at council. I'll sort something next week."

I followed Laura upstairs. It was not the office I had imagined. It had boxes all around the walls, a tiny window, an electric jug, a microwave and a grotty sink in one corner.

"You'll never get a management plan," Laura said. "You'll never get anything except what's wrong. Never what's right." She sat down at her desk and clicked the mouse on the computer. "Not that there's anything much right. I don't know how to work this program and neither does he, but he's always telling me to do it differently."

"Show me," I said.

"The inventory files are a bit strange," she said, "because mostly, with each new lot of stock, there are new prices, so I open new files. Dad said to do it that way, but now he complains that there are way too many files."

I leaned over her shoulder. There were forty-four files for Mustad hooks, size 0-one.

"Is there a cash flow?" I asked.

"Not really," she said. "Sit down." Laura pulled up another chair and we sat together at the computer. "It's all supposed to be integrated," she said, "like when they ring something up in the shop, it's supposed to go into the cash flow and out of the inventory. All the payments and wages are all in separate files and I dunno how to link them. The stuff we order goes into the cash flow, but I do the inventory manually, except then I have to change the sale into miscellaneous because it's already gone in from the register."

"Hang on, why do you do it that way?"

"Because the hooks are all different prices, depending on when they've come into the shop. Which is why there are forty-four files. Just for the Mustads. And sometimes, there's a bonus discount, and Dad says you can't put that on cash flow, because it isn't cash. And it's not profit till it's sold, but it's impossible to tell which ones are sold, so it's easier to do a separate file for each one."

I wondered if she was gifted and talented too.

"It's very complex," I said.

"I can never answer any of Dad's questions," she said. "The accountant says it's totally stuffed."

"And what's this one?" I asked. "Cars?"

She sighed. "On the weekends, you know, the markets are up the road. Dad has an agreement with a guy on council so we use the land next door for paid parking. And a car-wash. Which is mainly a cash business. I have to work here because Dad is convinced the boys will cheat him. But we can't put it all in the computer because the cars are a cash business."

"Cash?"

"They don't pay that much tax."

"And photographic?"

"That's the ballet studio upstairs. Dad rents it to Emmy's ballet teacher because she lost her booking in the school hall. And we do photographs of the little girls when they go up each grade, because we have it set up down here anyway, because some of the guys bring a catch in and they want a proper photo. We've got that little studio booth up the back. And that all comes through on photo 1, whereas the ballet is photo 2."

"Is there anything else?" I asked.

"Colour photocopying." She giggled. "One of the guys photocopied his bum last week. Dad was furious because he says it might be a joke, but jokes cost money." She clicked on another file. "There's an old guy who does some outboard repairs in the shed out the back on the weekend. It all comes through the business but then Dad pays him the lot because his wife has cancer."

"So why are you leaving?" I asked.

"I can't *stand* him," she said. "He's like – manic. And everything changes all the time. And he's terrified of me finding out how much he makes and telling Mum in case she wants more money. Except I did anyway, and now he hates me because he has to pay her more, except he can't bear to admit I got through his system because he doesn't like to admit I might have any brains."

I was itching to get the system working. Even Jeff, if he stopped talking about the dog and the ducks, could be managed. Same techniques you use with Year 5 when they decide they're grown up and can now run the world – flattery, common sense and some good hard discipline.

I felt a warm glow that all those months of study at the computer had paid off. My brain was already buzzing with the inventory problem.

"I've made loads of money here," said Laura. "I mean I work real hard, and Dad's not that bad. He's paranoid about the boys in the shop. I'm the one he trusts. But I'm off to London in a few weeks."

"And what are you going to do there?" I asked.

"Rage and spend his money." She looked at me, guileless. "I have got one big fat bonus for me in the payroll for when I leave." For a second, my heart went out to Jeff.

❀ ❀ ❀

Trudging with the peak-hour traffic racing past me, breathing in poisonous fumes (what are poisonous fumes compared to taut thighs?), I thought about my new job. I'd cleaned the sink and the desk, but it wasn't an executive office. It would be satisfying to sort out the files, but you wouldn't want to work in a job like that forever.

Taz had told me that to be a career person you had to eat, sleep, walk and talk your job twenty-four hours a day. She kept a pad next to her bed to make notes when she had midnight revelations about corporate structure or market penetration. Taz had always been totally focused. When we were little, we started collecting a series of twenty china horses. I paid for one, broke its legs and lost interest. Taz got the whole series. She told me later she didn't like them much, but she did it because she'd decided to.

Teaching isn't the sort of job that suits that sort of thinking. You think about teaching a lot, but in bursts like you think about being a mother. You don't need a notepad next to your bed. Getting the Hook Line and Sinker cash flow in order was interesting but would never have the pull of teaching. It was a complex technical problem, but when I tried to concentrate on it now, my mind went to Maggie and wishing she would contact me and wondering why she didn't like me. And then I was thinking about David and how nice it had been in bed, with a sudden pang of wondering whether Sam knew, and whether he was forever psychologically damaged if he did.

And then there was Gen and the fact that I'd made another tactless remark about Boaz and money to her and now she wasn't speaking to me. And how, all my life (now I'd turned off the main road and its poison fumes into the quietness of suburbia), I'd just wanted love and happiness in one of these nice tidy houses without the grass growing up over the fence in great feral strands. And how the Ex had deserted me, and maybe that's why the relationships with the children weren't as nice as I'd once imagined.

And then, when I got home, there was the Ex, sitting in my kitchen. The Ex! Who I had not seen for years, sitting there. As if he belonged. Cool as a cucumber. Just sitting, only a bit older than he used to be, but still very nice looking, with gray hair cut really short which suited him and no paunch. Which I was so used to in David that even though I could recognise the Ex was in fine shape, he looked just a bit pinched and mean, as opposed to David's rather more generous and expansive body. In fact, he'd lost a lot of the glam and glitz I'd always thought he'd had and I wondered if he had actually lost it; or maybe he'd never had it, and I'd just imagined it.

185

Sam was in his room, playing the devil worship music very loudly, and the first thing the Ex said, without introduction or explanation of why he might be in my kitchen, was, "I can't seem to get through to *him*."

"Stay another five minutes," I said. "You know, quality time." My smart mouth, my sore feet. This was the man I had longed for and wanted for so long. Although, to be perfectly honest, not the man I had in mind with my taut thighs.

"The place is looking a bit run down, Leah."

I was so amazed to find him in my kitchen that I didn't know how to react to him criticising me, wearing an Indian shirt and one of those annoying spiritual expressions, which didn't quite match his discontent at being where he was.

"Do you want a cup of tea?"

"I have chai," he said. "I've brought my own."

"So, you *have* been to India," I said. "Did you look for Maggie?"

"I couldn't track her down," he said. "But I had an amazing journey."

"Well, I've had a hard day at work," I said.

"I've surprised myself coming here," he said, as if he expected me to be equally amazed, which secretly I was.

"So Sam wasn't thrilled to see you?"

"No, he wasn't."

"It'll take a lot of time," I said, "if you're serious. But he does need a father, you know."

"You know I left Jackie?" he said, as he made his chai. It was funny, seeing him make the tea because it was so familiar, but unfamiliar too. He used to be a milk and three sugars sort of bloke, and he still had all the gestures, but I could tell he wasn't the same any more. The chai smelled different, but it smelled nice too. He made me a cup of ordinary tea with a teabag, as if he'd never stopped doing it.

"I've completely screwed up my life," he said, when he sat down. "And Jackie's."

I was tempted to add *my* life to the list of ruins and I was especially tempted to ask him about this latest break-up, but I refrained. "I'm worried about Maggie," I said.

"She's all right," he said. "She's been in touch with Jackie. She made her promise to ring every week."

My heart felt as if it were splitting. "Jackie!?" I said.

"They've always been close. Jackie lets her call reverse charges."

"Is she okay?" My heart was pounding with resentment and sorrow and relief.

"She's fine. Five months pregnant, I gather."

"So why wasn't I told this properly? By Jackie? Or given a phone number?"

"Jackie will barely tell me anything. She says the calls are between her and Maggie. I mean, I suppose she's got a point – Maggie's twenty-one. But that's partly why I went over. I had an address for Maggie but she'd moved on."

"So *this* woman," I said, "*she* knows where Maggie is, but she won't tell her father or her mother."

"Don't call her 'this woman'." He said it gently, more in sorrow than in anger, which was irritating.

"I can call her what I like. I'm past being polite about *her*. First, she pinches you. Now, she's picking off my daughter. And my grandchild!" I'd never thought of Maggie's pregnancy as really producing a baby who would be my grandchild, but now, the thought hit me forcefully. *My* grandchild! And my Maggie. "Why doesn't Maggie ring *me*?"

"Leah, you know you two have always been daggers drawn. She can't talk to you ..."

This went through my heart like a knife, but it was true. I'd been thinking of Maggie as my wildchild, my adventurous one. She was those things but, unlike Genevieve, she had never seemed to need anything from me. I wasn't even sure she actually liked me very much. It must have shown in my face.

"Leah, sometimes it's better when we face these things..." He patted my hand across the table. "When I was in India, I found out I couldn't be all things to all people. I just had to be true to myself. It's been really hard, this break-up with Jackie. When I left, I just felt so guilty. Breaking up something like that. But staying there, I was destroying myself."

"What about when you left *me*?" I demanded, lifting my head to give him my steeliest glance.

"I would never have left," he said gently. "You made me go."

❀　❀　❀

I was in a frenzy that night. *I* made him go? I *made* him go?

"*You* told me," he said when I'd questioned him further, before pouring out his chai and telling him to go, evidently for the second time in my life. "You said, 'I'm not having you in this house, contaminating these children.' Even then, I knew it wouldn't work with Jackie, but it was all I had."

"After your *holiday* with her," I said. "You wanted to come back to my loving arms?"

"It was before the holiday," he said. "You told me the marriage was over."

I denied all memory of this but then I searched my mind. Well, I had the memory, but I'd never meant it. I wanted him to be sorry, to feel the full impact of my upset. I hadn't wanted him to *go*.

The Ex and I batted this back and forth in my kitchen, the level of distress and the noise level equal to the original altercation more than ten years before. Sam had stuck his head in and said, "Oh shit." We were shamed into silence for a short time, then started arguing again. Finally, I insisted he leave.

When he'd gathered up his things, he'd said, "Leah, we really should thrash this out in a more spiritual way," and I'd made my vomit face which I had been famous for when I was about six.

I said, "Goodnight, sweetie," to Sam through his door in a pathetic way, and didn't get a reply, then got into bed and read my medical dictionary entry about intestinal parasites. In the middle of the night, in a frenzy of intestinal worm paranoia, I got up and dosed Sam again, and then myself, and got out the worm tablets in the laundry cupboard to give one to Jack and Lucy. I gave Lucy hers in a chocolate which she sat up and gulped and then, because the packet said "with food", gave her the rest of the chocolate, all the while thinking about the extraordinary revelation that the Ex had really not wanted to leave all those years ago and it was only my ill-chosen words that actually forced him out the door.

All the hurtful things he'd said to me came back like lines in a bad play that I'd written myself and had been rehearsing for ten years, thinking it was true. And at the same time, I was trying to gather myself to go back to my new career in the morning. I had fish hooks and computer screens running through my head, along with the picture of the intestinal parasites, convinced that by this time they must have reached my brain and were causing all this havoc, making me more paranoid about parasites than I needed to be.

I felt like a bad mother. Drugging a near adult child wasn't good parenting in anybody's book. It wasn't a good example for a seventeen-year-old boy, except he didn't know. Although he'd nearly woken up when I'd given him the dose. And I got to thinking there were a lot of unethical things I'd done, and lies I'd told in my time as a mother.

After that, I did some tossing and turning with maternal guilt and dreamt about Taz being cross about her money, and the Ex and Pouty Lips, until Sam appeared in my (real) consciousness, jumping around in a fury, holding the Combantrim bottle, and yelling that he knew what I'd done and I'd had no right. He quoted the UN Convention on the Rights of the Child that Boaz had told him about. I begged him to try and see reason and I apologised, but you should never apologise with the "for your own good" proviso which I used on this occasion, because that proviso simply doesn't go down well with your average seventeen year old. Then he slammed out the door and I thought, well, at least it got him to school on time for once.

❋ ❋ ❋

David called just before I set off on the long march to work (I wasn't letting taut thighs go, even if the rest of my constructed world was falling down around me).

"Leah," he said, "don't let these people get to you. I love you, you know."

"Your own flesh and blood never stop getting to you," I said. "They're worse than intestinal parasites. They *are* intestinal parasites."

He laughed. "Your Ex isn't flesh and blood."

"David, sometimes he feels like it."

Then there was a hurt silence.

"It's crazy, I know."

"I want to replace him," David said, "as flesh and blood."

I was going to thank him and tell him I needed less flesh and blood both literally and figuratively, but he told me a call was coming through from one of the subs and we'd talk later. I sighed and put on my shoes and tied up the broken latch on the gate to stop Lucy getting out of the yard and waved to Katie Bless You and headed off for my second day at Hook Line and Sinker.

❀   ❀   ❀

I thought the Ex would be back the next day, but he wasn't. Or the next week. He rang the following weekend, spoke briefly to Sam, who for once seemed pleased to talk to him, which was probably because Sam was still not talking to me because of the Combantrim episode. Then the Ex asked to speak to me.

"Jackie is prepared to pass a message on to Maggie," he said.

"Tell her to go bite her bum," I retorted.

"Jackie or Maggie?" he said and just from the way he said it, I could tell he was wearing his spiritual expression and probably the Indian shirt.

"Both," I snapped. "I'm not going to pass on a message through her."

"Isn't this a bit childish?"

"Maybe. Look, what sort of message am I going to give her? 'I love you honey and I'll support you all the way,' or 'Make sure you're taking your iron.' If she wants to talk to me, she can call me. If I send a message, it's just demeaning and you can be pretty damn sure it'll get re-interpreted and rephrased along the way."

"Leah . . ."

"Well, you can . . ."

"You know when we were talking about the break-up the other night, this is exactly the sort of thing I was going on about. You over-reacted to the situation. And before we knew it, we were divorced."

"And not a moment too soon," I said and hung up.

❀   ❀   ❀

"Whose fault was my divorce?" I asked Taz. We were sitting in her courtyard, sipping martinis. I'd come to give her an instalment of her money, but I was stalling, because I had to confess that she wouldn't have it all by the time she went to Bali. And I wanted to discuss the tissue of lies that we were both involved in over this money.

"I thought it was all no fault now," she said. "In law." She even had a mirror in her courtyard, and she strained to catch a glimpse of herself, and then carefully ran her finger over her eyelid to adjust the brown eyeshadow.

"Yes, but that's only law. The Ex came round the other day. He was saying he would have come back except that I made him go and insisted on the divorce. I mean, would you say he was right?"

"Pretty much," she said. "Remember he tried to get me

to talk to you, and I told him he had to do it himself. And then, when he did, you threw an apple at him, and gave him a black eye. I ended up driving him to the doctor because you wouldn't."

"I was upset," I said. But the tables had been turned, the truth re-configured. It still didn't feel right to me, but I knew that could have been because I was deceiving myself all those years. "Here's a cheque," I said, ferreting round in my bag. "Part payment."

"I need it all by the time I go to Bali," she said.

"If you'd thought about it, or I'd thought about it before this, we would have known I can't do that," I said. "Our form of lending and borrowing is a form of self-deception."

"What's that supposed to mean?" she said.

"It means the money is a game between us. You lend me money and tell me I have to pay it back by a certain time. I know I can't and you know I can't, but we never even think about that. It's just this sister game. Good sister/bad sister. Big sister/little sister."

"That's nonsense, Leah." She used her most snooty, company voice. "I wish you'd stick to the timetable that we agreed on."

I knew it was her as much as me. Even so, the big sister thing sticks with you a long time, maybe for life. I felt as if I'd made a rude gesture in front of a Virgin Mary statue. After all, we had an agreement (me and Taz, not me and the Virgin Mary). I'd signed up for life when I was about two years old.

"Thanks for the drink," I said. "I'll see you later."

❀   ❀   ❀

I worked so hard at Hook Line and Sinker at straightening up the accounts that my head hurt, but I was gradually getting the system running. I had a sense of growing mastery. This wasn't teaching, but I was good at it. I had a proper cash flow and had the inventory files in order. I was even playing round with a financial bottom line.

Jeff came in now and then. I emailed him reports about what I was doing and how I was getting the system in order. He never acknowledged them, but sometimes dropped in, patronised me, and then left.

I pointed out that his cash flow projections didn't look good.

"The overdraft won't carry you through next Christmas," I said. "If you look at last year's figures of what you ordered, it's going to put you over the limit."

"Leah," he said, "you're an office manager, not a business manager. Remember that." But at least nothing more was said about the dog and I had the feeling he was slightly intimidated by me knowing about his finances.

Day to day, my biggest problem was the men in the shop who continued to ignore me, even though I made a point of talking to Mike, the sales supervisor, and asking him about his life, however blank the reply. A technique learned from teaching. But it irked me how unresponsive he was.

"Hey girls." Mike stuck his head round the door one afternoon. "I need you two to come down and stick price stickers on the new shipment."

Laura started to get up, but I pulled her down. "That's not our job," I said. "We run the office."

"Laura always helps," he said. "It takes ages on our own. We gotta have the stock out for Thursday night."

I knew this tone from kids in second class. Before age

seven, they'll do anything you ask, however incompetently. After that, better nature ceases to be second nature and they do anything to avoid doing anything. This was where Mike was at.

"I'll phone Jeff and ask him if he'll pay you overtime to stay back and do it," I said.

"It only takes a couple of hours," whispered Laura.

"We're doing the invoices," I said. "I'll phone and authorise the overtime."

"Don't worry then." Mike grunted and went back down to the shop. Over the next few days, there was retribution in the form of botched invoices and cash entries that made no sense. I'd conquered a delinquent Year 6. I could do this.

"I'll be getting Jeff to look over the invoicing system when he comes in," I told Mike, "so we'll try and work out why all those mistakes are coming up from the shop. We might run a little training course, so everyone knows their job and how to do it from sales to invoicing." I said it with a smile and an implied threat, then I ordered them in pizza on Thursday night when the shop was busy, and the next morning, I had a heart to heart with Mike.

"I like you," I said, "despite all the shit you've been throwing my way. You do a great job in the shop, and I guess it's not your fault that you think the female sex is put on earth to do your bidding. But this is the twenty-first century and life is different now. Men are now on earth to do women's bidding and I'm the advance guard. Don't mess with me, or I'll kill you." They weren't the exact words I used, but he got the message, and I got peace and co-operation. A couple of them even developed a slavish devotion which I took to quite easily.

At Hook Line and Sinker I had the moral superiority card. At home, I'd given that away with the Combantrim. No amount of Eat U Rite choc chip muffins or pepperoni pizza would get it back for me. The devil worship music played night and day. There was little indication during a four-week study break that any study was being done. Sam had long talks on the phone to Boaz and three girls called Amanda.

"Sam, this year is very important. I think you could put in a little more effort," I suggested.

"Mum, I am studying. Don't hassle me."

"You're not. You're out most days."

"Well, I can't study here. You'll drug me."

"Sam, I explained about that. I said I was sorry."

"But you did it before, didn't you? The time I had that dream?"

"Sam, I get really scared of intestinal parasites. You read the medical dictionary. You'd be scared too."

"I'm scared of you. You're really crazy, you know."

I know what it's like to think your own mother is crazy. I was thinking it about my mother. Except she *was* crazy.

"Leah, I was on John Laws today," she rang and told me, "talking about the unemployed."

"What about them, Mum?"

"That they could all get jobs. Like you. I told them your story, how you never took the dole."

"But I did, Mum. How else do you think I lived?"

She sniffed. "Tania lent you money."

"I spent that on clothes," I said. In fact, I'd made progress on that front at least, taking out a loan at a sharkish rate of interest and repaying Taz in full. I could tell she didn't like it. She would have rather had the moral superiority.

"Leah! Really!"

"Mum, I have to have decent clothes. And feed Sam, and send him to school."

"You could get a sewing machine. I used to make all your school uniforms and Tania's formal . . ."

"I know Mum . . ." Fear and gratitude had been bred into me.

"I'm glad I didn't know the full story before I rang Mr Laws."

"You could always ring him back and explain."

"I'm going to ring him about the unmarried mothers soon. It's a disgrace. Do you know how many of these girls are producing innocent babies just for the money?"

I was tempted to tell her about Maggie, but it would have just been point scoring. She'd have to be told, carefully, and a storm would break when she was. I dreaded the whole thing.

❀   ❀   ❀

Jeff seemed to regard his elevation to council as a personal endorsement of his development project and anything else he wanted to do. I kept giving him cash flow projections and pointing out the bank had been calling about the excess on the overdraft. To which he paid no attention. Now Laura had gone, I understood why. Jeff was obsessed, amongst other things, about Emily and her education, in which he assumed I had a never ending interest. I was shown Emily's compositions, her spelling reports, her maths exercises and her drawings. Apart from his obsession with Emily's talents, Jeff had the attention span of a mosquito, but the same desire for blood.

"What do you think of that, Mrs J?" He bounced in one morning when I had especially tired taut thighs and presented me with one of Emily's poems. "Pretty good for an eight year old, eh?"

"It's nice," I said, and turned to the invoices.

"It rhymes!" he said. "I told her lots of poets these days can't do a rhyme."

"It doesn't scan though," I said.

"Well as long as it rhymes," he said. "Ninety-nine per cent of the population wouldn't know a scanned poem if they tripped over one."

"Don't take it personally."

He looked at me suspiciously, finally noticing my lack of enthusiasm. "Maybe you think Emily *isn't* gifted?"

Emily's giftedness and talent had become harder to take than Laura's sloppiness or Mike's hostility. I'd managed to make headway with those.

"I like Emily. She's really sweet. And incidentally, she's a very smart kid too." I started checking the invoices.

"But you don't exactly take it seriously, do you?" He was hectoring me. "It's like you're laughing at it or something." I kept on with the invoices.

"She's performing at least three years above her age group in English and four years in maths. You'd have to agree that's pretty impressive."

"Look," I said. "I'm pretty good at maths. I'm pretty good at computing too. I probably perform better than most people in the forty-five-year age group. I'm probably up there with the fifty year olds, maybe even down there with the eighteen year old hot shots. But I wasn't brought up with that idea in my head, Jeff. It's nice, but it's not important. I learned that as a teacher. Kids have other dimensions. They shouldn't be paraded like performing seals. Not that seals should be either," I added, probably detracting from my argument.

Jeff stormed off to his townhouses.

"Did you deny young Emily was the Sun Goddess?" said Mike, who'd come upstairs after Jeff had given him the poem to read on his way out. After Mike's treacherous praise, he had been given a scathing indictment of my failure to appreciate the gifted and talented. "I think that's grounds for dismissal."

"My big mouth."

"She's a sweet kid, but he's a deadshit," said Mike. "Anyone can see that."

"You like me to tell him that too?" I asked, and we laughed and he actually made me a cup of coffee and told me my new dress looked nice. Just like a Year 5 kid will do after you've broken their spirit.

I worked madly all day to prove my worth and Jeff came back in the afternoon and for the first time didn't mention the prodigious talents of his daughter. But it was clear from the careful way he explained things to me that he felt I'd dropped a couple of IQ points. He stayed around, shuffling through papers and sighing theatrically at what were presumably my mistakes.

I began to see that this job might not last until I got my five thousand dollar pay rise. It had been dumb to deflate the Emily bubble. I needed the job. Not forever, but for a respectable length of time, so I could get another one without looking like a complete loser. I knew that now I had the computer system up and running, I could do it. I had runs on the board, but I needed an employment record. It was a bad habit to tell employers what I thought of them. Just when I thought he was going to leave me alone, Jeff leaned back on the filing cabinet, looking very pleased with himself.

"My wife picked up your dog down at the reserve this afternoon," he said.

"What reserve?" I said. My heart was beating fast. The heart of a duck killer. Mummy goes a hunting. Images crowded my mind – my shame, the fear of exposure, rather than compassion for the ducks.

"The duck reserve. Out the back of our place," he said. "You didn't tell me you have a Labrador."

"Well, part Labrador," I said. "Not a thoroughbred." Why lie? She *was* thoroughbred, yet here I was, prepared to defame poor Lucy.

"They're hunting dogs, aren't they?"

"They're retrieving dogs," I said. "Who collect *dead* things out of the water."

"Well, you should keep her away from there. Once a dog gets a taste for blood ... the council has the right to destroy it."

"How does Susie know it was Lucy?"

"She met Katie Stenmark. We go to the Pentecostal church with Katie Stenmark. Well, we did when we were doing the election. Networking. We're not really religious." He laughed apologetically for Steve's benefit. "Not God botherers."

"Well, I'm a Catholic," I said. "And Lucy wouldn't have been chasing ducks." I don't know why I was lying. I don't know why I suddenly reclaimed Catholicism. I guess it gets bred into you at convent schools, along with the lying and the desire for confession. I wanted to throw myself at his feet and confess the sins of Lucy and beg for mercy.

"Time to close up," said Steve, and winked at me.

❀   ❀   ❀

I was stressed. The job, the Ex challenging my life story. Maggie not calling. Gen didn't like me. I didn't like Boaz. Sam still wasn't speaking to me, although he was deeply chummy with Boaz and the Ex. He'd even got a crew cut like the Ex, which looked weird in yellow with black roots. I'd done myself no good paying off my loan to Taz. She failed to acknowledge it and I was paying outrageous amounts of interest. David was the only light in my life, and even that became a little flaky one afternoon when I arrived home to find him talking to Sam. Sam seemed to have no problem with David and David had no problem with Sam, but somehow I felt I could not, despite David's protestations, take David into the former marital bed with Sam in the house, even allowing for the difficulty of getting the dog out. All in all, it seemed easier for us to have sex at Cockroach Towers.

"Sam knows what's going on," David said. "He's pretty worldly wise."

"There's a difference between knowing what's going on and hearing what's going on," I said.

"But we can't go on forever sneaking off to my place."

"It's okay for now."

"You're not letting me into your life."

"Well..." Maybe that was true. But the fact was, I didn't know him that well. We saw each other once a week at least, but when I'd been with the Ex, he'd phoned me twice a day and in the spaces in between, I'd phoned him. We'd lived in each other's pockets, knew what the other had for lunch, knew the names of the people we'd worked with, their good points and their bad, dictated to each other what we should wear on dates, played around with our future and our past. In contrast to this sort of intimacy, my relationship with David seemed casual. To me at least. Was this ordinary middle-aged dating behaviour? I didn't know the rules. I was at sea.

We always went out to dinner, although I suspected he longed for a home-cooked meal. For me, it was paradise, going to restaurants I'd never been to. And from there, we'd go on to Cockroach Towers, which he kept meaning to move out of, but never got round to. I didn't care. I liked the smallness and the intimacy and the makeshift feel of it all. It felt young and exciting. And we'd make love, which for me was somehow far more delicious and sexy in someone else's bed, free from my domestic chains.

"Your thighs are so smooth and so soft," he murmured, stroking my leg after sex.

"They're supposed to be taut," I said. "I walk miles every day in pursuit of taut thighs."

"Well, they're taut, but they're still soft," he said, and grabbed a handful of thigh to make his point. And even though he liked them and it was a nice male lie, it was a small death of the ego, knowing that if, after all that pain and suffering I still had soft (flabby?) thighs, that perhaps I never would be taut thighed.

He kissed me. "I'm serious about you, Leah. But I feel we're not going anywhere."

"Because we don't sleep at my house?" I hoped it wasn't the thighs.

"We don't seem to have become as involved as we could. You know, I've always got involved with a crazed sexual obsession. Now, I'm not sure how I should do it. But you're holding back too."

If he'd been crazed about other women, why wasn't he

crazed about me? "Is it me you're not crazed about or have you stopped being crazed in general?" I asked.

"It was something I was reaching the end of anyway," he said. "You know, I'd had this pattern of pursuing women, and then being unhappy. The wheels were coming off."

"So what now?"

"I think I'm in love with you," he said. "I feel like I want to marry you." Now I have to stop here, because I'm actually not sure what he said. I had the old roses and picket fence and clean kids in pyjamas rise up in my mind and obscure my whole perspective of the conversation. He may have said –

"I'd like to be married again sometime."

Or, "I'm looking for the woman I'd like to marry."

Or, "I have feelings for you but I'm not sure we should get married."

Or, "Have you thought of getting married again, but not to me, of course? What a hopeless joke."

I was overcome by feelings of insecurity and fear and not knowing what I was doing, which I tried to explain in a roundabout sort of way.

"Do you remember the first time we met?" I asked.

"Vividly," he said.

"You were in hot pursuit of Rosanna."

"But *I* remember meeting you. And feeling something different."

"Do you remember what we talked about?"

"Divorce," he said.

"And you were newly divorced and I was ten years divorce and I was ashamed I wasn't over it."

"I remember."

"I still have to get over it," I said. "Too many things happening. I really like you, but I can't say if I love you and I'm scared you'll disappear. But I have to work this out first."

"That's okay," he said, "I'll wait."

❀ ❀ ❀

Tookie sat at my kitchen table, late one Sunday afternoon. We'd already got through a bottle of wine and I was making up a pasta sauce for dinner. Cooking for Tookie wasn't stressful, because food was totally irrelevant to her life. It was just something you put in your mouth three times a day. Which was why she was scrawny and birdlike and why I was size sixteen and adding cream to the simmering tomato and basil sauce.

"Leah, you look so stressed," said Tookie. "I hope you're going to be all right for the court case."

Somewhere in my head I knew that the court case was about ten days away. I hadn't read all the material the Federation had sent me. I hadn't even asked Jeff for time off. I stopped chopping the tomatoes and sat down at the table.

Tookie, being a stern old socialist with more grit than most people, but with an ideal of kindness and sisterhood, put her arm round my shoulders awkwardly. She stroked my back, the way I'd seen her stroke distraught first graders.

"I think you'll find teaching is really your vocation ..."

But it wasn't the job. It was all those years I'd kept the fantasy alive about the Ex. It had actually felt as if there was somebody there, potentially if not actually. A comforter, a mate. I thought I'd been keeping it together, but in fact it had fallen apart.

"We're due in court on Tuesday week," said Tookie. "You got the letter from the Federation last week?"

"I got it," I said, although I wasn't sure. I did throw a lot of my letters in the bin. It was a form of denial. "But I've lost the details."

"I brought all the copies," she said. She obviously knew more about my housekeeping and my practice of denial than I'd given her credit for. "You really need to read through them carefully, Leah, especially your statement of what happened."

That night, after my very successful pasta that even Tookie had commented on, and after another bottle of wine, and after Tookie had gone, I lay down with all the papers she had given me. I had the very best of intentions, but sleep and the Labrador overcame me and when I woke up the next morning, they were all over the floor and I was no wiser. In a fit of responsibility, I gathered them up, put a rubber band round them and put them in a safe place. Exactly where, I can no longer quite remember.

Chapter 9

By middle age, the self-destructive loop which is built into our emotional lives is clear. The middle aged know they put off dealing with procrastination. They sense that they too quickly dismiss a tendency to impulsiveness. Leah knows that thinking about her taut thighs while eating Eat U Rite choc chip muffins is a small form of insanity, as is her continuing to view marriage through a romantic haze. Habits of thought become worn into the grooves of the brain, so that sudden insights turn out to be things your mother told you. Occasionally, though, shifts happen, unexpectedly, deep in the soul. It's that seminal moment in life, when maturity kicks in before the dotage.

My past had been stripped from me. *I* had left the Ex. And now I'd lost my current comfort zone around David. I think I had just been expecting David to hang around the periphery of my life, at least until I was ready for more, but now he had said something significant. Except his words about love and marriage eluded me. I'd just got into midlife dating. Anything more was daunting. And then there was plain old everyday reality to cope with. Sam didn't like me.

He quoted Boaz and the rights of the child relentlessly, bringing up the Combantrim episode as evidence against me. Instead of being the uncommunicative, unmotivated adolescent he'd been for the past four years, he'd become a hostile, motivated activist.

I needed to get my head around all this.

"Dad's going to the parent–teacher thing with me tonight," he said one morning with triumph. I was silent. I was pretty sure that the envelope containing his school report had gone the way of all the stuff from the Federation. Losing his school report cut the moral superiority from under me. Moral superiority is one of those things you lose if you use it the wrong way – the idea is nicely summarised in that car bumper sticker about butterflies and love.

"Don't you care?" Sam asked as he ate a slice of cold pizza.

"I've been to plenty," I said, with just a bit of moral superiority. "And *you* never seemed to care."

"Well," he said, "I've got my head round the school thing now. You know, with Boaz."

"Oh yeah," I said. "With Boaz."

"Boaz is a great guy. This is one of those times in life, you know, when you meet up with a person who, you know, is for real. Like the way he explains things. It's changed everything for me. He's like a life guide."

"Don't look at me," I said. "I'm just a mother."

"Dad likes Boaz too." He was talking in a super casual, pretentious tone which should have warned me something momentous was about to be said. This wasn't like Sam. He usually has a smart mouth, like me. "I'm going to tell you something, Mum, and I don't want you to go psycho."

At least he couldn't be pregnant, I thought. "I'm moving out on the weekend. I'm not living here any more. I've got a place."

They say that sometimes children want moral guidance and limits. "Forget it, Sam. You're not old enough. You need my permission."

"Or Dad's," he said. This pissed me off just ever so slightly. That the errant and absent parent was so easily forgiven. The errant and absent parent had given him permission to leave my home. So much for better fathering.

"You're going to live with Dad?" I said.

"No, Mum."

"So where are you going to live?" I asked. This was exactly the conversation that I had intended to undercut with my setting of limits. But it wasn't to be.

"With Gen and Boaz." He sounded genuinely happy.

"Are you going to finish school?"

"Of course. Otherwise I wouldn't be going to parent–teacher night with Dad."

"You and Dad are pretty chummy, aren't you? Now."

"He's cool." Fickle, fickle youth. "Mum, don't be upset. Dad's going to pay me the maintenance payment direct. I'll be out of your way. I'll come and see you –" He smiled at me, cocky. "– if you promise not to drug me or anything."

I was enraged. But I stayed silent, which took me and Sam both by surprise. I knew it wouldn't last, so I gave him a twisted sort of a smile and retired to my bedroom, where Jack was playing loony cat outside in the cotoneaster, swinging precariously on a twig. I knew how he felt.

The longer I lay there, the more I felt as if Jack and I

would both get by. Sam shouldn't be doing this, but I couldn't stop him. So I wouldn't. I'd just let it happen and have faith in the universe to resolve things.

✤ ✤ ✤

The next day, I felt I should do at least a few things to help the universe along so I called work to explain I had women's troubles (a term easily understood by the unreconstructed male) and I'd be in later. Then, I called the Ex.

"You don't think Sam moving out was something we should have talked over? You don't think, as his mother, that I should have been consulted?"

"It was his decision," he said with a weariness that implied that this would have been better, except that *I* was the mother. "But he's lost trust in you, you realise. He doesn't feel safe with you, Leah. Maybe we should talk about that some time, because you can have a very hostile sort of energy round you."

"Yeah," I said, "I can feel it coming on right now. But let's just talk about this unilateral decision you decided to allow Sam to make, and how we get him to come back home and finish his HSC."

"In a truly transforming adolescence you support the child through change, instead of opposing it."

"Yeah, yeah, yeah. But putting the philosophy aside, how do you imagine this is going to work? Who's going to make him do his homework? Who's going to feed him and clothe him? The child support you've been paying doesn't exactly cover all that."

"My child support will cover his rent to Gen. I thought you could contribute to the rest – seeing as you don't have to feed and clothe him." He had the grace to sound scared.

"Okay, so now I don't have to feed and clothe him any more, I pay to feed and clothe him. How exactly is that different?"

"Well, you won't have the hassle of doing it. But you'll still be contributing to his support."

"No way," I said. I had been conned into paying for things that weren't my responsibility for years. All in the name of staying on good terms with the Ex. "I wasn't consulted. I don't approve. This whole thing is nonsense."

"Leah, we're his parents. Legally, we're bound to support him. I'm doing some real estate work, but I'm not making a lot yet. He's moving out into the world. I think he deserves our support and I'm prepared to make a financial contribution. Which will involve a sacrifice on my part."

It was at that moment I really got in touch with my hatred for the Ex. "You sanctimonious bastard," I said. And full of hostile energy, I put the phone down.

I could have easily spent the day watching the *Bold and the Beautiful*, the *Young and the Restless* and *Dangerous Doctors Downtown*, but I decided to go to work. And seeing as I had pretend period pain and I was late, I left the thighs for a day and treated myself to a taxi.

"You okay?" said Steve, more sympathetic than I'd ever seen him before. Somebody had evidently given him a talk about women's pains being equivalent to a serious fishing accident.

"I'm okay," I said. I went upstairs into my little cubbyhole with my computer and my spreadsheets and worked on the cash flow. It was comforting seeing the numbers coming up and slotting into place. I realised that apart from being abandoned by Sam, undermined by the Ex and deceived by Gen, I was somewhere, deep in my soul, still okay. Maybe my heart had hardened up or callused over, but I felt able to cope with life at Hook Line and Sinker.

And even when Jeff came in and said, "Good morning, Mrs J, better now?" in a way that was jocular but seemed to imply I never had been sick (which of course was true), I felt less than my usual desire to throw myself at his feet and confess my dog was a duck killer who'd been bred up to it and aided and abetted by me. Later in the day, I approached him and told him that I'd need time off for the court case I was going to be involved in.

"Unfair dismissal," I said. "From the school."

"That legislation," he said, "is a disgrace."

"It has a certain charm though," I said, "when you *have* been unfairly dismissed."

"It's intimidatory," he said. "The employers in this country are held to ransom by that legislation."

"I'm going to have to take the time off," I said. "I told you that when I started."

He huffed and snorted and complained and explained how personally offensive the unfair dismissal legislation was to a person of his standing and importance. But then he looked at the cash flow figures for the month and was mightily pleased (with himself) because he saw the graph go up from last month (Father's Day blip!) although we were way below the official overdraft. He was still not returning the calls from the bank. Then, with more huffing and puffing, endowed with a sense of his own generosity, he gave me permission for time off after all.

Sam left home that afternoon when I was still at work. Obviously, he was worried by my reaction because he stacked the dishwasher, which made me go all mushy when I realised that he had actually gone, which was hard to tell because he'd left most of his clothes behind and a good number of his school books.

The next day Genevieve phoned to say she'd be round to pick up his clothes and discuss the "matter". Which was why, several days later, we were to be found facing each other across the table over a pot of tea and a plate of Eat U Rites – my peace offering.

"Mama," said Gen in her sweetest, softest way. "This business about Sam." She sat there, looking totally ravishing.

"So, Genevieve?" I said. Cool, but cross.

"We need to discuss this like adults."

"Yes."

"He needs his clothes."

"They're in the laundry and in his room. You can take them, if you dare to venture in there, or you can send him round."

Genevieve wrinkled her nose a little. "If it's okay then, I'll send him ..."

"Of course it's okay. I'm not going to bite him."

"You seem upset about it."

"Yes, but I'm not going to go through all my reasons, and have *you* tell me they're wrong. I'll just keep it to myself."

"Mum ..."

"Gen, I think it's awful you and Sam and Dad did this behind my back."

212

"He said you were drugging . . ."

"You believe him? Come on, Gen, I had to!"

"Boaz says that the UN convention on the rights of the child absolutely prohibits it. You can't do it. It's like you with me, all criticism, no support. Boaz says that Sam needs a sense of autonomy."

"I see I'm the only one not in Boaz's thrall," I said. "And I don't remember all criticism, no support. I was the one who threw the party for you when you got into medicine. I'm the one who paid for your text books for five years."

"Mum, I'm in love. What *have* you got against him?"

"He's vain." I'd decided I wouldn't say another negative thing about Boaz, but it popped out anyway. "And he has no substance."

"I'm going," said Genevieve. "Dad's right. You've got no respect for other people. I was going to ask you for some money for Sam, but Dad said you'd dug your heels in about that too."

"That too," I said. I had a momentary impulse to apologise to Genevieve, but I'd been apologising to Genevieve all her life. And the thing was, I was right about Boaz.

❀   ❀   ❀

I had a sense of gradually shedding some of my burdens (although not a substantial mass of my thighs) and I began to dream different dreams, a different life. Not practical options, but "creating new psychic realities", a topic I had heard Taz and Rosanna hold forth on. I began to dream of living on a tropical island. Perhaps it was a tropical fantasy because Taz and Rosanna had gone to Bali. My dream island was wonderfully peaceful, without Sam, without Gen, even without Maggie. I felt as if motherhood had been a kind of death, and without children, I could be myself again, with taut thighs and a personality to match. In my dream, strangely, the Ex was safely back with Pouty Lips and I sent him to her with my blessing this time. I was tired of the complications of this non-existent marriage of mine. David floated in the background of my warm and tropical life, in love, wanting me, but not demanding. Jeff had completely disappeared. Lucy was safe from duck temptation. Jack was in the cattery. The court case had never ever been thought of. Drinks and delicious snacks were given to me by people with flowers in their hair and soft smiles. My toenails were painted a vulgar pink and I could see my tanned knees because I had a concave stomach.

During the day, I was groping for some sort of new reality on a more practical level and sometimes I felt the old despair. How could I change my life if I couldn't even control my thighs? Or my Eat U Rite eating habits? It was as if I was giving away the old, not understanding or trusting the new.

Normally, I would have asked Taz what to do about Sam, the Ex, Gen and their conspiracy against me. But Taz was sunning herself in Bali, buying high Balinese artworks, having drinks by the pool and generally enjoying *my* island. David was on some journalistic junket for two weeks. Which left me to my own loopy devices, to re-order my life. I washed up religiously every evening and took all the junk off the kitchen benches, and sorted the cupboards in the kitchen and chucked a lot of my clothes I hated, but also watched a lot of late night TV I hated too.

Letting go of my motherly responsibility for Sam

definitely had its upside, but it was hard too. One night, I went into Sam's room and had a final little cry about the ingratitude of children. Something between us was finished. I needed something physical to demonstrate it to myself and to him. I had a burst of energy. I tidied the room up and put all his things away. I went through all the junk on his desk, which included a half-smoked packet of cigarettes. I put these in a prominent place, but in a casual way (which took ages to get right) for future use as emotional blackmail and moral superiority, to say nothing of using it in my standard health lecture.

I put on the Beach Boys *Pet Sounds* album and started the washing machine going. I scrubbed collars. I dug out old boxer shorts from the side of the bed. I retrieved unbelievably high smelling socks and separated them from food particles. I did load after load, wash, dry and iron, wash, dry and iron, wash, dry and iron. I felt in control. Waiting for the last load to dry and be ironed, I dug out an old suitcase from the shed and washed it inside and out, and began folding Sam's neatly ironed clothes into the suitcase.

It was three in the morning when the last load came out of the dryer. Half past three when I finished ironing it. I wasn't finished with Sam, but I was finished with his childhood. I was about to close the case but, with a last piece of genius inspiration, I ran back into my room and rifled through my top drawer. There, a photo of him and me, when he was ten, a fond and smiling pose in a nice wood frame. I grabbed the Combantrim, put it and the photo tenderly on top of the clothes, and carefully shut the lid.

I slept like a baby.

The next night, I still had unfinished business and dialled my mother's number.

"Terrible things are happening," I said. "*Terrible!*"

"Don't exaggerate," she said.

"Maggie's pregnant and lost in India."

There was a gratifying silence at the other end of the line.

"I told you that you should have given them a *religious* education," she said after a while. "But at least she's in India."

"She rings her stepmother," I said. "She doesn't tell me the important things."

"People never tell their mothers the important things," she said. So she had noticed. "Maybe it'll blow over."

"Pregnancy doesn't blow over," I said.

"I meant hating you would blow over," Mum said. "But they do have them out of wedlock these days. It's quite wrong in *my* book, but things are different now. It's awful, Leah," she went on, "but it's no use crying over spilt milk."

This common sense cliché seemed too restrained. I had expected the emotional catharsis of her outrage.

"Sam's left home," was my next announcement. I was telling her the important things now. "The Ex gave him permission and is paying him child support direct and he's gone to live with Gen and that awful Boaz."

"I don't approve of this so called 'living together'," said Mum, "but you wouldn't want Genevieve married to him, would you?"

"No Mum, it's Sam I'm worried about. It'll wreck his HSC. And he's blaming me for *everything*."

"Children do," she said.

"He'll ruin his life."

"Leah, don't exaggerate. He wasn't about to shine, was he?" she said. "It's not as if he was another Genevieve."

"Thank God. But I was trying to get him motivated . . ."

"So now you don't have to," she said. "You ought to be on your knees, saying a prayer."

"Mum . . ."

"Look dear, I know Sam's a problem, and I know you were doing your best, but he's a nice young man and he'll come good in the end. But really, I think you've let those children drag you down a bit. I certainly never thought I was responsible for *your* happiness."

"No you didn't," I said. But for once I wasn't bitter. I actually thought my mother was quite sensible.

"And I missed you and Tanya when you left, but I have such a lovely life now."

"Which was all we ever wanted . . ."

"Of course your big mistake was putting on all that weight after Sam. That's when it started going wrong, didn't it?"

"Mum, you've got to stop blaming . . ." I took back thinking she was sensible. She was judgmental and moralistic.

"I've got to go, dear. Mr Bonham's here and we're going to watch *The Bill*. Goodnight."

"Night, Mum."

I couldn't watch *The Bill,* but I sat with Lucy and we put on a tape of the Ronettes, and then I started dancing to it, which was spoiled a bit by Lucy barking at this strange activity, but even so, I thought, "I'm alone, I'm alone, all by myself." And I stopped dancing and I rang up the Thai takeaway and ordered stuffed chicken wings and Tom Yum Gai soup, and thought how nice it was I didn't have to have pizza. When the food came and Lucy got the bones from the chicken wings, she became reconciled to the Ronettes and to my dancing and we had a very happy evening, and even Jack came and sat on the couch and made a noise remarkably like purring.

❀   ❀   ❀

"I thought that was very manipulative," said Genevieve. "Washing all Sam's clothes and putting that photo on top of them." I presume she didn't mention the Combantrim, because it was so far beyond the pale.

"It was a joke," I said.

"A very tasteless one."

"Well, I never had much in the way of good taste," I said. "Which is just the way I am. But it was also goodbye to this stage of his life. I won't be doing cooking and cleaning and that sort of thing any more."

"Boaz had to debrief him. Boaz thinks that deep down he feels very rejected."

"Sam's not a deep down sort of person," I said. "What you see is what you get."

"You really don't understand," she said.

"Is that all you rang up about?" I asked.

"No," she said. "Maggie is back in Australia. She's living with Jackie up on the Gold Coast. I know it will drive you crazy, and God knows what mad thing you'll do, but I decided to let you know."

"Thanks so much," I said. "What's the number?"

Genevieve was right. It did drive me crazy. I was jealous, furious at Pouty.

But somehow, I kept my cool. I held my fire and two days later, I called.

"Hullo." It sounded bright and breezy. "This is Jackie's home and Maggie's living here too. The beeps are coming. You know what to do and how to do it."

"Hi Maggie," I said. "I hope you're well and happy. Please ring me when you want to. I'd love to hear from you. Love you."

I did allow myself a minute of controlled crying after that.

❀ ❀ ❀

Of course I missed Sam in a way that wasn't made up for by having the house to myself. I'm not sure I was made for a house full of kids, but I wasn't made for long nights with a Labrador either.

Work kept me going. Even though I knew Jeff didn't like me any more and that Lucy was on his list of duck-killing suspects, and I was regarded as the Anti Christ of the gifted and talented child, I was doing a fabulous job. Jeff couldn't admit it, because if you really looked, the business was in deep trouble. With Laura gone, I gradually cleared up all the mess in the system and found logical, easy ways of dealing with the irregularities. I developed a system of monthly reports, which gave feedback on slow stock and margins. I worked with Steve on ordering and invoices. I integrated the ballet photos and the photocopy charges. I produced reports for the accountant. The bottom line and I were one. I was enjoying myself. I couldn't stay in this job for long, because of Jeff, but I wanted to hang in at least till I could get a reference.

Jeff made endless digs about the court case. "There are laws against harassment too," I muttered and he descended into surly silence. Taut thighs were still on my agenda. Relentlessly, I walked to and from work.

"What a pity," said my mother, "that you ever put it on. I mean after Sam. If you'd have been able to lose it then, things would have been different ..."

"You've lost weight," said Genevieve. "Have you checked your breasts?"

"I'm fine," I said.

"Well, I'm worried about Sam," she said. "He's got dreadful habits you know. I can't sleep either. I'm terrified he'll set the house on fire or something. And he's very expensive," she added.

"I'm amazed," I said.

But motherly kindness got the better of me and I sent him a T-shirt and some vouchers for pizza, but I knew I was really in his bad books because he didn't ring to thank me. Sam was usually a very grateful child, unlike his sisters.

"Leah," stammered Twisted, standing on my doorstep. "You look different."

"It's my new work environment," I said, "which is very supportive." And began to wonder *why* she was standing on my doorstep.

"Can I come in?" she asked.

There's something about headmistresses. Despite her complete lack of natural authority, or even credibility, I felt I had to ask Twisted in. And once she was in, I was embarrassed by the state of my kitchen, which by my usual living with Sam standard was actually impeccable. But when she cast her eye over the dark corners, I had to resist the temptation to apologise.

"So, Leah," she said. "You don't miss teaching?"

"I miss teaching dreadfully," I said. "I miss everything about Grevillea Public. And you know, there was no other school in the district which wanted me as a casual. It was really odd," I added. "Not one single school had one single vacancy." And gave her my best beady-eyed glance I usually reserve for naughty Year 3 girls, but without any of the usual potential forgiveness in the look.

"So," she said in a high, not so Twisted sort of voice. "How do *you* think this court case will go?"

"It's become very political," I said. "Which sort of avoids what actually happened, doesn't it?"

"But we wouldn't want to bring *that* up, would we?" I detected fear and shrugged my shoulders.

"The important thing is to make sure *you* say things to improve the rights of casual teachers. But I mean, we wouldn't want to bring up those little (squeak again) *personal* matters, would we?"

"Well, apart from the rights of casuals, I'd really like to be able to work as a teacher again." As I said this, I felt it was at least partly true. Being a computer genius was okay, but it was hardly teaching. And I couldn't resist a dig at Twisted. I was pleased to see that Jack was biting her feet, and she was too scared to complain. I felt my power, although I wasn't quite sure how I could exploit it.

"I'm sure, *whatever* happens with the court case, that I'll have a vacancy for a *casual* next year. As long as there's nothing *personal* said." Her voice squeaked even more. "You see my *sister's* coming to the court case."

The deal was clear. In my years at Grevillea, I'd heard lots about Twisted's sister. She was the head of a high school, one of the more prestigious ones and was the star in the Twisted family firmament. The sister was the one, the only one, to whom Twisted was hopelessly devoted, the one she looked up to, quoted ad nauseam, believed in implicitly and whose approval she clearly wanted above all else. The deal she was offering me was that I could have my job back as long as I didn't make any nasty remarks about her, as long as I didn't hold her up to ridicule in front of her sister. That was more important than how she struck the judge, her peers and the general public. For that, she was prepared to somehow squeeze me back in at Grevillea Public, whatever the cost to her personal pride. On the other hand, it was no skin off my nose. After all, I'd already promised Jason and faithful Tookie that I'd restrain myself when it came to Twisted's character. And standing there, puffing and wheezing, getting redder and redder, she no longer looked like a headmistress.

"I'll stick by you. You stick by me."

"That's what friends are for," she said. And without even a cup of tea, she went.

❊　　❊　　❊

When David came back from his two weeks of travel journalism, Sam was no longer in the house. I no longer had to rush home from the Cockroach Palace. We could go to sleep together, wake up together, have breakfast together, watch late night TV together. I still only saw him once or twice a week, but now he called me every day.

I was no longer the middle-aged single mother of three worrying about launching the last of them. Even if Sam came back, it would be different. I felt like an ex-mother, a thoroughly modern woman with (undefined) prospects.

"Why don't I move in with you?" David asked one morning.

"Because Sam might move back."

"You don't have to take him back."

"I don't want to have to choose between him and you."

"Leah, this is silly."

"It's not. It's practical. I have to be sure. Okay, my kids are grown up, but they still matter. And we have to know more about each other. We have to find out what we're about. We probably even have to have a few fights."

"But that's what's wonderful about us," he said. "We never ever fight."

At which point of course, we did, and as with most fights there was lots of heat and not much light, and he stormed off, and even though it didn't feel like the Ex leaving, it felt sad. I wondered if I was full of self-pity. Then, I felt even more sad to be afflicted with self-pity. I pulled myself together. There was no need. People had fights, and this was just a little one.

❋　　❋　　❋

I'd had suspicions about Lucy and ducks but had turned a blind eye. Muddy paws, a blathering sense of excitement, a determination to jump the gate no matter what barriers I erected, extraordinary tiredness, irregular hours, very healthy appetite, and finally, another duck. Lucy was a killer. I found the duck in pieces all over the backyard. A frenzied killer with bloodlust.

I'd coped reasonably graciously with Sam leaving and Maggie not calling me, but the combination of having a killer dog and Katie Bless You leaning over the fence – "Oh dear. Leah!" – made me feel defensive and aggressive – flight and fight.

"If you tell a soul, I'll lose my job. I'll be completely washed up and I'll be publicly humiliated. I'll lose my credibility in this court case and casual teachers will never get a fair go!"

I think Katie took in the tone rather than the substance of this remark. But being neighbourly, she rushed in and helped me pick up the duck parts from all over the yard, even though she had to let Lucy (with the low growl) keep some feathers. Then she came inside with me and we washed our hands and she sat me down and we had a cup of tea and she even rushed back to her house and got some Eat U Rite freshly baked choc chip muffins.

"It's nice when you can do something for a neighbour," she said. I always knew she was crazy. All I could think of was me on the unemployment scrapheap again.

"*You* can't do anything for me," I wailed. "This requires lying and deception and keeping the dog in, and those things are completely beyond you."

"I meant helping clear up the mess," she said. She was a little cold. "You'll have to get a higher fence built, Leah."

"I'm going to lose my job," I said, "if you tell Jeff Smith." The Evangelical church seemed to have a prayer meeting or a fellowship discussion every night and Jeff was pretty busy with their God, only because there were key votes on the council who also attended and he'd been running foul of the planning staff.

"Why would you lose your job?" she asked. (The right response would have been "Why would I tell Jeff Smith?")

I threw myself on Katie Bless You's mercy. "I'm throwing myself on your mercy," I said. She looked at me open mouthed, as if she had just had an erotic experience.

"Pardon, Leah dear?"

"I'm throwing myself on your mercy," I said, "because I told a lie so I could get a job and feed and clothe Sam."

"He's not here any more, is he?" she asked, so I

knew what I'd always suspected – that she kept tabs on who came and went. "I do see another fellow coming and going."

Another fellow? Lover, David? What did it matter? Now wasn't the time to lay bare my sex life to Katie.

"Sam's living with his father, and I've got a boarder." The trouble is lying feels really natural to me. It's not as if I plan lies. They're spontaneous. But it is true what the nuns said. They do cause moral (and other) complications. Of course, so does *not* lying.

"What did you tell the lie about?" asked Katie.

"I lied about Lucy's car accident," I said. "That morning I had to bring her back from the park, and I told you she was all wrapped up because she'd had a car accident."

"I knew she hadn't had a car accident," said Katie. "There wasn't a scratch on her." Which confirmed my suspicion that Katie snooped. "I saw her the next day. She was trying to jump the fence."

"I had to lie to get my job at Hook Line and Sinker." It sounded lame and apologetic. "And I need you not to say anything about it."

"Leah," she said, suddenly theatrical. "You should pray. You must pray. God has a solution for all these things. Truly . . ." She clasped my hand, I swear. "Jesus helps all we sinners. Truly Leah. Truly."

Now I have to admit that Katie Bless You, apart from continually blessing me, had never tried to convert me, even though she was pretty well known for putting her best foot forward for Father, Son and Holy Ghost. She thought I was making some sort of bizarre confession, that I wanted absolution, not collusion. "Pray Leah," she repeated fervently. "God forgives sinners."

I put on my very own pious face. "I did pray," I said, "and the answer from God was that it's best if nobody says anything. Especially to Jeff."

I could see all the neighbourliness drain out of Katie Bless You's face, and all her hidden dislike of me flood in. I could see her mind clicking over all the snide remarks I'd been forgiven over the years, all the dreadful music she'd had to endure out of Sam's windows, the unkempt garden next to her own perfect one, the helpful hints she'd given me, the cups of tea, the tossed muffin. It was all there, writ large.

"Please don't say anything, Katie," I said, now truly penitent. (I was sorry I'd been sarcastic to her because it had clearly blown up in my face. But I was also truly sorry for hurting her feelings.) "I'm not asking you to lie, I'm just saying, please don't say anything."

This was sincere but it touched a raw nerve. "I'm not a gossip, Leah," she said. I'd never said she was (or at least not *to* her), but obviously somebody had. "I wouldn't dream of saying anything, but certainly, if the subject comes up..." And with that, she swept out of my kitchen.

❀　❀　❀

I guess the subject of Lucy and ducks came up that very evening between Katie Bless You and Jeff while they were all at a prayer group, because it was certainly hanging there when I went into work the following day. Not directly, but in the form of a conversation between Jeff and Steve about people you could trust and people you couldn't, and people who told bald-faced lies to further their own ends and people in positions of responsibility, who didn't admit basic things about their lives, like owning a hunting dog. Hunting dog? I almost said something, but I thought about Sam saying, "The truth, Mum, the truth." I resolved to have more confidence in reality and the way things are, rather than trying to improve them in a theoretical sense, which is what lying really is.

But I knew also that Steve didn't give a stuff about dogs killing ducks, and Jeff didn't either, except for wanting to improve the value of his house by having a pretty reserve behind it. And Jeff told terrible lies to the tax department and Steve pinched money from Jeff on the parking racket. I could rest easy at least on those two counts.

When Jeff went off to do a deal with the council building inspector about the plumbing for his townhouses, Steve gave me his best boyish grin to let me know he was just bullshitting with Jeff and he needed me to continue to turn a blind eye to the parking money, which was fine by me. And then, to stir me, he told me that Jeff didn't mind his employees taking liberties (parking money?), but what I had done had sent him psycho and the consequences for myself and my future were looking bad. Steve really felt for me, and if he could do anything he would, because Jeff was a bastard and the way he'd treated Laura and her mother, to say nothing of his years of exploitation of the good Steve himself . . . Et cetera.

While all this was pouring out, I realised that what I had lived in fear of had come to pass. I could handle it. Later, I'd sit down and think about it, and if I did that, instead of lying compulsively, I'd come up with a solution.

But Steve couldn't let it alone. "I reckon he'll sack you, you know. I mean *I* know you've done a fantastic job, but *he* won't give you a reference. You're stuffed, Leah."

I had a lot of strings to my bow, but I wasn't about to fire all my arrows. "I guess I'll have to think about it," I said, "but I don't really have to worry for a week or so. Because I'm taking time off for that *unfair dismissal case* I'm involved in."

I knew he'd pass the message on.

❋   ❋   ❋

I forgave Katie Bless You, I forgave Sam, I forgave Gen, I forgave Maggie, I forgave Steve. All on my taut thigh walk home. I forgave Jeff, but in my heart, I still wanted fate to strike him down. Which was pretty much the same as for the Ex.

I gave Katie a cheery wave as I walked up the street. I knew she was peeking out the curtains of her front room. She rushed out, unable to contain her silly self and wanted to have an emotional scene on the pavement about how she'd actually sought Jeff out to tell him about Lucy and how she'd repented because she'd seen later (too late) that she'd be driven by anger, not God's will. I told her it was fine, it happened to we sinners. That's religion for you.

Lucy was overjoyed to see me because she'd been locked in the house all day with nothing to think of except ducks. We sat on the bed with an Eat U Rite choc chip and had a long talk. I was through lying (as much) and she was through with ducks. I was having a whacking great fence erected the following week, with no holes, and if necessary, I told her, I'd employ an armed guard. And I explained that while this behaviour was natural to her, it was not acceptable in polite society. I promised her other walks, and retrieving things other than ducks. We'd grow old together and the children would come home for

Christmas. And we'd both be nicer to Jack and she wouldn't eat his food when I wasn't looking. I swear she shed a few doggie tears.

And what happened then was that David came in with his standard bunch of substandard daffs. And he danced round the kitchen and told me he was happy because he was in a new phase of his life and he adored me so much. And he had tickets for a concert that night for a piece of music called *Carmen Burana*, by Carloff, which I kept in my mind to impress Sonny and Rosanna. It turned out to be the theme piece of an old coffee advert on TV! I had always liked the ad, even though I couldn't remember that much of it, but when he asked me if it conjured up images and feelings, I could truthfully say yes, seeing in my mind's eye sophisticated people drinking instant coffee, and wonderful pictures of coffee beans. It *had* made the music much much better.

And then we went back to my place and made delicious love so I didn't think about the court case at all until it was there, staring me in the face on Monday morning.

Chapter 10

The idea of life as a rehearsal permeates the first part of life. Next time, we are certain, it will work. After we leave school, we will shine. If not, then after failure in the workforce. A revelation of brilliance, after plodding mediocrity. Next time, next time. The career, the relationship will work. The children will succeed.

Next time, next time, next time. We never quite examine next time – it doesn't bear examination. It is there, all the same.

In middle age, it slowly dawns that there is no next time. This is it – with all our inadequacies, out stupidities, our hopelessness. This is a crucial moment – the time for the complete retreat from reality, or a leap to embrace the world as it is.

You're supposed to feel guilty when you walk into a courtroom. For a moment, I wanted to plead "Guilty your honour" to duck murder. "Guilty your honour" to flabby thighs, although a definite improvement there, your honour. Guilty of being unkind to Katie Bless You. Guilty of getting fat. Guilty of motherhood failure. And the cat (kicking), if you please, your honour. I accept the Apprehended Violence Order on behalf of the cat. Guilty, guilty, sorry, sorry.

I pulled myself together. Okay, there's all the majesty of the law in the dark panelled court with the coat of arms and the picture of the Queen. But this wasn't *Alice in Wonderland*. This was my life. I was involved in an unfair dismissal case and I had been unfairly dismissed.

But that was the rub. I hadn't read the stuff Jason from the Federation had sent me. Nor had I read the summaries Tookie had made, because I wasn't a fan of the version of the truth they presented. Those great piles of paper were full of evasions and half-truths. These would have normally invoked my Year 1 "*Recycle or die by my hand before three o'clock*" lecture, thereby stopping these legal blokes dead in their tracks.

"Don't worry," David had said the night before. "I'll make sure my reporter hits the industrial tribunal tomorrow. I'll get you on the front page." When I'd told him that the story had been reconstructed, he'd laughed. "Happens all the time." Now, I imagined the headlines.

TOTALLY INEPT TEACHER LOSES THE BATTLE FOR CASUALS IN FIGHT FOR JUSTICE.

Or just, STUPID WOMAN MAKES COMPLETE FOOL OF SELF.

But after the initial panic, I started snoozing from boredom during an argument as to the admissibility of clause 123 paragraph 4b from the *Simmonds v Wilson* case. I could have, in other circumstances, given them the Year 2 "*Sit up straight and face the front with your hands on your head for fifteen seconds.*" It turned out it didn't matter what had happened in other cases, as each one was to be judged on its merits, and this one really turned on how casual is casual and whether you can be unfairly dismissed from a casual job.

Twisted kept throwing smiles at me, which was like being eyed off by a hungry tiger. She was sitting with a woman I took to be her sister, who looked just like I'd imagined a Twisted older sister might look – steel-wool hair and a face to match. In spite of the promises I'd made Jason and assurances I'd given to Twisted herself, I still really loathed her. I might tell lies for the sake of the greater good, but in my heart I would have liked to tell the truth, the full truth and nothing but.

Tookie was there as the union delegate to support me. I suspect the sort of support she had in mind was for when I needed to be scraped off the floor to testify. She and Jason knew I still didn't want to say that Twisted was an excellent person whose actions against me had been entirely involuntary and impersonal.

"We'll get you your job back," said Jason, with a hint of a threat. Tookie must have kept him up to date with my career difficulties at Hook Line and Sinker. He was involved in an interminable argument about *Simmonds v Wilson*, turning on the point that although the case couldn't be a precedent, it could be taken as an example. Which then set a precedent. Finally the judge got into deputy principal mode and stopped the nonsense.

The first witness was from the Department. She went on about the amount of latitude Twisted had as a principal, especially in terms of firing me. My total employment at Grevillea was only ever a series of short-term contracts, which had, purely by chance, ended up as years of employment. And the conditions of my employment, which were basically that I could be terminated at the end of any contract before starting the next, were made perfectly clear to me by the Department. Both the witness and the barrister seemed to shape their mouths so their voices bounced and echoed. I started to get a headache. I didn't read the little notes Jason was passing me, which I could tell was annoying him.

We went out to lunch, which was a sandwich in a cheap café, which reminded us this was about the union, not big business. Jason was getting quite sharp with me until Tookie intervened and told him I was nervous. I was, but I think Jason liked the sort of person who gets nervous energy, whereas I had nervous lethargy. Tookie seemed to believe I had read the reams of notes she had sent me, which made me even more nervous, especially as when I was going back in, a young fellow came up to me and said, "David Moloney asked me to drop in here. Is there anything interesting going on?" His name was Simon and he was a journalist on David's paper.

I started to explain how casual teachers were exploited and I was only one of many, and it was a test case, but I'd been a dedicated teacher almost all my life and now, by a whim of fate, I was out of my chosen profession. Calling Twisted a whim of fate was stretching a bit, but telling him seemed much more productive than what was going on inside.

I was in mid-sentence when Jason yanked me away and told me not to talk to the Murdoch press as he was sure they'd be hostile. I didn't tell him I was sleeping with one of them.

But inside, I told Jason that he didn't have to be so superior just because he was a lawyer and I was a teacher.

They were just jobs after all, not measures of personal worth. And although he looked at me as if he suspected I was an old-fashioned communist like Tookie, he apologised, and explained it was his first big case and he was a little nervous, which made me feel forgiving and motherly. I dreamed my way through the next part of the proceedings thinking that maybe Sam would become a lawyer, or at least pass his HSC at a level that allowed him to pursue some gainful employment.

At the end of the afternoon, there was just a shiver of excitement when Twisted was called to the stand, but then the judge announced we'd adjourn and continue on the morrow. The morrow. He actually said that. I didn't want Sam to be a lawyer if that's the way they talk.

❀　❀　❀

Tookie drove me home. She was on fire about what Jason had said to the Department and what the Department had said to their counsel. Apparently there was lots of lying and lots of drama which had gone over my head. But I hadn't missed anything vital. It was along the lines of what he said to her and what she had said to him, like the staff room at school, except the content was less interesting.

"Miss Siskay is determined to have you back teaching next year," Tookie told me. "I don't know how she'll do it, but she says she will."

"It's a bribe, Tookie. She's scared of what I could say." Sometimes Tookie who was so smart about politics didn't get personal stuff.

"She's had a lot of trouble in infants, Leah. I'm a bit out of touch, teaching Year 4, but the infants has been unstable."

"Well, Twisted isn't stable," I muttered.

"You can't be an effective head and be liked by everyone."

"Don't try and make me like her," I said. "You can't be a good head if everyone despises you. Just because she's fallen on the right side ideologically, she's got you onside. You've got a very narrow world view." She used to say that to me when I refused to go to union meetings. We pulled up outside my place.

"Look," said Tookie. "This is worth mending bridges for."

I had far less faith in the court process than she had, but I let it go. "Come in and have dinner, Tookie. Thai curry leftovers. I ordered too much last night."

"Love to," said Tookie, who lived on boiled eggs and Vegemite toast. As well as the leftover curry, we got stuck into some cheap wine and started talking about the year we'd done team teaching, until I began to think it *would* be good to go back to Grevillea Public and have riotous times in kindergarten again. It was only the vision of Twisted and her fixed smile that prevented me truly embracing the possibility. And Twisted was more than a vision. She was a real live witch. Lucy joined us for dinner, scoffing the leftover leftovers, and forgave me for having the monster fence erected. And Tookie kept giggling and saying we shouldn't get too drunk because we shouldn't have hangovers for the court case the next day.

Of course we kept on drinking.

It was a lovely evening, except when I remembered the evidence I had to give about what a nice person Twisted was. But we swapped a few Twisted stories and I could see Tookie really didn't like her, although she said,

"Not a word against her in court, Leah. Not a word, you promised."

Then Taz and Rosanna turned up, having just arrived back from Bali that morning, and Taz was happy and having fun and talking about her trip and being truly spontaneous in a way Taz hadn't been for years. Rosanna looked beautiful in a white sarong and magenta toenails and Taz had a gorgeous green dress which looked a million dollars, but had cost about five.

"And you look wonderful," she said. "You've lost weight."

"Self-discipline," I replied. "That's all you need."

"I had an *affair*," she said, giving particular emphasis to *affair* (when it should have been on *I*). "Really Leah, it does wonders for the soul. Not to mention the body."

"You mean a proper affair?" I asked. "With sex?"

"Of course with sex," she said. "Otherwise it wouldn't be an affair."

"I thought sex was like beaches."

"The beaches actually weren't that good," she said. "Most of the time we were up in the mountains in Ubud."

"But the sex *was* good?" I pressed her.

"Of course it was," she said. "He's Italian. He's coming out here next year to live for awhile.

"So it might go somewhere," I said. I was always foolishly thinking of marriage as the ultimate goal, although my sister had made it clear she had no interest after the first disaster with Dreary Malcolm. "You ought to have an affair, let your hair down a bit," she added.

Which of course made me wonder what she thought David and I were having, and my happiness for her drained down into envy and I felt that stab of depression about Taz always assuming I had such a terrible life. I poured her a big drink, which turned out not to be such a good idea because it loosened her up sufficiently to rip into me.

"I heard about this business with Sam and Genevieve," she said. "Really, Leah."

"What do you mean *really*? And who told you?"

"Mum told me. You shouldn't have let it happen."

"Just how could I have stopped it?"

"You know Mum never lost control of us."

"That's because there was nothing to lose control of. We were good little Catholic girls."

"Exactly. Because we were brought up to be."

"I've never heard you giving applause for *that* before. And anyway, you can't bring kids up like that now. It just doesn't work."

"You should have stopped him going. You should have read him the riot act."

"I did. And *he* quoted me the United Nations' Declaration on the Rights of the Child! He had international law on his side. *And* his father becoming all nurturing and fatherly lately. It wasn't exactly a fair fight."

"It should have never been a fight at all. You should have just laid down the law or appealed to his better nature."

"He hasn't got one."

Tookie was looking at me sympathetically. Unlike Taz, who has an idealised view of children, especially mine, Tookie knows that they are monstrous beings, even though she also loves mine (and many others).

"Why are you so unsympathetic about Sam when you were so nice about Maggie?" I asked Taz.

"Sam's still your responsibility. Maggie getting pregnant is hardly your fault."

"Well I don't think Sam leaving home is either."

Of course all this sisterly bickering meant that Taz showing her holiday snaps wasn't quite as much fun as it should have been, in spite of me pointedly pouring more big drinks. The big drinks didn't have their usual effect of releasing me into a land of happiness and little care. I wondered whether I should have laid down the law to Sam, and why the United Nations wasn't on my side for once. And of course it was far too late to ask Tookie what she'd written in those notes and retain any shred of credibility.

Then David arrived, and seemed both pleased and embarrassed to see Rosanna, and mildly pleased to see me, who he had admittedly seen just that morning, but who he had perhaps wanted to marry. And after the big sister/little sister spat with Taz, I felt in the grip of my adolescence, at a time in my life when I should have been gearing up for hot flushes. But I was jealous of Rosanna in her white sarong and magenta nails. And I thought if I was over lying (except for the awful court case where I'd given a solemn undertaking to lie), then surely I could get over jealousy. But I couldn't help myself from then on giving both David and Rosanna mean-sized drinks.

David asked me all about the case and told me they were keeping an eye on it. Rosanna and Taz grilled him about his new job and I began to realise that David's description of himself as a Murdoch underling wasn't accurate, and he was in fact something of a high flyer, who I had met at a low point. I'd seen him as an underling because that's the way he'd described himself, but also because of his badly co-ordinated clothes, but as Taz had explained to me, all journalists are badly dressed unless they're on television, and sometimes even then.

I told David that Jason had warned me not to talk to the Murdoch reporter and he laughed, and I felt things were more normal. But then, everybody left, and David left too because he had to go back to Cockroach Towers. I peeked through the blinds, or what was left of them, in Sam's room, and I saw him kissing Rosanna. Well, not kissing, as in long kissing, but giving her a kiss, which could have been brotherly, or not quite so much.

I went to bed and tried to read. Then the phone rang.

"Leah, it's me."

"Hi," I said.

"Did you think I was running away with Rosanna?"

"You didn't see me peeking out the blinds?"

"I did, she didn't."

"Do you think it's totally pathetic?"

"The way Rosanna comes on, I think it's totally understandable. I have a confession to make."

"God, please make it that she's not there in bed with you," I said.

"No way. But the thing is that until tonight, I didn't see how predatory she is. I mean I could have very easily had her in my bed tonight. Because she's not like you. She's desperate, and unscrupulous, and basically everything from the porn star hair-do to those sparkly toenails, is saying, 'Have me, take me, fuck me'. But she's not what I want."

He couldn't have known how happy I was to hear him refer to Rosanna's hair like that. But that was just jealousy dying a slow death. The thing is I realised he really did like me. He might be a hot shot and speak Italian and not understand about the Beach Boys, but he liked me.

After we stopped talking, I explained to Lucy I was in an emotionally heightened state, due to drink and the state of the world, and she did her sympathetic Labrador thing (snuggling in very close) and finally, we went to sleep.

❀ ❀ ❀

The next day in court, Twisted seemed nervous as all get up and kept looking at her sister with moonie eyes. The sister dispensed a sort of steely approval with a stern look and a mouth that relaxed from its usual fish-bum position into something resembling a fish mouth, which I took to be a smile.

At first, Twisted was all humble your worship, but once she got going, she gave way to her tendency to lecture.

"What you don't *understand*," she told the Department's counsel, "is the *responsibilities* a Principal has."

"What exactly, Miss Siskay," he asked smooth as the silk he was, "is it that I don't understand?"

"Look," she said, when questioned about my dismissal, "there's a lot of *responsibility* on a principal. I have to *run* the school, and I *have* to follow the Departmental directives."

"So you see a conflict between the two things?" he asked. "Running the school, and following the Department's rules?"

Which got her into a right mess, because she couldn't remember what she was supposed to answer.

"You're asked to do *this*," she said. "But they expect *that*, and then your staff want one thing and the parents want another. So *I've* always stuck to my principles."

"Even when they go against the designated requirements of your job?" He was like a snake charmer.

Twisted shot a look of desperation at the elder sister. The sister shot back a moral fibre ray from which Twisted seemed to gather strength.

"There *isn't* any contradiction between the job and my *principles*," she said.

"So running the school, following Departmental directives, pleasing the parents, and keeping the staff happy and in line; that all falls into line with your principles. Almost miraculously, it appears."

"Well, I have to *explain* it to people," she said.

"What about personal conflicts?"

At this point, Siskay didn't say anything. She just went a nasty purple, swallowed then took a deep breath.

"Beg pardon?" she said like a small girl.

"Personal conflicts. You wouldn't say that personal conflicts between you and your staff, or even, say, between you and any parents caused you to act in a way that perhaps went against the requirements of your job?"

She looked to her sister again. The sister sent out more moral fibre rays, but they weren't such good ones this time. "My *feelings* are *never* in conflict with my *principles*," she said. "Never." There were beads of sweat on her brow. Also on Jason's. He didn't like this line of questioning (or answering) any more than she did. "Never," she repeated. "I couldn't live with myself if they were."

The silk went on then at some length about the alleged perfect harmony of Twisted's universe which he tried to probe, but her mind, and her mouth, had closed like a trap. Then he probed her about the perfect harmony of her relationship with me. He asked her about the perfect harmony of her relationship with Miss Baker, my replacement. We all knew that he knew what had really happened. Someone had found out a lot more of the truth than Jason had expected. But Twisted stuck to her guns. Under the influence of her sister's moral fibre, she idiotically insisted she was a sphere of perfect harmony in her thoughts, principles, feelings, and in line with the directives of the Department. There had never been any trouble, never any conflict. She had done what she was told, always. Which was why she had fired me. She couldn't remember what she had been told in relation to me, but she'd done it anyway. She'd never made a mistake. She'd followed the rules. No, she hadn't tried to keep me or get rid of me. How I'd stayed at Grevillea Public so long was a mystery to her. Why I'd been fired was also a mystery, but it must have been the right thing, seeing as she always followed orders.

She would have made a good war criminal. Jason sat with his head in his hands, probably seeking divine guidance.

The stupidity of her stance dawned on her sister, who gave her a withering look as she sat down. Which surprisingly got a sympathy vote from me, knowing as I did the power of sister looks.

There was a lot more shuffling of papers and approaches to the bench and learned muttering, which in a different setting would have had Tookie and me taking them out into Macquarie Street for fifteen minutes of jumping to music so they could burn off all that energy and then settle down and concentrate. But of course they were learned judges and learned counsel, so we couldn't perform this simple trick which worked like a charm on the five to six age group. Instead, the shuffling and muttering went on interminably. I whispered to Jason I couldn't stand it and I was going out for a while. He told me sternly I had to be back in half an hour.

I walked along Macquarie Street and went into a coffee shop where I saw David's reporter, Simon, also having a coffee. I asked him if he was coming along to cover our case.

"No,' he said. "There's that big blackmail case on. You know, the one where the guy threatened to tell the husband the wife wasn't a virgin when he married her."

I knew the case from watching it on *A Current Affair*. "So you think *that's* more interesting than unfair dismissal and the rights of casual teachers . . ."

He didn't get it, but he *was* very young and earnest. "It's what sells – you know, sex and blackmail. People think teachers are always complaining."

"Well, I guess we are," I said. "Maybe we need sex in our case. Or blackmail."

He was a polite young man and after we'd chatted about the virginity blackmail, he asked me how our case was going, and I told him, but explained first he couldn't quote the libellous bits about Twisted. I asked him if he'd quote the non-libellous bits in his paper. He laughed and said maybe, if I got lucky, they'd take the virginity blackmail case off page one and stick it on page six and put our case on page one. I told him how depressing it was, because casual teachers had a raw deal, and because we were such a fringe group, no-one took the slightest notice. I told him what I used to earn as a casual teacher with no holiday pay and no sick pay. As I was talking, I got it all straight in my head because apart from being earnest, he was also one of those truly curious people who want to get to the bottom of things by asking probing questions. Which produced in me a random worry about my own son, given the only thing Sam ever wanted to probe was the peanut butter.

And then I noticed I'd been gone an hour. Simon realised he was going to be late for the virginity blackmail case and I rushed back into court to find Tookie on the witness stand. I wasn't sure why she was there but Jason gave me a note saying the Department had her on their list and had decided to call her.

"Given the clear contradictions in Miss Siskay's evidence," said the Department's counsel, "where on one hand she had to balance all the requests of all the different parties concerned with the school, and then her assertion about the total harmony of thought, feeling and action, can you tell me whether in your opinion, Mrs Jarrett's dismissal was for personal reasons due to a conflict between her and Miss Siskay, or because it was a departmental regulation?"

"Departmental regulation," said Tookie.

"So there was no *personal* reason why, after such a long period of casual employment, Miss Siskay decided to fire Mrs Jarrett?"

"None that I know of," said Tookie. Despite myself, I felt a stab of admiration for this performance. She had trained herself for when the revolution came.

"So there was no personal animosity between Miss Siskay and Mrs Jarrett?"

"There were professional differences," said Tookie. "But we all have those."

"To the extent where Miss Siskay might dispense with Mrs Jarrett's services?"

"That wasn't the reason. There were professional differences, but they weren't the core of the matter."

"What was?" asked the Department's silk.

"I didn't make the decision," said Tookie.

And so it went on, Tookie maintaining that Twisted merely followed orders, and that there was no personal animosity.

"Is this what I'm supposed to do?" I whispered to Jason.

"Yes," he said. "Any conflict was merely a professional difference of opinion."

I suppose most court cases are just versions of the truth, but this felt as if the true substance had gone and that we were just shadow boxing. By the end of proceedings, I felt as if I was watching a play in a foreign language. Experts in law gave opinions. Argument is the essence of the law, but I began to feel that this was a boy's game that should be broken up before it turned nasty. I dozed, much to Jason's disgust. I ignored Tookie's prods and pokes.

That afternoon, Tookie drove me home. "I won't stay for dinner, Leah," she said. "You have to be fresh for your turn in the box tomorrow." She made it sound as if I would be performing magic tricks.

We went home via the school, and Tookie stopped off for a moment to do some stuff in her classroom. It was still light so I went and sat under the trees near the bubbler and watched the currawongs fossick for scraps the kids had left from lunch. It was cool and quiet after the madness of the day, but I felt a sort of fury for letting myself get involved with this. I should have refused. It wasn't right and it wasn't working.

I was sitting there with my gloomy thoughts wondering what the hell Tookie was doing pottering around in her classroom, when I noticed someone coming across the playground. It was the clever Miss Baker, the Miss Baker who had replaced me. She didn't look half as smart as she had when I'd first seen her. She was carrying a great load of books and papers.

"Hi," I said to her. "How's it going?"

She looked at me with that *not another bloody parent lying in wait* look, but smiled, very uncertainly.

"I'm Leah Jarrett," I said. "You replaced me."

"Oh God," she said.

"Tough year?" I asked.

She nodded. "But you'll be back next year." She sounded bitter.

"Maybe," I said. "I don't know."

"I hate her," she said. "I can't tell you how much I hate her."

"Why?" I didn't have to ask who. This was a woman on edge, the very place Twisted was so good at putting people. Here we were, virtually strangers, but with one almighty common denominator.

"She begged me to come here. She was really happy to have someone with my qualifications. I wanted to come. Then she wanted everything done her way. I had to teach exactly how she wanted me to teach — her methods, her texts, even her award stamps! And then she undermines me to the parents, the children, everyone. She virtually tells me to resign, and hints that in spite of what she calls my bad performance, she'll give me a recommendation for a country school. Maybe. Then I find out she's getting you back. Personally, I think you're crazy to come back here."

"What about the kids in your class?" I asked. "How are they doing?"

"Okay," she said. "Look, I've got all the theory, and I like kids. But I've never had to deal with a classroom before. Miss Took and Mrs Andrews have given me a lot of help, but Miss Siskay is busy telling the parents I'm hopeless. Maybe I am hopeless. Maybe I can't teach. I've had some magic moments, but it's really been horrible." She had tears in her eyes. "I'm sorry," she went on. "I shouldn't bombard you with all this stuff. I know you've got this unfair dismissal court case. Miss Took told me it was all political. You know, I almost feel as if I've got a case for unfair dismissal. Or harassment. Except she's got everyone intimidated."

❀　❀　❀

Lucy Labrador and I stayed up almost all night. Even though I'm a champion thrower out, there are some things I keep. I don't claim any more virtue in those I keep than in those I throw out, but it allowed me to trace year to year, with some gaps, my work arrangements at Grevillea Public. There were times when Twisted should have got a permanent, instead of keeping me, times when she had found jobs to keep me at the school. There were reminders of things she had promised, deals she had done. Date, times, facts!

"That year, I got offered a block at Northside," I explained to the Education Department barrister the next morning. "But Miss Siskay begged me not to take it. She only had three terms, but she said she'd fit me in the fourth term as the RFF — that's the relief from face to face."

"And the following year?"

"Someone was on maternity leave."

"And the year after?"

"We'd had a big intake of new teachers and she needed an experienced person to teach infants and ease the new graduates in."

"Were you aware that this was an unusually stable position for a casual teacher?"

"A few people said so," I answered. "But I'd never been a casual before, so I didn't realise."

"You *did* realise you were a casual?"

"Miss Siskay made that very clear."

"She made what clear?" he asked.

"That I was there by her grace and favour if you like." Jason was shaking his head at me, and Tookie was looking despairing.

"Did you *want* to leave Grevillea Public School?"

"No. It suited me. I live close. I know a lot of families. My children went there. There were times I wanted to leave, but in general, I was happy to stay."

"Due to grace and favour?"

"I didn't like that. No. But she behaved like that with everyone. It annoyed me though because I never had an opportunity to do courses or go to seminars."

"Did you want to?"

"Very much. I paid to do a reading methodology course myself, because she wouldn't sponsor me for an inservice."

"Was that because you were casual?"

"I don't think so."

"Can you explain why Miss Siskay refused to allow you to do an inservice course?"

"She had her favourites. They are always the ones who go to these courses."

"You were not a favourite?"

"No, I was grace and favour." I felt quite calm saying all this. I had glanced at Tookie, who looked shocked. Jason had his head in his hands and Twisted was giving me the evil eye.

"So when it came to your dismissal, you feel these same sort of criteria applied."

"Yes."

"What is a mystery to me is why Miss Siskay employed you for so long when she didn't like you." The barrister looked genuinely puzzled. He'd obviously never worked in a school, or dealt in office politics.

"She had a group of her favourites and then there was a group of untouchables. She rewarded her favourites by denigrating untouchables. She handed out favours to her favourites and she handed out horrible jobs to people she didn't like."

The barrister cleared his throat and smiled. "It's very descriptive language, but you need to give me specific examples, Mrs Jarrett."

"I was on playground duty four days a week, while there were teachers who did none at all. I took two classes for sport even when I was teaching infants, who don't do the sports' afternoon. Things like that."

"Then the mystery is, given she didn't like you, but she needed the untouchables, as you have so quaintly named yourself, why she ever got rid of you." I could see this man was on my wavelength, even if he was technically the opposition. He had a twinkle in his eye which made me think he understood Twisted and her ilk. I felt further emboldened when I saw David and Simon the cub reporter taking seats up the back. I resisted the temptation to wave.

"When I was first there, my husband had left me..."
I hesitated a moment before realising this was not the
place to air the issue of whether he'd left, or whether I'd
told him to go. I continued. "So I had to go back to
work. I was grateful to have a job near to home. And she
liked me being grateful. She made a lot of patronising
remarks about me being a single mother, to show how
good she was to have one on her staff. I stopped being so
grateful after a while, and she stopped being charitable.
We had a lot of different views, but you could never
discuss it with her, because she was right and that's all
there was to it."

"So you became an untouchable?"

"Yes, and a nuisance."

"A nuisance?"

"Well, parents liked me. I'd help them if they were
trying to get something for their kids. And there were a
few of us who resisted her picking on particular kids from
particular families."

"So you thwarted her?"

"I stood up to her. But she had the power."

"So you were a thorn in her side?"

"Yes."

"For how long?"

"Quite a few years."

"So why didn't she dismiss you quite a few years ago?"

"She was struggling to keep up the enrolments and
because I'd taught the kindergarten kids for ages, parents
would send their younger children if they knew they'd
be having me. I mean, it wasn't that many, I guess, but
sometimes one or two make all the difference as to
whether you get another teacher or not. But things got

worse. I'd encouraged a mother with an autistic kid to send him to the school, which Miss Siskay didn't like. I'd given the parents a copy of the departmental guidelines so they could make their case. And then the Department had other guidelines for equity, which some of us put forward as a draft school policy – on how we could implement it – and she accused me of trying to mastermind a revolution. It escalated. She got a new teacher with special reading skills and then told me publicly, in a very humiliating way, that I wouldn't be coming back."

"Was that a relief to you?" he asked.

"Public humiliation?" I said. "No thank you."

"I meant not going back."

"It was totally demoralising the way it was done."

"Would you go back now?"

"Miss Siskay," I said, looking very deliberately at Twisted, "offered me a deal, if I didn't reveal any of this. To go back next year. She's been hounding her reading expert out of *her* job now."

"So really," said the barrister, "summing up this whole sorry saga, you'd have to say that your dismissal had nothing to do with the Department, but with Miss Siskay's peculiar prejudices." This was the key question. For a moment, I thought I'd ruined Jason's carefully constructed case, but then I realised that I hadn't at all.

"No," I said. "Not at all. She could treat me that way *because* there isn't any protection from the Department for casuals. You don't have rights, even if you've been there ten years. And in the end, the Department is my employer, not her."

After that I was stood down, which was the official phrase for leaving the witness box. Then there was a lot of argument about whether the case should be heard in the industrial tribunal at all. The barrister from the Department, who had understood me so well, argued fiercely that I didn't have a case and it was an internal disciplinary matter between myself and Miss Siskay. Jason argued just as fiercely that the Department had been aware that I had been at the same school for a long time and had an obligation towards me. The judge reserved his decision.

When I got out of court, I expected the cold shoulder from Tookie, but she came up and hugged me and said, "Well, you stood up against injustice," in her proper school teacher voice, and then added, "Good on you, Leah."

Jason gave me the evil eye, and said, "You *never* read my notes, did you?" looking as foul as a man would when his first big career move was torn to shreds by an idiot.

David and Simon came up and David squeezed my hand. Simon said, "That was almost as good as the virginity blackmail." And then we went and had a drink and I told them lots of other good stories about Twisted which were far too libellous to print, but also gave them my spiel on the unprotected nature of casual employment, which Simon scribbled down on his cub reporter mini laptop.

The case did Jason's career no end of good, not only because we won, but because what I'd said about Twisted got a lot of attention in the press, because it was so personal and undignified (for her). I got my hair and my make-up done courtesy of *A Current Affair*, plus an interview on the plight of casual teachers, and Taz rang me up and said, "See what happens if you make an effort. Really, you looked fabulous, Leah."

And my mother rang me up and said, "I didn't know you were in the *union*, Leah," with enormous distaste.

Tookie took up Miss Baker's fight to make sure she would get a good transfer the following year and we hoped Twisted would be sent to Siberia, or at least the western third of the state.

For me, this was enough, so it was an incredible bonus when the judge gave me fifty thousand dollars.

"Mine. The whole fifty thousand?" I began to shake.

"The whole fifty Ks," said David.

I went into nervous shock for about thirty seconds, but I actually adjusted quickly and smoothly. I'd owed fifty thousand in my time, but I'd never had fifty thousand. Fifty thousand! I could do anything! Anything, everything.

"I've sent you some brochures on superannuation," said Taz, "and the number of my financial adviser."

"Oh God no," I said. "I'm paying off the Mastercard and the mortgage and then I'll go and stay in a five-star hotel for summer."

"Leah ..."

"Do what you like," said David, "but she's right, think about it."

"Do you think I'm an idiot?" I said. "Of course I'll think about it." In fact, when your financial arrangements are as simple as mine, it doesn't take much thinking. I came back to the basics – the Mastercard, the mortgage and Sam's fines at the video store.

I might also afford the dream island holiday where I could drink a lot and buy presents for my ungrateful children. And myself. And my sister. And Tookie. And even my mother, though I couldn't imagine what I could buy that wouldn't provoke her deep disapproval. And they say that money doesn't buy happiness. That's only because they give it to the people who already have it. For people like me, money does buy happiness. And I was ready for happiness. Life had begun to feel different before the case. I'd found out that awful things could happen and I would still survive. None of my children seemed to like me much, but I would still survive. Not having a job, I'd still survived, and then got one, of sorts.

"Are you going back to teaching?" asked Simon.

"Can't wait," I said, but that was for public consumption. I said I'd be having "discussions with the Department", which was so pretentious that I repeated it to other reporters, and then, of course, the whole thing faded into obscurity and oblivion. It had been my five minutes of fame and I still wasn't sure what I was going to do.

It was gratifying though how fame and money enhance. Taz regarded me as more interesting in my own right than she ever had before. My mother, once she got over the shock of my belonging to a union, chuckled with John Laws about what I had said about Twisted and I felt her approval flow through me, via the radio.

"What a star!" said Genevieve, but I wasn't sure if she was being sarcastic or not. Things between us hadn't actually thawed. "And you know what, you know you were right about Sam." She said it almost accusingly.

"In what way?" I said.

"Well, he should be living with you."

"What about his rights under international law?"

"Boaz and Dad take his rights very seriously, and they've taught him how to stand up for himself which is a good thing. But he should be home with you. You'll notice the difference. He's stopped dying his hair. He's much more mature now."

I patted my own "More Beautiful in Ten". "Then he shouldn't be living with his mother." I knew where this was leading.

"Mum, your relationship with him will be totally different now."

"*You're* sick of him," I said, "even though he's been trained up by Boaz, the source of adolescent wisdom and the King of Yellow Circles."

"See," she said. "you're just the same."

"Have you been trying to reform me too?" I asked.

"Well, it would have been a bonus." She sounded bitter. "A miracle actually."

"I don't want Sam back," I said. "You decided, he decided. That was your commitment."

She looked at me, slightly hysterical. "Mum, I can't have him here any longer. You know he can't possibly pass his exams. He's driving me crazy."

"Better you than me."

"Mum . . ."

"He told me he's very happy with you and Boaz . . ."

"He *is* happy," she said. "But I know he misses you, Mum."

"I don't think he should just move around willy nilly. He needs stability." This was like a fast game of ping pong. But the truth was, I couldn't bear the thought of losing my freedom. The more noble truth was that I wasn't sure that Sam and I could live together again. The punitive truth was that I wanted Genevieve to understand she was partly responsible for this.

"I'll ask Dad," she said.

❀   ❀   ❀

After the court case, the judgment and all the media attention, it was as if my life emerged into a parallel but improved universe. Having money made a difference. Standing up for what was right gave the warm glow the nuns always promised for honesty. I felt as if I'd been through the long dark night of the soul and emerged into the dawn. Seeing justice was done felt fantastic. But it was a lot more than that. My new universe didn't suck me in and spin me round three times and stand me on my head and say, "Stay there!" My new universe stopped dropping cats on my head and removed midnight fears of intestinal parasites.

It was only the dawn though, not a full day of sunshine. Although the Ex should have been stuck in my old universe, he poked his head into my new one. I wasn't holding on to the rosy romantic dreams of our life together any more. It was more that I felt their failure was my fault. My kids didn't like me either. I had no idea where I was going with David. In other words, my life still conformed to chaos theory.

Chapter 11

The Old Moralists believed life was a serious matter, in which every decision had to be carefully weighed to avoid mistakes. The New Agers pose an alternative explanation – that life is a game, in which playfulness and experimentation are at a premium.

The middle aged are handicapped in play by wrinkles and bad backs. It is no surprise when things go wrong. Despite the dire warnings of the Old Moralists, it is clear that few mistakes are fatal. Life is difficult but there can be a sweet acceptance of beginnings and ends.

"Hi Mum."

"Maggie!"

"How you doing?"

"I'm fine. Maggie, I've been longing to hear from you."

"Well, now it's me and this squirmy thing in my tummy."

"Are you still on the Gold Coast?"

"Yeah, at Jackie's."

I took a deep breath. "Maggie, why didn't you ring me back? Why didn't you let me know what was happening? I was worried sick."

There was silence. "Maggie?"

"Mum." A catch in her voice. "Mum, I know."

"Okay." Maggie never had a catch in her voice.

"Mum, I get so tangled between you and Dad. You were supposed to be friends and it was all supposed to work for us kids, but somehow, I knew you wanted me on your side and he wanted me on his side. And I was so confused about this baby that the last thing I wanted was two points of view and nobody listening to me. And I know you hate Jackie, but the thing is, she never says a thing about you, or about Dad. You and Dad are so highstrung, but she lets me be." She sighed. "And Mum, this place up here is very nice after backpacking round youth hostels when you're pregnant. I mean, I love home, but with Sam and Lucy and Jack and you, it's like a youth hostel you know – you have to fight to get breakfast. At home Gen would be on my back, and Auntie Taz would have words with you. And God knows what Grandma will say to me. I really love you all, but right now, I need my space."

"Well," I said. I did some deep breathing. "Okay. But things have changed a bit. Sam's not here any more. We could fix up Gen's room for you. You always liked Gen's room."

"That's exactly it, Mum. It'd still be Gen's. Like a shrine. You know Gen. And with Dad down there, I couldn't cope."

"Your father and I aren't really friends any more," I said. "If that makes it any better."

"You never were! That's why I'm staying here!"

"Can I come up and see you?"

"Okay." Tentative, but an okay.

"I'll be up on the weekend."

I got off the phone and thought of Pouty Lips, who was giving shelter to my Maggie. And I felt ashamed that poor Maggie had felt all this about the marriage breaking up. You think you know everything about your children, but often, you don't know much at all. And I remembered I'd forgotten to tell her about iron supplements and not getting too fat (although apparently the man had left when she was thin, so there's a moral in that). I had a cup of tea and threw the remains of the Eat U Rite muffins to Lucy, who caught them neatly and even licked up all the crumbs.

❀   ❀   ❀

After the court case, I had to go into the Federation to sign legal documents. Jason greeted me warmly.

"What's happening to Twisted?" I asked him.

"Miss Siskay's on stress leave," he said.

"*Stress* leave?"

"Actually," said Jason, "that's the official story. After the case, quite a few people have made complaints about her. Predictably, it's sent her into a rage. The Department can't have her on the loose, but they can't sack her until these allegations have been investigated, so the easiest thing is to put her on stress leave."

"Those complaints never get anywhere."

"She'll most likely get a quiet job and early retirement," said Jason. "When are you going back to work?"

"I'm supposed to be going back to Hook Line and Sinker next week," I said.

"We really need a photo of you going back into Grevillea Public," he said. "With some kids," he added as an after thought. "Publicity for the case."

I wasn't sure. There was something about going back to Grevillea Public, even if Twisted wasn't there any more. I'd had a taste of the wider world. Grevillea Public was too easy, too safe. Not that I longed for rods and fishing tackle, although I'd have to tidy things up there, but I wanted more challenge than Grevillea Public would give me. I was even prepared to cut back on my TV time.

"I'm not sure I want to go back there," I said.

"Just for a while," he said. "It's all fixed up. But go and talk to this woman." He scribbled down a name on a piece of paper and a phone number. "She looks after this sort of thing in the Department. She'll tell you where you are as far as getting to be permanent and that sort of thing. We've all reached a pretty fair compromise, although we'd never say so publicly of course."

"I don't want Jenny Baker's job."

"Whose?"

"She was Twisted's latest road kill."

He looked at me with exasperation. "I'm sure you can sort it out, Leah. You know I thought this case was going right off the rails, but you did okay in the finish."

"I know," I said, "and you didn't come out of it too badly either."

❀　❀　❀

"Leah, Leah, Leah." David kissed my stomach and stroked my thighs. "Leah, Leah, Leah."

We had just made love, and I twirled my finger round his furry little nipples. There was something animal about him. Not animal in the raging bull way. Something animal in his responsiveness, the shiver that went through him when I bit him, his big bear hug, his strong barrel body. It was so far from the conventional masculinity of the Ex that it had taken me a long time to see I preferred it, and actually found it more compelling and deeper. There was no fakery about David. The reality versus a story. I used to like stories. In fact I still do, the ones you read though, rather than the story of my life, re-configured in my head.

I had bought myself a midnight blue, fake satin nightie from Target at an excellent sale price, and I slipped this on. It was suitable après sex wear, and to tell you the truth, I loved the feel of my breasts through it. The nightie surface was definitely superior to bare skin, unless you were Elle McPherson. David rubbed my breasts and my bum, and then we started kissing. And then we realised we were far too exhausted to be making love again, because we had already made love twice, which is enough when you're forty-five, even if you are keener on sex than a teenager.

I felt totally comfortable with David lying there in the post-sex haze. It felt deeply companionable and deeply easy. With the Ex, I'd often felt a sort of tension and embarrassment, a sense that things could have been better. Maybe there was another woman out there who was better than me, who he desired more, who didn't have stretch marks or who had shaved her legs more recently. Those anxieties popped up when I should have been feeling beautiful and desirable.

And the Ex had had a way of niggling those doubts. When I got out of bed, he'd comment on my body, in a jokey way, but with a mean edge. He'd rub my leg and point out I'd missed shaving the hair from the dimples behind my knees. I never felt I had the right of reply.

Whereas David always seemed to like what he saw. It made me like him.

Which is all a long-winded way of saying that when he said, "Leah, did you think about marriage?" that I stopped feeling paranoid and insecure and didn't need to ask whose marriage with whom.

"I have," I said, although that wasn't strictly true. It had churned through my head as a possibility, a rose-covered possibility that would get me away from where I was, a bit like my island fantasy. But with the word "marriage", my mind became cluttered with ideas of what it should be and what it shouldn't be, what I'd wanted and not had, and what I'd had and not wanted.

"Please, please, please. I need to be married to you." He started kissing me again. "Please. Marry me, Leah. I need you, love you, want you." He tumbled off the bed and knelt there, looking both grand and pathetic. The naked lover, asking for my hand in marriage. My heart melted. I felt a great sense of love sweeping through me. "Leah?"

But it wasn't right. I was being swept away by passion, but it was his, not mine. And I was delving into that hidden childhood hope of the great love I had wanted my father and mother to have. And the fantasies of me and the Ex.

"Leah ..."

"There's no rush." That sounded a lot more sensible than I felt.

"Do you love me? Do you care about me? Do you want me?"

I was painfully aware that he loved me more than I loved him. I was holding back. If I married him, I would be the object of desire, not the desirer. I'd often wanted to be the object of desire, like Rosanna. But now it felt unbalanced. He jumped back into bed and kissed me again.

"Leah ...?"

I was forty-five. He was about the same. We weren't in a rush.

"Maybe. Some time. I don't know."

❀　❀　❀

Flying is one of the things you don't do much when you're a single parent, but I decided before I returned to Hook Line and Sinker that I'd fly to Queensland and see Maggie. I went in the guise of supermother, determined to convince my daughter of my goodness and my honourable intentions, determined to bring her back into the folds of the maternal bosom, which actually had one or two many folds. I was on a mission.

She was thin and pale with a big belly – a classic case for dosing with Combantrim, which I'd forgotten to bring. She had dark circles under her eyes and skinny legs. She needed iron and folic acid. I realised getting fat when you're pregnant is not such a sin after all.

It's a lovely feeling hugging the long lost child in the airport lounge. It beats living with a child and it beats having the other one drop in every so often and lecture you. And it beats living with little kids or with teenagers for that matter. We both stood there, crying, our arms wrapped round each other. I felt warm, motherly, tender and affectionate.

But of course all good things come to an end. The hug did, and as soon as we got into the taxi, I was at her about iron supplements and Combantrim and folic acid (which is motherly, but in a way children never appreciate). She retreated into sulky silence.

"You could ask me about India!" she finally blurted out, when we'd settled ourselves in the coffee shop attached to the budget hotel where I was staying.

"Darling! What about India? What was it like?" I sounded as if I genuinely wanted to know about India, even go to India, live in India.

"I don't mean *that*," she said. "I mean about the baby's father."

"Who is he?" I asked.

She relaxed. "Lucas. I'm still in love with him," she said. "That's the problem."

"You mean the problem is that he's not still in love with you?"

"I'm not sure. We broke up, *then* I found out I was pregnant. He doesn't even know, because he was back on the road. I've got an address for his parents in England, that's all. I don't know what to do, Mum."

"Has he got any money?"

"That's a terrible question."

"Not when you have a child to support, it isn't."

"Really, I've got my pride."

"You've got his baby too."

"But he never wanted a baby."

"Did you?"

"God no."

"Do you now?"

"Sometimes. But I can't get it out of my head that he'd come back if he saw the baby. So it's all mixed up with that." Maggie, a romantic? This wasn't like Maggie at all.

"Your dad didn't ..."

"Leave you and Dad out of this. For once ... this is different."

"Exactly how is it different? Man fathers child or children. Man leaves."

"Well, he doesn't know he's fathered the child. And

he hasn't got any money. And he's in England. And he's already had two years working holiday in Australia, so he can't get a working visa unless we got married or something . . ."

"Don't go down that track."

"But I'm so in love with him."

"Marriage isn't all it's cracked up to be." At this point we had a little breather as I remembered that recently I had almost accepted a proposal of marriage, with its attendant fantasy of rose-covered cottage, new Labrador puppy (treachery, but it was only in the very back of my mind), family unity and so on. We also had a little breather because the waitress brought us cheesecake with ice cream. Unlike Gen and I, Maggie and I have identical tastes in food. Except she didn't appreciate my comment about the cheesecake being good for her because it was full of calcium.

"Mum, don't kid yourself."

"About the cheesecake? Or marriage?" I was now a potential consumer in both departments.

"Cheesecake. It's made of pig fat or something. I read it in a magazine. I don't necessarily want to marry him, that's just an immigration thing but I feel as though we were supposed to be together. You know, we broke up over a misunderstanding . . ."

"Like your father and I . . ." I murmured.

"Mum!"

"Okay." We sat in tense silence while I ruminated over my intestinal worm lecture, adapting it for pregnancy and finally deciding it wasn't the time. More tense silence. I was bristling with advice. Advice about marriage, about the young Englishman, about iron supplements and getting

enough rest, about ginger for morning sickness and short-
term romance and long-term relationships. Much of which
might have its place in my own life, if I thought about it
carefully. But it was of no interest to Maggie.

"Life's hard," I said to her. "But you've got a lot going
for you, you know." And squeezed her hand. "You'll be
okay, Maggie. It'll work out."

❀   ❀   ❀

"Mum, I want you to meet Jackie." Maggie dropped the
bombshell at breakfast the next morning. While it was true
that I was no longer imaginatively planning Pouty Lips'
demise, I could see that this would be complicated.

"Darling," I said. "Why don't we go to the markets and
get some cute little baby clothes? That's what I'd like to do.
And talk to you about coming home."

"I'm not coming home," she said. "Jackie's fine with
lunch. She's making it right now. Please Mum, please."

"Why? What's in it for me? Or for her for that matter?"

"Ex-wives Club." She grinned. "Mum, you have so
much in common."

"You know what I think of her."

"But she's not like that. Anyway, you don't really think
it any more. You haven't even give me your standard Pouty
Lips blast."

"So why don't we leave it and you and me go to the
markets?"

"Because she's making lunch."

I was about to reply how I'd made beds and meals for
the Ex for years and he'd never turned up because he was
with Pouty. I was about to tell her the story yet again how
Pouty had stolen the Ex. Except there was another version

of the story in his head and my head now, which I couldn't quite dislodge. A sadder story of my own foolishness, telling him to go. Had I really done that?

"Okay," I said. "But it better be a pretty good lunch."

❀   ❀   ❀

She didn't have pouty lips at all, they were quite thin. Of course I was tempted to believe she'd had the silicone lip implants removed because they'd collapsed, but I had given myself a stern lecture on doing this for Maggie, and being openminded. As well as the stern lecture, I was also trying to stop my fear – fear that I'd like her, fear that I'd say what was on my mind, fear that she'd attack me, fear, fear, fear.

She didn't look at all like Maggie, except they had the same sort of build and were dark and had sweet, chunky, and determined faces and almond-shaped eyes. But past that, nothing.

She had a great flat which overlooked the ocean at Surfers Paradise, and an enormous stainless steel kitchen unsullied by children or Labradors, which was exactly as I'd imagined it all those years when Taz was telling me I shouldn't lust after the vulgarity of Paradise, the Surfers variety in particular.

Jackie, as I awkwardly called her, did not, being totally objective, look that much better than me, at least not the time I was on *A Current Affair* and they had improved my looks considerably with make-up and a misty camera. But if you'd had Pouty, sorry Jackie, bear three children, and put on two stone, we would have been roughly equal. This was going through my head as we chatted about the lovely view. Lovelier than mine at home, but I liked my garden, although I didn't mention the dog holes. I said that she must have excellent shopping here in Paradise. She pointed out how cosmopolitan Paradise had become to which I could make no parallel claim in regard to Grevillea, except for the ubiquitous descendants of bog Irish (me included) and adolescent multi-racial gangs. But it was all lovely, lovely, lovely. This verbal air kissing was getting wearing so we dropped a notch when we sat down to lunch.

Food releases inhibitions, and her food was extra good. Which made me want to cry at the thought of my takeaway pizza and Eat U Rite choc chip muffins with Combantrim to follow every three months. No wonder the Ex left!

"So, how did you seduce and bewitch him *and* get him to desert me and the children leaving us with a single parent income, *and* get him to come up here and buy you this luxury flat when I had to squeeze maintenance out of him, which the bastard, (and you by implication), still owe me?" This isn't verbatim. I'd only had one glass of champagne and Maggie was kicking me under the table, so my venom was conveyed in a polite code.

Pouty made her reply (also in polite code) along the lines that I was a fat bitch playing the sympathy card over three kids with big eyes and brattish manners. All the time she'd worked hard to support herself and put up with my brattish kids and look how Maggie (traitor!) loved her and she spoke often to Gen, and yes she'd had trouble with Sam, but then, hadn't I? From what she'd heard at least. And probably, it was hard for me, not having much drive, to go out and earn a squillion dollars and lavish it on myself and said brattish children. God! And how could I stand having a dog, the filthy animal? The Ex had sent that thing to me because she wouldn't have it living anywhere near her.

Lucy, poor, innocent Lucy had also been a pawn and victim in this divorce.

This is a only a version of what we each said. God or the United Nations were with me for once, and maybe with her too, because it just came out as tense politeness, interspersed with some of the bitterness we had savoured for each other over the years.

Then I said out loud, "When he left me, did you get the idea that I'd driven him out? That," and this was hard to phrase (you were a last resort? he had nowhere else to go? he needed a woman, any woman?) "... that he was very conflicted about leaving me?"

"He hated losing his family," she said.

"What made him go?"

"He never told me. He just did it."

The white wine was flowing now, and the dessert appeared and Maggie got that sudden black tiredness of pregnancy and went to lie down.

I told Jackie how hard it was being a single mother, and how I'd wanted to stay friends with the Ex, how I'd blamed her. And she told me how she thought it would be paradise, but he always made it hard with the kids, and it was like I was forever present in their lives and he always wanted to talk about how difficult I was. He was a lazy slob, so she always worried he might be with her for her money. They'd had a business partnership and she'd dissolved it because he wasn't doing his share. That's when he started working when Sam came to stay, to show her he was working and had to sacrifice his relationship with his one and only son to do so. Evidently, he never understood real estate, and he bullshitted people. She hated that. She began to suspect he was lying to her about other things. She felt she'd wasted her life, because she'd wanted kids. He'd had a vasectomy, and now her biological clock was ticking. Anyway, with an experience like the last ten years, she felt seriously over men.

"He did a lot of damage to the kids," said Jackie. She was Jackie now, in my mind. "He'd go over the divorce, tell them how you got everything, how you were trying to turn them against him. Not straight out, but Gen got it right away. She called them 'your mother' stories."

"I had 'your father' stories," I said shamefaced. "But the kids told me you never said a word."

"They weren't my kids," she said. "That makes it easier."

"Still," I said, "I didn't say very nice things about you. I'm sorry." Wine and honesty can be a good combination.

We left the table and sat staring at the surf rolling in. We were like an old married couple (which I guess we were except we'd both been married to the Ex rather than each other). "I'm sure he told you a lot of lies and I know he told me a lot of lies, but he did say one thing before he left that was probably true," she said.

"What's that?"

"That he'd always loved you."

"Funny way of showing it."

"But I think it was true. Don't you? When I kicked him out, it wasn't like a body blow, except where his lifestyle was concerned. And maybe that's what attracted him in the first place."

270

I gazed out at the surf. "This beats Grevillea on a teacher's salary."

"Does he want to come back to you?" she asked.

"Nup," I said. "See, that's where I think you're wrong. He's been round to my place and stirred up Sam because I told him he was a lousy father. And then he told me that I made him leave in the first place."

She sat up, excited. She did look like Maggie. "That's his technique. The guilt trip he lays on you. All in the name of emotional honesty. Now he's on this spiritual journey that makes him *totally* poisonous. He gets to you, undermines you, offers you a few sweeteners and then he has you exactly where he wants you. And because you've had to support yourself, you've probably got *things* he wants."

I laughed. "Not my things, I don't think." But as I looked around the apartment, I thought of Grevillea more fondly. It wasn't smart and it certainly wasn't sophisticated, but it did look as if real people lived there.

❀　　❀　　❀

The cat attacked me when I came back after my Gold Coast weekend and Lucy danced round and round as if I'd been gone for a week. Katie Bless You leaned over the fence.

"How's dear Maggie?"

"Six months pregnant." Short, sweet and to the point. But evidently not quite clear enough.

"So she got married in India?" Katie's voice rose to an excited pitch. "You never told me that." I was over having to be sarcastic to Katie Bless You. I was probably as irritating to her as she was to me. Or maybe I was Katie's version of X-rated entertainment, with a healthy dose of moral superiority (hers and mine) thrown in.

"She's an unmarried mother," I whispered. If I was going to be X-rated I may as well play to the gallery.

"Oh Leah, how terrible for you." Her eyes filled with tears. "You never think it can happen to your own. I pray every night, you know."

"Me too," I said briskly. "But God moves in mysterious ways."

I bustled round at home, turning on lights and opening windows. I made myself a cup of tea and realised I had no Eat U Rite choc chip muffins. For a moment I was tempted to rush back and beg some from Katie, but it was just loneliness. Loneliness and disappointment that Maggie wasn't coming home.

When I switched on the answering machine, I realised I wasn't alone at all. I had nine phone messages. Unfortunately, they were mostly from my mother, with varying degrees of hysteria.

"Leah, Tania tells me you're getting married. Of course I would have liked to have you tell me something so personal, but I do hope it turns out better than your first, especially since you have lost some weight."

"Leah, of course I don't know who this man is, but I do hope you have chosen wisely this time."

"Leah, Tania tells me this fellow is a journalist. They're always putting things in the paper and then you find out they're not true."

"Leah, this is Taz. Sorry. David saw Rosanna at that music afternoon and she grilled him on what was happening with you and him. He told her about wanting to marry you and Rosanna told me and I take full responsibility for telling Mum because I

thought you would have told her. Actually, I thought you would have told me."

"I may be old fashioned, dear, but isn't it common courtesy to inform your mother that you intend to marry? And an introduction really would not have gone astray."

"Leah, David here. Your mother just called me and told me off. I told Rosanna I'd asked you to marry me and she assumed you'd said 'yes', which would have been a good thing. She didn't tell me that she thought it was all a done deal, but treated it like hot gossip, which I suppose it was if you had said 'yes'; and she told Taz, who told everyone including your mother. She seemed to think I'm a monster corrupting the innocent. I lost my cool a bit and we had words. Sorry. Hope you had a good time in Queensland."

I rang David and left a terse message on his machine about bumping into Rosanna however innocently, and then telling her his intentions and letting her assume I said yes. Rosanna probably thought I was desperate enough to say yes to anyone which, as he knew from personal experience, was far from true. In fact, I might get even more choosy. And then it was all out of my system.

The last message was from the Ex.

"Sam just told me you're getting married again and Gen's completely hysterical. I mean it's one thing to go up to Queensland and stomp all over my territory, but I do think you could have had the common courtesy to let the children know your intentions."

I watched the lights go out next door in Katie's bedroom. I lay on my bed, Lucy next to me. I kicked off my shoes and pulled off my pantyhose. I thought of being married to David, all the potential sweetness and fun. I thought of all the nonsense on the answering machine.

It was strange to have other people being more hysterical about my life than I was.

. I was exhausted and I promised Lucy I'd have a shower and clean my teeth in the morning. That's one of the compensations of living alone. There's only the Labrador to set an example to.

❀   ❀   ❀

The signs were there. On the window of Hook Line and Sinker. *Closing down! Under receivership. Bargains galore!* Steve was there, black as thunder.

"You haven't got a job," he said. "We're closing."

"Okay," I said. "I can see that. But it's not my fault."

"Just ask Jeff," he said.

I went out the back to see Jeff. "I'm sorry it's folded," I said.

"Sorry!" he said. "Sorry? The whole thing's folded and you're sorry. Those cash flow figures, they put them on to this. I could have extended the overdraft. Now the development's gone, this is gone, the whole bloody thing has gone. And you're *sorry*." He was crazy. "You and those figures. You're mad. I should have known after I found out your stunt about your damn dog."

"I lied about the dog, which was a mistake," I said. "But those figures were right. The cash flow is just the money that's coming in and going out. So you can't judge it in the same light as ducks."

"Bloody ducks!" he exploded. "My wife says we can't live in that house because they're in there all the time shitting on bloody everything and chasing the cat. And I can't even get a permit to shoot the things, even though it was *me* that made it into a wildlife refuge!"

"I came down here to resign," I said, "which I don't need to. But I do need a reference."

As expected, he got red in the face and looked mad and threatening and started talking about a feminist plot against him. I was quite relieved that Steve came in, although Steve wasn't the sort of bloke who'd automatically spring to the defence of a woman in distress.

"I need you to say that I was very competent using the program," I said. "That way, I wouldn't need to get involved in all that stuff that's coming out in the local paper about bribery of the building inspectors. Or anything about tax evasion."

He suddenly saw reason.

"I'll write it," I said. "And you can sign it."

I went upstairs and collected my coffee mug and wrote myself a nice reference. I knew the local paper had all they needed on the building inspectors. Jeff would be in plenty of trouble with the tax department without my help. I printed the reference out, took it downstairs and got Jeff to sign it.

"Steve," I said on the way out. "Do yourself a favour. Get another job."

"There's still the parking," he said. "On a Saturday."

"Forget it," I said. "The tax department. Get out while you can."

I went home and called the woman at the Department whose name Jason had given me and made arrangements to go and see her.

"Only for one term," I said. "That's all I want."

"Are you sure?" she asked.

"Absolutely."

❀   ❀   ❀

I went back to Grevillea Public to teach Year 3, who were charming and whom I'd taught in kindergarten. Emily was in my class, evidently withdrawn from her private school due to the collapse of her father's business. We became great friends.

We went down to the duck reserve and studied the local ecology, including the problem of duck poo, a study which was extremely popular, and the problem of roving dogs versus ducks. I told them the terrible story of Lucy's crimes. I even wrote a play about a two-headed duck escaping from a Labrador, the performance of which was only marred by the two ends of the duck forgetting their stage directions and exiting from different sides of the stage with a heart-rending split. We wrote stories about ducks and decorated the ceiling of the room with a flock of painted ducks. We ran a cake stall and raised money for the guide dogs as a counterbalancing activity. It was restful and just a little too familiar.

Of course school was a lot more fun because Twisted had gone and we had a human head for a change. I had my picture taken as "Sacked teacher goes back to school" on page three of the papers, although I didn't make the TV this time. I helped the poor Miss Baker get ascendancy over her tots and she showed the makings of a good teacher, although she was more serious about it than you need to be. I could see she'd be a principal sometime, dedicated and sincere, with no idea of how much fun it is.

And I started to remember how much fun it is myself, even though it's hell on your feet and your voice.

❀　❀　❀

"Sam's decided to stay home today so he can do some work for his exams," said Genevieve. "Boaz has made sure he's extremely motivated." We were all at Taz's for lunch to celebrate my birthday. It was elegant and wonderful, except that David and I failed the elegance test. Taz had relented further on this front and invited Mr Bonham, who seemed unnaturally familiar with Mum. Free and easy almost.

"Yes, but is Sam *doing* any work?" I asked.

"He's got his confidence back," said Boaz. "And his trust in people."

"You make him sound like a cat you picked up from the RSPCA," said Taz. Taz had lost confidence in Boaz since Rosanna had told her he had moved onto blue squares.

"Not rectangles," Boaz told Mr Bonham confidentially. "People can live with rectangles. They actually like something longer than it is high, or higher than it is long. They can't cope with the absolute perfection of squares."

"Television is square," said Mr Bonham, "and I can cope with television." Then he spoilt his argument. "Books too. Youngsters today never ever read."

"So when are you getting married?" Rosanna asked David. "To Leah?" As if this needed clarification.

"Don't know," said David. "I'm on trial at the moment."

"How long a trial?" asked Rosanna.

"Don't know," said David.

"*We* don't know," I said, "if we're getting married at all. We're just friends."

"I hardly think that can be right," said Mum. "Trial marriage."

"It's not trial marriage," I said. "It's not marriage at all."

"Well, I'd never marry again," said Mum. "Not after your father."

At this point we were usually silent, out of respect for the widow's grief.

"Was that because it was so awful, Gran?" asked Gen. "Or so wonderful?"

My question had finally been spoken.

"Neither," said my mother briskly. "It's just too much bother."

Late that night, after David had gone to sleep, and Lucy had crept onto the bed, I had a think about marriage being too much bother. And it wasn't only marriage. It was life in general. David's feet were a bit sandpapery, so I had to draw my feet up in bed, although I liked the way he put his arm round me in the night, stilling my fears of intestinal parasites. Lucy, burrowing between us, engendered fears of intestinal parasites. I worried about the cat pouncing on me in the garden. About Sam getting his confidence back, Gen with blue squares, Mum and Mr Bonham watching *The Bill* together and Taz having the Italian affair in Bali. I slowly sank into my tropical island dream. Now that was life.

Chapter 12

In youth, we are attached to constructs of eternal love, of passing fancies, of soulmates, of free love. We use these constructs to shape each passion, as if we're afraid that without a framework, it will collapse against the difficulties of real life.

In middle age, the dimming of ideals combined with a dawning acceptance of reality gives us more realistic expectations.

Leah, our heroine, finds happiness with the marriage of her ideals and reality.

I lay, Rubenesque, across the double bed, the new golden satin sheet draped tastefully across my hips, in such a way as to outline the tautness of my thighs, but at the same time hiding the varicose veins. All of which was lost on Lucy, who scratched at the door to be let out, so that when I got back to bed and David came in I wasn't quite as exquisitely draped.

He threw himself onto me, not seeming to mind the disarray in drapery.

"Maybe we should go and live in another house," he said. "I could afford something now I've got this salary and I'm out of Cockroach Towers. We could get something together."

"Which would be bigger than getting married and Ben Hur put together," I said.

"So then, let's get married and avoid Ben Hur," he persisted.

"I have to work out *why* I'm getting married."

"Because I love you and you love me. And because your mother doesn't like me."

"It might just be infatuation," I said, kissing him, "arising from the fact my mother doesn't approve."

He did a bit of toe kissing, like the royalty does. I liked that. We have the *Woman's Day* to thank for putting us in touch with that particular type of erotica.

"Why won't you marry me?" he said.

"I'm not sure. My first marriage went so wrong. It devastated me for ten years. I still don't understand it. It worries me the same thing will happen."

"How can the same thing happen?" he asked. "We're different people. Different situation."

"I'm the same person," I said. His head was under the sheet, nuzzling my breast. I raised one leg, to check the shapeliness of my thigh.

"Mum! What are you doing?" It was Maggie, enormously pregnant, enormously shocked.

I dropped my leg back down and pulled the sheet over me. "I'm having a rest," I said. "And this is my friend David." I pulled down the sheet to reveal the back of David's head. "He's having a rest with me." It's the sort of excuse you'd use with a four year old. "You should always knock," I added breathlessly as Maggie retreated and David and I struggled into our clothes, unable to meet each other's eyes. I came out into the living room to find Maggie on the couch, in the embrace of a tall, blond man. She looked tearful and embarrassed. It wasn't much of a homecoming, but we were saved by the young man.

"Hi," he said. He got up, full of bravado, as if nothing had happened, and shook my hand. "I'm Lucas, father of the baby, your Maggie's fella. I don't know why, but I think Maggie expected to find her dad under that sheet." Lucas had a Cockney accent and I could see he was going to keep talking until we were all over the embarrassment. "That fella's probably very nice, maybe even nicer than her dad from what I heard about *him*, but Maggie was taken by surprise. And embarrassed and all."

"I'm sorry, Mum," said Maggie. "I shouldn't have barged in like that. But I didn't expect . . ."

"That's right," said Lucas. "Just shut up, Maggs. You'll get off on the wrong foot, telling your mum you never would have thought someone of her age would have had sex, or liked sex or be interested in it. You look, you can see the light in yer mum's eye. My God, she's a beautiful woman, in the prime of life, just like you, my darling one." And he fell back on the couch and put his arms round Maggie. "Don't take it to heart, Maggs. God, I once found my old man shagging my auntie up behind the pub, about ten minutes after me mum had had me little sister. This is nothing."

"Well, I wouldn't call it nothing," said David, who had just come in. He was good at this male banter, which of course turned into beers and Maggie and I went into the kitchen and she told me that she and Lucas would like to live with me till the baby was born.

"I felt like coming home, Mum," she said.

"Ring next time."

"You know I did sort of think it would be Dad. I don't know why. I've always expected you and Dad to get back together."

"It's not going to happen."

"I know that, Mum. Really, I do." She patted Lucy, who was squirming ecstatically round her feet. "You know why I came?"

"No." I was hoping she would say something about the wonderful emotional support I could give her, or the mother–daughter bond.

"I'm going to need help with the baby. I don't want to be totally tied down. And Jackie doesn't have a clue about babies."

❊ ❊ ❊

"I won't be coming back to Grevillea Public next year," I said to Tookie as we sat in the staff room late one afternoon. The sunlight fell across the battered brown staff table. The stale whiff of the end-of-week tea towels wafted through the room, with the acrid metallic smell of the photocopier, relieved by the scent of the bottle brush outside the window.

"But Leah," said Tookie, "I'll be acting deputy. I need you. You're not going back to that awful shop again, are you?"

"No, no, no. I wasn't tired of teaching. A teacher is what I am. I was demoralised by being treated so badly by Twisted. But even if she'd been halfway reasonable, maybe I've been at Grevillea too long. It's too predictable."

"So where are you going?"

"West. The cutting edge. I applied last year when Twisted was letting everyone know how wicked I was and the school I applied to didn't even answer my letter. Now they've seen me on *A Current Affair*, they like me."

"But the travel!"

"I don't mind. It's one of those great big infants departments with hundreds of kids. Half of them don't speak English. I'm starting an ESL course. The woman in the Department has organised a couple of inservices for me. And I'm thinking, how do you get the parents involved in a great big diverse community like that? And how do you make the playground feel safe for the little ones at that size school? How do you cope with racial tensions between kids? It'll be totally new."

"It's still teaching."

"I'm not actually going to be a teacher," I said. "They get a lot of new teachers who've never taught before and I'm a support person for them. Somehow, they've got the funding. Which means I get paid holidays too. All these kids like poor Jenny Baker won't get swallowed up, spat out, then give up in despair. I give them the grounding and some emotional support and encouragement, see what they're good at. It might drive me crazy, but it'll be really interesting."

"My God," said Tookie. "You make me feel totally backward."

"I'm going to do a unit at uni too. Psychology. I reckon you could set up a program and work out what the main factors that make people leave and what keeps some teachers teaching. I mean apart from the holidays and the money."

We both laughed.

"But won't you miss us?" said Tookie.

"I don't think so," I said. "You and I will go out to dinner at least once a week, and I'll call you and you'll call me, and I'll come to the school play. Besides, being deputy, you'll probably be very glad to have one less troublemaker on your staff."

"I'm really sad," said Tookie, raising her tea cup. "But here's to the revolution."

"The revolution," I said. It occurred to me I'd never known which revolution Tookie was talking about.

❀   ❀   ❀

I walked home every afternoon from Grevillea Public and though it wasn't long enough to be a taut thigh walk, it was a lot more pleasant. It was strange to be back at the school and to recall my months searching for employment, then my time at Hook Line and Sinker. I'd learned lots. But I had never belonged to that world. I am a teacher. I groan and moan and complain, which is part of it, but there's something fantastic about those kids' faces, about their idiocies, my own, about the strange processes we go through, about the hopes for a six year old, the worries of parents, the timelessness of it all, the rhythm of each term, of each year, the gratitude and the ingratitude.

And I felt good about it. Taz wasn't the successful sister any more, the one who'd done better. My God, I thought, poor Taz couldn't teach to save her life.

❀   ❀   ❀

The upshot was that I had full house again, with David and Maggie and Lucas. Maggie and I talked a lot about families and babies and bringing up children and the hurts of childhood, and tried to understand each other better than we had before. And David and Lucas talked and laughed and joked and drank a lot of beer. Which is pretty much how life is, I guess.

Lucas professed a desire to live in Australia, which was somehow mixed in with his love for Maggie. "I love 'er," he said, "but she isn't actually an angel. With Maggie and the baby, I reckon I should have the points to migrate."

He was happy engaging in a battle with the Immigration Department, but he was also happy working illegally and buying a basinet and a cot and a pram second hand and doing them up. He was irrepressibly cheerful, and so much better than Boaz.

David slipped into family life as easily as Sam had slipped out of it. Sam was now living, in a considerable state of tension, with his father, Gen having finally got sick of his slovenly ways. Sam came home for an occasional pizza, having begun to realise that I was more tolerant and a softer touch than his sister or his father, except in the matter of him living with me again.

Life was in a rhythm, but at the same time the birth of the baby loomed as a watershed. After that, life would be different again. But not too different. Maggie and Lucas would move out eventually, and David and I would be on our own. Every morning, before setting off for the last days of term at Grevillea Public, I walked Lucy to the duck reserve. She was in no danger of killing ducks because there were no ducks there any more. It had become an ordinary suburban park, and I understood the reason why when I met Jeff Smith down there with his two new hunting spaniels.

"Morning Mrs J."

"Hello Jeff. No ducks down here any more?"

"Wildlife has to be compatible with people," he said.

"And compatible with dogs?" I replied, glancing at his spaniels.

"People keep pets. It's part of our traditional lifestyle in the suburbs."

"Traditional lifestyle?" I'd heard a rumour he was going to run for mayor. With a line like that, he'd probably make it. Lucy had a go at his spaniels and we parted in a flurry of dog fur.

❀　❀　❀

"I've already bought the puddings," said my mother triumphantly as she and Taz and I sat on a lounge in the furniture department.

"Well, you can use those for your Spare Parts Club," said Taz. "I refuse to eat those puddings."

"I've ordered the pork too," said Mum, "after the fuss you made last year."

"Mum, Christmas is hideous enough without you interfering," said Taz.

There was a sort of collapse of my mother's face when Taz let fly with this. "You've always blamed me," she said. "Always!"

"You told him to get out!" said Taz. "You told him you couldn't stand the sight of him a minute longer."

"Your father was drunk," said my mother. "He'd been drunk for a week. I *couldn't* stand the sight of him."

"But you let me go with him. I was only four."

"It was a bush track. I didn't know old O'Donnell would be out there playing bullfighter. Those two were as bad as each other. Best drinking buddies. He shouldn't have been on the road."

"Well, neither should Dad," protested Taz. "We never saw him again."

"You would have never seen him again anyway," said Mum. "I'd made arrangements to leave. We were going to live in Queensland. He knew that. We'd agreed, in a rare sober moment of his."

Taz became wide-eyed. "Maybe he committed suicide. Maybe he couldn't bear the thought of us leaving."

My mother looked old and disintegrated. "I've thought of that," she said. "I think of it often. I wonder if it was my fault."

"I'm sure it wasn't, Mum. You never meant it to happen."

And I felt finally that I was old enough to be told, and old enough to understand.

❀　　❀　　❀

Maggie's baby started coming early evening. She and Lucas were committed to nature's way and had ignored my hints about the compensations and pleasures of childbirth drugs, but by the time we got to the hospital car park, Maggie was demanding an epidural.

"Oh Mum," she breathed, ignoring Lucas, who was still advocating natural birth. "You'll get me the drugs, won't you?"

"Of course, darling." I took Lucas aside. "It's her body and her pain. Your job is to support her whatever she does."

"They said not to call it pain."

"It doesn't matter if you call it green bananas. It still hurts," I said. And found the nurse, who fixed up the gas and phoned the anaesthetist.

"You're fantastic, Mum," said Maggie when the epidural took effect. "Ohmigod. It's so much nicer when you can just watch the contractions on the monitor."

"You're doing fabulously, Maggie," said Lucas, who was glued to the monitor as if it were a football match. "That last one was huge. I wonder if they let you keep the printout."

"No," said a nurse sternly, "just the baby."

The Ex poked his head round the door. "How are you, Maggie? I'll be outside." He came over and kissed her and then darted out. He'd always been scared of birth.

We sat and talked. Lucas fell asleep for a while, probably because of too much laughing gas. It was past midnight, and the hospital was quiet, just Maggie and I chatting. The Ex came in, and then David arrived.

"Gen rang," he said. "She's started her shift, so she's on her way up."

A minute later Gen arrived. "My God," she said, looking at the printout from the machine. "These contractions are all over the shop. Is it beginning to hurt?"

"A bit," said Maggie.

"I'll get a nurse," said Gen. "I'm supposed to be on in casualty. It's quiet now, but I'll have to go down if anything comes in. I'd like to see a birth all the way through."

"*A* birth?" said Maggie. "You're an aunty to this one."

"From a technical point of view," said Genevieve. "For experience."

"You're jealous, I know," said Maggie.

The nurse came to examine Maggie, so we all went out into the corridor. Lucas ambled sleepily after us. "I need a smoke," he said. "I gotta go outside."

"I hope he's okay," said the Ex. "I mean I hope he sticks with her. I'd hate to see her struggling to bring up this kid on her own." I couldn't think up a coherent and masterful reply, so I made my hissy vampire face for which I'd been famous when I was eight. I don't think he noticed because David and Gen were staring at him. "I mean, she's very young," he added.

"Yes," said David, squeezing my hand. I held the hissy vampire face without even having to think about it.

"Do *you* remember?" Genevieve said to the Ex, "leaving Mum to bring us up on her own?" I looked at Genevieve. She isn't one to show her emotions like Maggie, but she was doing a slow burn. I guess the Ex didn't catch it, because he went on.

"Your mother *made* me leave," he said. "I wouldn't have just gone." He glanced at Genevieve and realised he had made a big mistake.

"So you would have continued the affair with Jackie, and used Mum to bring us up, totally humiliating her. But because she had the guts to make you go, you think it's fine *she* had most of the responsibility and the financial burden, while you sponged off Jackie."

"It wasn't like that, Gen."

"It was exactly like that," she said. "Maggie and I have talked about it. We asked Gran and we asked Taz and we asked Jackie because both of you parents talk so much crap. We wanted to know. Even Gran finally admitted it wasn't just because Mum had put on weight. And okay, Mum mightn't have done such a fantastic job with Sam, drugging him and everything . . ."

"It was only worm medicine," I interrupted.

"Worm medicine!?" she said. "He never told me that."

"Oh don't worry," I said. "I'm sure the United Nations is against worm medicine too."

She turned back to the Ex. "You should be down on your knees thanking her for what she did for me and Maggie."

"Look, I am sorry," the Ex said to her. "I'm trying to make it up to you all now."

"What about Mum?"

"I am sorry, Leah." And for once his silly spiritual expression looked right for the occasion.

The nurse stuck her head out the door. "She's in second stage," she said. I sent David to find Lucas. Gen and I went back in.

The epidural began to wear off. Maggie demanded to go home and then vomited and the pushing started in earnest. Another midwife came.

"My God, it's hurting!" yelled Maggie.

"Push down," I said. "Push with it."

"I'm going to die," she sobbed.

"Only the good die young," said Lucas. "Push with it, like your mum says."

Gen came back from casualty. She took in the lights and the drapes and the concentration of people round Maggie and looked panic stricken.

"It's okay," I said to her. "It's only childbirth."

"I can't do any more," said Maggie.

"One more push and it'll crown," said the midwife. "Pant when I tell you."

The baby's head was crowning, a thick thatch of dark hair. Maggie, pushing, then panting. Lucas, intent on her eyes. Genevieve, arms folded, watching beside the midwife. Me, holding Maggie's hand.

"Mum," she breathed.

"You'll be one any minute, darling."

"Pant," said the midwife. "Shoulders are coming. Pant."

The baby slipped into the world. Small, crying, dark. Very dark. Indian dark.

"Bugger me," said big blond Lucas. "'E's black."

"She," said the nurse, looking away from him, as if embarrassed by his blondness. "It's a girl."

"Let me see," said Maggie. "My God, she's gorgeous." She looked at Lucas uncertainly. "She's pretty dark."

The baby started crying. I was crying. Gen was crying. The midwife wiped away a few tears.

"It's wonderful," she said. "Your first baby."

"It's a girl, Dad," Genevieve called out into the corridor. You're a grandpa."

"You too," I called out to David. "A step-grandad."

"Do you want to cut the cord?" the nurse asked Lucas.

Lucas took the scissors and did the honours. The nurse swaddled the baby and handed her to him. "My little girl," he said.

Gen nudged me. I leaned over and kissed Maggie. "She's beautiful," I said. "You did very well."

Genevieve persisted. "Lucas, do you think this is your daughter?"

He laughed. "Shouldn't think so. But it's all the same to me." He winked at me. "And to immigration."

"Give her to me," said Maggie. Lucas kissed her and put the baby tenderly in her arms. "My girls," he said.

Epilogue

A year later

I wore blue silk. Well, it looked like silk and it felt like silk and it was on sale. It was long and floaty and very romantic, and as a little touch of something too much, as my sister put it, I wore a black lace veil, and had my hair flaming bottle red, which after fussing round with high quality hairdressers seemed the best colour for me. Certainly my Year 3 children agreed.

We got married on a cliff top, to symbolise the precariousness of love, overlooking rocks (the hard pathway) and sea (the depth of our love). It was on the edge of a golf course, the symbolism of which escaped me. I thought afterwards it was about life being a game. It was at dawn, the symbolism of which was quite clear, and impressed upon me by Sam yawning loudly, Gen looking at her watch, and Maggie and Lucas and baby Bettina huddling together for support. Mr Bonham and my mother still refused to acknowledge their co-habitation, my mother emphasising she had picked him up from his own home at five o'clock, to get a taxi to the ceremony by five-thirty.

Sam gave me away, which was appropriate, because as he said, we'd had enough of living with each other, although he had tears in his eyes during the ceremony. And he'd started dying his hair again. We were matching redheads. Taz and Tookie were our witnesses and we had a pro forma ceremony which sounded okay when we first saw it, but when the celebrant read it out I saw Taz wince with embarrassment. I knew she'd tell Rosanna later that it sounded as if it was written by one of those people who write the rhymes in sympathy cards. Lucy behaved badly and the ceremony was interrupted by her sniffing dangerously close to the edge of the cliff top and me calling, "Lucy, here girl, here girl. *Here!*" She also made disgusting dog noises as we exchanged rings. There were gusts of wind and rain, which botched the sunrise a little, and brought up goosepimples on my bare arms. Which disappointed me because the blue silk wasn't the sort of dress you couldn't wear more than once, even if it was on sale. Which made you want the once to be perfect.

We staggered back across the golf course, passing round a magnum of champagne David had brought and avoiding the early morning golfers, who were a lot more appropriately attired than we were.

David was chatting to the celebrant in a polite way, and I fell in behind with Taz and Tookie.

"You know you're awfully lucky to get married at your age," said Taz. "Hardly any women do."

"Including you," I said. The Italian lover from Bali had never showed up.

"Well, I've got very high standards," she said in a very up herself way. I poked her in the ribs and we both laughed.

And when we got to the car, I felt awfully, awfully in love with David, which may have been him or the champagne.

That night, we had a dinner for all our friends and family. I asked Katie Bless You, who declared herself "thrilled". "Bless you, Katie Bless You," I said. But from the smile on her face she obviously thought I'd said, "Bless you, Katie, bless you."

"Taz has discovered sex," Rosanna was telling David, "but she's the sort who only has to have it every two or three years. Not like me." I swooped between them, and almost knocked Rosanna off her feet. There are some advantages in being size sixteen.

We played the Beach Boys singing, "Wouldn't it be nice?" and David and I made ourselves ridiculous trying to dance to it.

The next day we took off on the cheap tropical island deal. It rained for the whole two weeks, and they didn't serve drinks with umbrellas in them. But otherwise, it was pretty much how a honeymoon for a middle-aged couple should be.

Acknowledgments

Many wonderful people helped me with material for this book. Thanks to all, especially three fantastically funny women – Kathryn Bendall, Dawn Fenech and Sue Craig.

More than the usual standard thanks are due to my family – my daughter Sophie who laughs in the right places, and has a mean critical eye; my husband Steve, who makes the best coffee in the world and has a calming desk-side manner when a plot tangles; and my son Patrick, who tolerates and enjoys having a mother living in a parallel universe.

My thanks to Tim Curnow, not only for his input into this book, but his many years of work as my agent, and the generous friendship that went with it.

In this book, I used two characters, with their real names, mainly because they can't sue. Jack the cat is every bit as mean as he is portrayed. Lucy, our dear labrador, died as I was writing the final draft of the manuscript. She had been my constant companion during my writing for many years, as well as a wonderful and complex personality in her own right. She wasn't much of a critic, but she knew that retrieving *must* be a cure for writer's block, and that a wet nose in the armpit was bound to cheer a person up.

Lucy's relationship with ducks is portrayed with total artistic licence. She never killed a duck in her life. She may have frightened one or two, but then, they might have frightened her too.